CW01641953

RIGHT OF SANCTUARY

A totally gripping mystery full of suspense

NICOLA CLIFFORD

THE BOOK FOLKS

Published by The Book Folks

London, 2021

This book is a work of fiction. Names, characters, businesses, organizations, places and events are either the product of the author's imagination or are used fictitiously. Any resemblance to actual persons, living or dead, events or locales is entirely coincidental. The spelling is British English.

ISBN 978-1-913516-38-3

www.thebookfolks.com

To The Prison Phoenix Trust

Prologue

6.30am – HMP Heatherlea

Click, click. Greta stirred in her sleep as the irritating sound wormed its way into her consciousness.

Click, click. Unable to ignore the noise she woke fully, stretched under the covers and opened her eyes.

Click. Florescent light suddenly flooded the room and she slammed her eyelids closed. Click. The light was extinguished. She rubbed her face, stared at the bed springs above her and grinned. This was the last time she would wake in this place, endure the early morning switch-clicking, the sounds and smells of institution, the shouts and screams of others. Tomorrow she would wake in a different place, in a comfortable bed with a duvet and two pillows, not blankets and stained sheets covering a thin mattress.

She slipped out of her bunk, dressed quickly, poured a splash of water from the plastic bucket to the bowl and washed her face, cringing as frigid water came in contact with half-asleep skin.

Different noises filtered through the door, squeaky footsteps of staff in the corridor, rattling keychains, clanging and banging of metal doors. Her door suddenly swung open and a screw peered in. Greta picked up the bucket and hurried to the sluice room at the end of the corridor, passing other rushing women, eager to be first in, and retreating quickly before the small room became crowded.

Ten minutes later Greta's bed was stripped, the linen – if it could be called that – folded, bowl and bucket stowed away and her belongings packed. She perched on the bed and gazed around the depressing cell. The walls were painted blocks, a dingy cream colour marred by dried blotches of toothpaste – prison Blu-Tack – the dark grey tiled floor scuffed and pitted. On the wall opposite the bunk was a noticeboard, bare now as she had removed her photographs and posters last night. The narrow window was grubby, inside and out, and overlooked the rear of a potholed haulage yard. Each morning for the last three months, the growl of diesel engines and clanking of metal on metal penetrated her dreams before the clicking light switches. Tomorrow she would hear none of it. In a little over an hour she would walk through the prison gates, return to the real world outside the walls, pick up her life where she'd left it, and the fresh start she had planned.

Greta's pad-mate dangled her legs from the top bunk and dropped to the floor, yawning and stretching. She shuffled out of the cell and headed down the corridor as screws ordered inmates to line up, ready to be escorted to the dining hall for breakfast. A wing was eating out this morning.

Greta followed the slow-moving gaggle of pallid, weary-looking women as they threaded their way through the maze of corridors and endured the laborious process of passing multiple barred gates. The dining room was as drab as the wing, although the windows were bigger and outside was the exercise yard, the view little better than the one from her cell.

Eventually all inmates had been served with rubbery toast, soggy cereal and over-brewed tea, all of it barely edible. Greta didn't bother with anything other than the tea. She'd soon be on-the-out and able to choose her own food.

'GJO619 Holtz,' the principal officer yelled.

Greta stood.

'You packed?'

Greta nodded.

'Grab your stuff then, I'll take you down to Reception.'

* * *

Ninety minutes later, Greta was escorted to the main gate. The civilian staff unlocked the barrier and she walked out – free! The feeling was truly sensational. She stood on rough tarmac, face turned to the sky. Raindrops sprinkled her skin and she took deep breaths of damp morning air.

Parked on the opposite side of the road was a brightly coloured minibus. Greta smiled and waved as doors opened and the occupants spilled out, a mixture of happy men and women, dressed in brightly coloured clothes. A tall, slender man dropped out of the driver's seat. He was dressed in a black, tailored suit with a collarless jacket, white linen shirt beneath. A gold cross hung from a chain around his neck, a single diamond sparkled in his right ear, and a heavy pocket-watch chain looped across his belly. His skin was creamy, raven-black hair hung below his shoulders and matched dark eyes. He raised an elegant hand in greeting.

'Greta!' he called. 'Fantastic to see you. Are you ready?'

'Yes, Adam, I am. More than ready.'

'Then load your gear in the back and we'll take you to New Eden, your new home, where the rest of your life will begin.'

With help from her new friends, Greta stashed the plastic HMP property bags in the storage area and climbed in the side door. Adam fired up the engine, pulled away from the kerb and within minutes the prison buildings were lost from sight. Greta would never have to see the place again. Her heart twitched with excitement, joy and the overwhelming sense of freedom.

Chapter one

DC Heidi Holtz stretched languidly beneath the duvet and flopped an arm across her partner's body, DS Erica Bevan, both members of Dyfed-Powys Force. Erica groaned and snuggled closer.

'Morning, snoozy,' Heidi said and brushed a lock of Erica's dark hair from her face. 'You up for some breakfast before we leave?'

'What time is it?' Erica mumbled.

'Six fifteen. We need to be away by seven, mustn't be late.'

'Ten more minutes.'

'No chance. We've already had ten more minutes.' Heidi squirmed away, grabbed a corner of the duvet and flipped it off the bed. Erica curled into a tight ball trying to ignore the sudden chill. 'I'll meet you in the back kitchen,' Heidi said. 'Don't go back to sleep.'

Heidi rubbed a hand over her short, almost white hair, pulled on a pair of boxers and an oversized rugby shirt over her slight frame, padded out of the high-ceilinged room in Milebrook Manor, her father's home, and down the wide staircase to the ground floor. Her toes cringed on contact with icy floor tiles in the hall as she scurried towards the kitchen. By the time Erica appeared, a pot of strong coffee rested on the scrubbed wooden table next to a full toast rack.

'Help yourself, love,' Heidi said. 'I'll go and get dressed.'

At exactly 7am, the couple climbed into a black Land Rover. Heidi started the engine and pulled away from the imposing, yellow-stoned, Milebrook Manor buried deep in the Cotswolds.

'Didn't your pa want to come with us today?' Erica asked.

Heidi shook her head. 'No, Freddie isn't best pleased with Sis. Told me last night he'd be happy to leave her rotting in jail, but it's all bluster. He hangs around with too many government right-wingers and can be a dreadful snob. You know what he's like.'

Erica giggled. 'I'm always surprised he's prepared to put up with lesbians under his roof.'

Heidi laughed. 'OK – so he's a broadminded rightist.'

'What's your mum like? You never talk about her.'

Heidi shrugged, reached the end of the long gravelled drive, turned onto the main road and headed towards HMP Heatherlea.

'OK,' Erica said, 'so tell me about Greta. You never talk about her much either.'

'For a start she looks nothing like me. You'd never guess we were sisters. She's tall, nearly six foot, nowhere near as skinny as me, has very dark hair and is definitely the black sheep,' Heidi said as she negotiated a sharp bend. 'Got herself in some fearful scrapes when she was young. Hates authority and the establishment, even though she's part of it, and adores demos. If there's a march anywhere for anything she supports, she'll be on the front line, shouting the loudest and carrying the largest banner. Always managed to avoid prison – until now.' Heidi sighed. 'She could have stayed out this time if she'd accepted the fine rather than verbally abusing the judge and being sent down for contempt. Maybe this will calm her wild side a little. Smacking coppers is never a good idea, even in self-defence.'

'Do you two get on?'

'Most of the time, we are sisters after all, but I can't say we share much common ground. She's the good-time girl, I'm the studious, boring one.'

Erica rested a hand on Heidi's thigh. 'I like studious and boring.'

'And I'm delighted you do. How are we doing for time?'

'Quarter to eight, perfect.'

A mile or two further on, a sign announcing the presence of the prison appeared by the side of the road and Heidi pulled into the car park.

'Let's meet Greta at the gate,' she said. 'She should be released any minute now.'

The women wandered across the tarmac arm in arm and waited near the tall metal gate. A small crowd had congregated close to the entrance, ready to greet their loved ones and eventually the Judas gate opened. A handful of women shuffled out, some smiled broadly, others looked exhausted and all shouldered plastic sacks containing their belongings. A little girl burst from the waiting pack, dashed to the gate and hurled herself at a dumpy woman who swung her high in the air as the child laughed and screamed, delighted to be reunited.

Erica nudged Heidi. 'I wonder how long they've been apart.'

'Too long judging by their reaction,' Heidi grouched. 'Don't misunderstand me, I'm all for prison for the right people, couldn't be a copper if I wasn't, but we lock up far too many non-dangerous individuals – mainly women.'

'Sounds as though you could be a rebel too.'

Heidi grinned. 'Don't get me started.'

The flow of released prisoners dwindled to nothing and the small door slammed shut.

'So where's your sister?' Erica asked. 'You better not have dragged us out of bed on the wrong day.'

'As if!' Heidi strode across the tarmac to the gate and hammered loudly with her fist. 'Oi! Open up. I've come to collect Greta Holtz, so where is she?'

Not receiving an instant response she booted the bottom of the door, hammered some more and stood back when she detected movement on the far side. The door opened and a burly prison officer stepped out.

'What's all this fuss?' he grumbled. 'Move away from the gate.'

'I'm here to collect my sister,' Heidi said. 'Greta Holtz GJO619.'

'All prisoners due out today have been released. You must have missed her.'

Heidi took a deep breath and yanked a piece of paper from her pocket. 'I wasn't late and they haven't all been released.' She flapped the paper under the officer's nose. 'Holtz's release date – today! Now, off you trot and find her. Quick as you like.'

'You need to calm down,' he warned, 'and stop ordering me about. Who do you think you are? If you don't leave I'll have no choice but to call the police.'

'I am the bloody police,' Heidi snapped and flapped her warrant card next to the release form. 'DC Holtz and DS Bevan, Dyfed-Powys force. Our boss is DI Ben James, check if you like. Now, go and find my sister!'

'You'll have to wait here.'

'I don't care where I wait, just get on with it before I lose my patience.'

The door shut with a bang and Heidi leaned against it.

'Bloody screws couldn't organise a conga in a holiday camp,' she grumbled. 'Useless, the lot of them.'

Erica looped her arm in Heidi's. 'He was right though, you do need to calm down. They'll sort it, we just have to wait a while.'

The while lasted ten minutes before Heidi attacked the door again. The same officer opened up looking uncomfortable.

'Where is my sister?' Heidi asked coldly.

'You'd better come in,' he said. 'Governor Hughes has asked to see you in his office.'

'Greta is OK, isn't she? Hasn't been injured or got herself in trouble? If she has, her family certainly haven't been informed.'

'No, nothing like that. The governor will explain. If you'd both follow me.' He held open the door. The women squeezed past and into a secure area behind a second tall gate topped with barbed wire. Heidi jiggled her feet impatiently while the guard waited for the barrier to be unlocked then led them across the exercise yard to the office block.

'Why can't you tell me what's going on?' Heidi asked. 'What's with all the secrecy?'

'As I said, Governor Hughes will explain the situation.'

Heidi opened her mouth to give the man a further piece of her mind, but Erica's warning hand on her arm encouraged her to keep quiet.

The governor's office was at the end of a long corridor. The guard knocked smartly and pushed open the door without waiting for an answer.

'DC Holtz and DS Bevan to see you, sir, from Wales.'

The man behind the desk stood and held out a hand in greeting. 'Ladies, do come in. Would you like coffee?'

'No, we wouldn't,' Heidi said, ignoring his outstretched hand. 'I want to know where my sister is and why you haven't released her this morning. Is she in any sort of trouble?'

'No,' Hughes said, 'but we do have a problem, I'm afraid.'

Heidi glared across the desk and waited for him to continue.

'Your sister has already been released, three days ago. The outstanding fine was paid and she was discharged.'

'Who collected her? She couldn't have walked away, it's three miles to the nearest main road and then you're still in the middle of nowhere.'

'You're right, of course. She was picked up by The Church of New Eden.'

'Who?'

'They're a Christian group, visited the prison last week. We often organise events with them, they bring the inmates some hope and comfort. Our chaplain arranges the visits. I'll give her a call. She can explain things better than I can.'

'Just get a bloody move on,' Heidi growled, 'and I warn you now, sir, this had better be good.'

Hughes frowned as he reached for his phone, bridling at Heidi's manner.

Five minutes later a short, rotund woman dressed in a black cassock bustled in and took a seat next to Hughes. She resembled an overweight mouse, twitching and fidgeting on the chair as she introduced herself and fiddled with a large silver cross hanging from a chain around her neck.

She said, 'I'm Maria Cole, chaplain at Heatherlea. Governor Hughes tells me you're here for your sister, Greta Holtz.'

'That's right and you'd better have some answers. I'm beginning to lose my temper and trust me – you do not want that to happen.'

Erica tapped Heidi's ankle with her toe, warning her to keep her emotions in check.

The chaplain swallowed nervously. 'I believe Mr Hughes has already told you Greta was collected by The Church of New Eden at the start of the week.'

'Yes, I've heard that. What I want to know is who these individuals are and where they've taken her.'

The woman hesitated before answering, 'I'm sorry, I don't know.'

'You don't know what?' Heidi snapped. 'Who these jokers are? Or where they've taken Greta?'

'They're not "jokers", Ms Holtz, they are a Christian community and do great work, especially with those who have experienced incarceration.'

'So you say. Where have they taken her?'

'That's what I don't know,' the chaplain admitted, sitting back in her chair as though her part of the conversation was over.

Heidi exploded, 'You don't know! How can you not know? The women in this prison are under your care and you just let one walk away – with no word to her family – to an unknown destination.'

'Your sister is an adult,' Hughes pointed out. 'New Eden paid the outstanding fine and picked her up on Monday. Holtz left of her own volition and we can't hold anyone over their release date. Once the fine was paid, she was free to leave.'

Heidi dragged out her phone and tapped the screen. A search engine displayed a list of entries relating to The Church of New Eden and Heidi's eyes widened as she read. She passed the device to Erica, not trusting herself to speak.

Erica scanned the page. 'The Church of New Eden, included on a list of new religious movements operating in the UK,' she said. 'You allowed a cult into your prison. A place full of vulnerable, unhappy women and, worse than that, you handed one over. What were you thinking?'

The chaplain protested, 'They're not a cult. I've told you, they're a Christian organisation. They regularly visit prisons and bring comfort to those in detention.'

'No!' Heidi shouted, unable to contain herself. 'Let's get this right. They come into prisons with your blessing, to recruit. How could you have been so bloody stupid?'

'You can't talk to me like that,' Maria said. 'The group has been thoroughly vetted by the church. How dare you call me stupid?'

'I dare because that's what you are. Give me the contact details for this bunch. You may not be concerned about my sister's well-being, but I most certainly am and I tell you now, never let these people inside your jail again.'

'You can't tell me what to do,' Maria muttered. 'You don't have any authority here.'

'You're right, I don't – not much, but if you ever allow these charlatans to snatch a woman again, I will make the rest of your life a misery and that's a promise.'

Chapter two

'What do you mean, the prison lost her?' Frederick Holtz raged. 'The whole point of prisons is to keep people in so we know where the criminals are.'

'OK, Pa, calm down,' Heidi said. 'Greta was bought out on Monday by a group calling themselves "The Church of New Eden", and neither the governor nor the chaplain know where she's been taken.'

'Outrageous!' Freddie growled. 'Nothing in this bloody country works, everything is going to pot around our ears.'

Erica giggled. 'Maybe you and your Whitehall cronies should try a little harder.'

Freddie glared at her, belatedly realised he was being teased and grinned. 'You're probably right, my dear. So what do we do next?'

'Track her down,' Heidi answered. 'Shouldn't be too difficult.'

'Then what? Arrest those who took her and charge them with abduction?'

'Nowhere near as straightforward as that,' Heidi said. 'If Greta went willingly we'll have an impossible job bringing any charges. No laws have been broken.'

'I've never heard of the group before,' Erica said, 'but that's not surprising. There are over a thousand active cults in the UK with new ones springing up all the time.'

'A cult?' Freddie raised an eyebrow. 'Are you saying Greta could be in danger? I remember that dreadful business in Waco, Texas, during the early nineties.'

'Cults are usually bad news, but not necessarily all as twisted as the Branch Davidians. As I said, this is a new one on me, so let's not panic until we learn more.'

'What can I do to help?' Freddie asked.

'Not much really,' Erica said. 'Let us spend a couple of hours online and see what we can find out. Rest assured, if we need your considerable clout we'll ask for it.'

'OK,' he agreed reluctantly. 'In the meantime I'm going to ring the prison and give the governor a piece of my mind, followed by the Department of Justice.' Freddie swept out of the room and slammed the door behind him.

Heidi chuckled. 'I almost feel sorry for the inadequate Hughes. By the time Pa's finished with him, he'll wish he'd chosen postman as a career, not prison governor. Let's get to work. Hunting down this posse of idiots shouldn't take long.'

* * *

Greta heard her name called, glanced up from the row of carrots she was harvesting and spotted Eleanor making her way from the far side of the garden.

'Hey, Greta, it's nearly lunchtime.'

Greta stood and stretched her aching back. 'Doesn't time fly when you're having fun?'

Eleanor laughed, a tinkling, almost musical sound. 'If "fun" to you means digging up carrots in the rain, I'm definitely asking Adam if you can work in the garden with me. I can always do with willing helpers.'

'Fine by me,' Greta said. 'I enjoy gardening, especially the vegetable kind. Roses and gardenias are all well and good, but you can't eat them.'

'You really didn't need to start work as soon as you got here,' Eleanor said. 'Adam would have given you time to settle in. We haven't even found you a bed yet.'

'It's fine, I wanted to get stuck in. This "new life" business is so exciting and I'm massively grateful to be granted a place here. I'm pretty sure Pa wouldn't have welcomed me home with open arms.'

'This is home now,' Eleanor said firmly. 'You shouldn't think about your old life, but strive in the new.'

'How long have you been here?'

'Three years – just about.' Eleanor retied her long dark hair. 'Adam found me in a bad space and brought me here. I shall always be thankful.'

'What sort of bad space?'

'I told you – live for now, not for then. The past is gone and can't be changed.' Eleanor smiled, green eyes shining, and she bent to pick up an overflowing trug stuffed with carrots. 'These are lovely, I can smell the freshness. By this evening the kitchen girls will have them tucked away in the freezer. Winter approaches.'

'That sounds odd, "kitchen girls", like they're workers or something. Aren't they part of the church?'

Eleanor laughed. 'We're all workers, but for ourselves – not someone else. No one's forced to do anything; you offered to help in the garden. You're still thinking old world and this is New Eden. Everything works differently here… better. We live gently, simply and happily, providing support and love for each other. You'll see. Now, let's scoot, lunch is waiting and you can meet the others.'

Greta lifted a second laden trug and followed Eleanor along brick paths between the raised beds towards the house; a twelve-bedroom Victorian monstrosity complete with a crenulated tower, masquerading as something much older. A large central hall was ringed by outbuildings, a couple of barns and three small cottages. Eleanor pointed out an extensive herb garden on the far side of the house from which the church earned its living and Greta was looking forward to a full tour.

The estate was secluded, tucked behind a couple of acres of woodland a few miles from any main road. The buildings were constructed with yellow Cotswold stone. Greta briefly thought of Milebrook Manor and her family before pushing the thought from her mind. If she was going to fit in here, make her new life work, she must listen to, and learn from those around her.

Eleanor guided Greta to the rear of the building and in through the kitchen door. Three young women were busy filling serving dishes with mounds of vegetables and two lads ferried them out of the room. One of the girls glanced up from her work and smiled.

'Hey, you must be Greta,' she said. 'I've heard about you. Welcome to New Eden. I'm Pixie.' She wiped her hands on a tea towel and embraced Greta warmly. 'Really good to have you here with us.'

Greta was surprised, but tentatively returned the hug. 'Good to be here.'

'I hope you're hungry,' Pixie said. 'We've been cooking most of the morning, there's nothing like fresh veg. Out of the garden and in the pot before any of it knows it's dead.' She laughed. 'Take Greta through, Eleanor, and don't go empty-handed, take some plates as well.'

The dining hall was large with tall windows and a high ceiling. The room was tatty around the edges, wallpaper peeling in places and ancient carpeting threadbare. A long wooden table surrounded by people, young and old, male and female dominated the space. They all smiled broadly, some waved and called out greetings. Greta hesitated in the doorway, suddenly nervous, uneasy with the amount of attention. Adam stood at the head of the table and beckoned to his new acolyte.

'Everyone,' he called. 'Here… is… Greta.'

'Hello, Greta,' the group chorused.

'Greta has joined us today. I want you all to welcome her and support her while she transitions to our way of life, her new life.' He raised a glass. 'To Greta – you are most welcome.'

The others got to their feet, raised their glasses and repeated the toast. Greta blushed and felt uncomfortable, unsure how to respond.

Adam called, 'Greta, come. Sit with me. Eleanor too.'

The women seated themselves, food was served and Adam bowed his head to deliver the grace.

'We thank God for the sunshine on our plates and in our hearts. We thank Him for bringing us Greta and for the daily gifts He provides us all. Amen.'

Adam covered one of Greta's hands with his and looked deep into her eyes.

'Thank you for helping Eleanor in the garden,' he said. 'I am grateful, but this afternoon, no work. Eleanor will show you around the estate and find you a bed in one of the dormitories. I sincerely hope you will be happy.'

'I'm sure I will be,' Greta said. 'It's very beautiful here.'

'We love it,' Adam said. 'Such a spiritual place. Being tucked away from the madness of society helps us grow. I've always thought personal development is so much more important than rising stock markets and the constant struggle for financial growth. All each of us needs is enough.'

Greta was nodding, agreeing. All her life she'd had more than enough and wasted most of it, couldn't even remember what she'd wasted it on. Adam was right. As long as she had a roof over her head and enough to eat, what more could she want? She tasted some of the vegetable bake, discovered it was delicious and quickly dug in, glad she had refused breakfast at Heatherlea. She relaxed, already knowing in her heart she was going to be happy at the commune and hoped she'd never have to leave.

Chapter three

Freddie Holtz hunched over the computer in his study as Heidi shared what she'd uncovered about The Church of New Eden.

'I haven't been able to find out as much as I hoped,' Heidi began. 'They are remarkably cagey, but I've had some luck. The group was founded just over three years ago by a bloke called Adam Inverdale. He has self-identified as a "messenger", but not provided any clues who he's working for.'

'Some sort of a god I would imagine,' Freddie said, peering at the screen.

'More likely himself,' Erica muttered. 'Until we started looking into this, I didn't appreciate just how much money is involved for those at the top. Some of these organisations are worth billions.'

'Anyway,' Heidi interrupted, 'Adam was running self-improvement seminars for five years prior. A sort of therapy cult. This manifestation works much the same as all the others, but over a shorter period of time and they don't tend to go in for communal living. A four day, very expensive course is about the average.'

'Doing what?' Freddie asked.

'The first three days is usually taken up with confessions and finger-pointing while you're repeatedly told how rubbish you are, how it isn't your fault but your family's, and lots of other crap besides. Then they love-bomb you on the last day and you're hooked.'

'Love bomb?' Freddie queried.

'Exactly as it sounds. Three days breaking you down until you reach what is known as the "snapping point", followed up with a day of love, or "love-bombing" and you belong to them.'

'Sounds like brainwashing to me.'

'That's exactly what it is, Pa, and it's very effective. After five years of seminars, Adam Inverdale disappeared from the scene for twelve months or so then popped up again and founded New Eden.'

'Where is he based now?'

'I'm still working on his location. It appears as though the only way to contact the group in the first instance, if you're not directly recruited, is via the internet and I'm not ready to do that. I don't want them knowing anyone's interested until I'm more clued up.'

'Any closer to finding your sister?'

Heidi shook her head. 'Not yet, but Erica and I are back at work tomorrow, so I can conduct a more in-depth search when I have access to my systems in Brecon cop shop.'

Freddie chuckled and poked a finger in his daughter's ribs. 'They're still putting up with you then?'

'More the other way around,' Heidi grouched, 'but I'm gradually getting used to them and they don't seem to want me out so I'll stay for now.'

'I was chatting to one of my contacts in Wales a week or so ago,' Freddie said. 'Seems you've impressed the powers-that-be with your recent performance so you must be doing something right.' He peered at the screen again. 'Anything else about this cult business I need to know?'

'Yes, Pa, there is.' Heidi took a deep breath, knowing her father didn't like to be told what to do any more than she did. 'If Greta should ring, you must not give her a hard time. Don't say her beliefs are wrong or crazy and don't tell her she's been brainwashed or anything. What you must do is make sure she knows you love her and bite your tongue if she says anything unkind or provocative. In two words, Freddie, be calm.'

'That's ridiculous! I'll demand she comes home, that's what I'll do.'

'And she'll stay away.' Heidi handed her father a folder. 'Read this stuff. I printed it out so you'll know what to do if Greta does get in touch.'

Freddie flipped through the papers and frowned. 'This all seems way over the top to me,' he grumbled. 'It's probably just a phase and she's had heaps of those over the years. Have you turned up any bad news about this group?'

'The odd rumbling here and there, nothing majorly alarming, but we need to be sure what we're dealing with. Don't worry too much, Freddie, Greta has been in prison for months and was able to look after herself inside, plus she's not stupid. I'll have more to tell you tomorrow. In the meantime read through the file in case she contacts you.'

* * *

Heidi and Erica walked into the squad room armed with a bag of pastries from the local bakers on the High Street. Tegan Hedges and Oliver Langdon – recently promoted Detective Constables – were working at the far end, immersed in a stack of paperwork.

Tegan looked up and smiled. 'Hey, you two, good break?'

'Yes thanks,' Erica said. 'What have we missed?'

'A bunch of travellers turned up to squat the main car park in town, but they've gone now, and another *Big Issue* seller was mugged in town a couple of days ago,' Tegan said. 'A Polish lad got beaten up by two blokes. Cash, magazines and a mobile phone stolen.'

'How is he?'

'Still in hospital. Broken jaw and cheekbone, three cracked ribs and the rest of his body is covered in bruises. Looks like a patchwork quilt. He was properly worked over.'

'How many is that now?' Heidi asked.

'He's the third this month.'

'I don't think this is a simple mugging,' Erica muttered, 'too much violence. Muggers only want to stop their victims chasing them, couple of whacks usually does it. I'm sure this is something else. Who's working it?'

'Me and Ollie,' Tegan said. 'We've asked the uniforms to keep an eye out, but haven't really got much to go on. Generic descriptions of the attackers from all three victims, no witnesses and very little in the way of CCTV. We're wondering if there's a racial element; all three were European migrants.'

'Could be,' Heidi mumbled and switched on her system, fingers twitching with anticipation. 'What's your next move?'

'We've an appointment at the magazine's offices later this morning,' Oliver said. 'We're going to talk to the vendors, warn them to be careful and ask if any of the others have had problems. You know how reluctant people can be to report crime. We'll pay our victim a visit in hospital on the way over.'

Heidi glanced up from her screens. 'Either of you ever heard of The Church of New Eden?'

'What's that?' Tegan asked.

'A new religious movement apparently – a cult, in common parlance. They removed a female prisoner from HMP Heatherlea a few days ago without her family's knowledge.'

'How can you remove someone from prison?'

'Pay the outstanding fine and they're free to walk.'

'How did you get involved?' Ollie asked.

'The woman they removed was Heidi's sister,' Erica told him. 'We went to collect her and she'd already left. We haven't been able to find out where she's been taken yet.'

'That's dreadful,' Tegan said. 'You must be really worried. How's your dad dealing with it, Heidi?'

'Like he does everything,' Heidi said. 'Lots of fuss and bluster with a handful of righteous indignation.'

'Can he do anything to help find her?'

Heidi chuckled. 'Plenty, but how much would be useful…' She rattled the keyboard and woke up her computer. 'What time was your *Big Issue* seller attacked?'

'Just after eleven at night. No idea why he was out so late.'

'Trying to pick up trade at closing time?'

'Yeah, maybe. Poor sod got more than he bargained for.'

'OK. Give me the papers and leave me alone for a while to get up to speed. Have we got any forensics to work with, Tegan?'

'Some very patchy CCTV footage, nothing else.'

Heidi nodded, immersed herself in cyberspace and began work.

Erica stood. 'Let's make the visits, Ollie. Tegan, you stay here and man the phones, give Heidi some space to work. If we're lucky she might find something on the security cameras.'

Chapter four

Erica and Oliver were directed to the third floor of Brecon County Hospital where they found the victim tucked away in a side ward. He looked up when they walked in. Erica gasped, appalled at the state of his face.

One eye was swollen to the size of a rounders ball, lids gummed together, the other barely cracked open. His cheek was a colour of vermillion Erica didn't think she'd seen before and his jaw a mixture of purple and yellow. A bandage covered his chin. He raised a hand, also heavily bandaged.

'Are you Alex?' Erica asked.

The man nodded slowly and painfully.

'I'm DS Bevan and this is DC Langdon. We'd like to interview you about the attack. Are you well enough to speak with us?'

Alex nodded again and waved his hand towards two plastic chairs by the side of the bed. The officers sat and Oliver flipped open a notebook.

'I know this is a daft question, but how are you?' Erica asked. 'Is there anything we can do for you?'

'I need nothing,' the injured man mumbled. 'I only need to get out of here.'

'I'm sure they'll let you leave soon. The nurses say you're doing very well considering the pounding you took. Do you have a last name?'

'Just Alex. You don't need to know me. When I leave here, I go home. UK not as good place as I thought.'

'Where is home?' Oliver asked.

'Poland.'

'Did you see who attacked you?'

'It was dark. I see two men, nothing more.'

'Can you give us any description at all?' Erica asked. 'What they were wearing? Were they tall? Short…?'

'I tell other police. Two men. Medium tall. Dark shirts, army trousers and big boots.' He winced. 'Very big boots.'

'Did they say anything to you? Was there a reason for them to attack you?'

Alex shook his head. 'Nothing. I sell magazines. The men come, they hit me, kick me on floor, take my things and go. I know nothing else.'

'Anyone else see them?'

'I don't know. Young girl find me, she call ambulance.'

'Do you know her?'

'No. I never see her. She save my life. When can I leave here?'

'I'll ask the nurse, but they won't keep you in any longer than they have to, trust me. Do you live in town?'

'I have place.'

'We'll need the address,' Erica said gently.

'No, you don't need. I tell you already. I get out, I go home.'

'When we catch these individuals we'll need you to give evidence in court, be a witness so we can lock them up in prison.'

'If you catch them. If! Two others beaten like me. Two! You haven't caught thieves yet.'

'Did the same men attack all of you?'

'How I know? I only there for one attack.' Alex sighed heavily. 'I know you try to help, but I'm tired. Please go and ask nurse when I can leave.'

Erica nodded and got to her feet. 'You rest now, but if you need us, just call the station.'

The officers walked down the corridor to the nurses' station and passed on Alex's message before heading to the car park.

'That poor lad,' Erica said. 'He got a proper working over.'

'Be helpful if we knew his surname and where he spends the nights.'

'It would, but he doesn't have to tell us and he's a *Big Issue* seller so probably doesn't have an address.' Erica sighed. 'I'm even more convinced this isn't a straightforward mugging, this is something else.'

'Could just be a couple of locals who had too much beer on a Saturday night and rounded things off with a punch-up, this is Wales. Maybe they thought Alex was English. There's parts of North Wales where it's still legal to shoot the English after midnight.'

'Don't be daft, Ollie.'

'That's true that is. My granddad told me.'

'Just drive us to the magazine's offices and stop talking crap.'

* * *

The acolytes gathered in the old ballroom for a group meditation. This was the first service Greta had attended and she was excited. It was an odd feeling, like her bones were fizzing. She realised nothing had really energised her for years, not like this anyway.

The large room was thick with the sweet scent of incense from bundles of sticks in burners. Wispy blue smoke curled languidly towards the ceiling, illuminated by weak sunshine, filtered through narrow, stained-glass windows. The walls were covered with bright hangings, eastern looking, exotic, and large parlour palms stood in the corners. At the far end of the room was a raised platform. Adam sat cross-legged in the centre of the dais and smiled as the group assembled in front of him. He lowered his arms and the congregation sank onto red cushions, faces turned towards their leader.

Greta gazed around the room trying to take it all in. With the hangings, the incense burners and coloured glass windows, it was more like being inside a church than a ballroom, and Adam sat on the altar. Nearly thirty people squatted on floor cushions, all smiling. More than smiling, they looked rapturous, entranced. Pixie pulled Greta to the left and pointed to a space. Greta sat, crossed her legs, rested her hands in her lap as the others were doing and looked up at Adam.

'Friends.' Adam began in an intense whisper. 'Welcome.' He smiled and the congregation smiled back. 'Here is peace. Here is love. Here is contentment.'

The others repeated the phrases like a chant.

Adam continued, 'Everything else must be left beyond the door or shared in this room.' Adam glanced at his audience, eyes settling briefly on each face until they reached Greta. 'Greta – our newest member – we welcome you to share with us.'

Every eye turned towards her and for an awful moment Greta thought she might faint. Adam had no idea how she hated being the centre of attention. This was too much and it wasn't fair. She couldn't be expected to say anything in front of so many people she didn't know. She struggled to her feet and panic bubbled in her throat. Pixie placed a hand on her arm, Eleanor did the same and squeezed encouragingly, but still Greta baulked. What was she supposed to say? Adam obviously wasn't asking for a happy story, a peaceful story. What could she tell a room full of strangers about her life? How to begin?

Greta opened her mouth and blurted, 'I whacked a copper and was rude to a judge who sent me to prison.'

Adam clapped his hands from the platform and the others joined in, a few made whooping noises. Greta was encouraged so added more detail. 'The copper deserved it and now I come to think about it, so did the judge!'

A ripple of laughter ran through the assembled company.

'Cause and effect,' Adam said loudly and recaptured their attention. 'A form of instant karma which nearly always catches us out so I ask, is this story really funny?'

The room fell silent and the congregation shifted uneasily on their cushions.

'Greta, why did you hit the police officer?' Adam asked.

'He pulled my friend's hair,' she said. 'We were at a demo and things got lively. The police overreacted and scuffles broke out. I saw one of them rip out some of

Mandy's hair, so I whacked him on the nose.' She paused. 'Surely that was his "instant karma", or whatever you call it?'

'Quite possibly,' Adam agreed, 'but in the process you stored up some for yourself. Violence can never be justified. Not content, you cheeked a judge and he handed you a six-month custodial sentence. Instant, but long-lasting karma.'

The disciples tittered and Greta felt her face burn with shame. Everyone was staring at her and she didn't know what to say. She shuffled her feet and gazed down at Eleanor, but she was looking at Adam; so was Pixie. Greta was suddenly very alone in a room full of people. She wanted to cry and her lip trembled.

'Look for the good in the bad,' Adam intoned from the front of the room. 'Don't despair, Greta. Karma isn't bad, it's just necessary. Without the policeman and the judge, you wouldn't have found your way to New Eden. Was the price you paid worth the benefit?'

Greta felt herself nodding, as tears ran down her cheeks. Relief and understanding flooded through her soul, and once again the people in the room applauded.

'Life only sends you the lessons you need to learn and grow,' Adam said. 'Recognising those lessons, that's the trick. Well done, beloved. Does anyone else have anything to share?'

Adam looked around the room expectantly and Greta relaxed, knowing she wouldn't be called on again. She sank to her cushion, curious to hear some of the others speak.

A dark, skinny lad got to his feet. He looked like a gypsy, a young David Essex look-alike with a thick gold earring in one ear, dressed in jeans and striped shirt, a red neckerchief tied at his neck.

'Felix,' – Adam smiled broadly – 'what do you have to share with us?'

Felix shifted his weight from foot to foot, reluctant to speak and when he did he mumbled, 'I rang Mum.'

Greta heard a gentle intake of breath as though the room had sighed. All faces turned towards Felix who looked even more uncomfortable. Greta wondered why contacting his mother had garnered such a response. Adam said nothing and continued to smile encouragingly.

'I wanted to find out how she was, you know?' Felix said. 'It's been nearly three years since I left and wanted to let her know I was OK; find out how things were at home.'

'Was she pleased to hear from you?' Adam asked.

'Yeah, she cried. I cried too. It's been a long time.'

'Was she happy for you?'

'No, not really, told me I should go home, said she was missing me and I must go back. She told me that…' he hesitated.

'Go on,' Adam prompted.

'That this place was bad. That I was stupid and had been brainwashed.'

A few of the group protested and Adam held up his hand for quiet.

'What did you say?' he asked.

'Not much. I told her I left because of her and wasn't going back. That my life was here, in New Eden. She yelled then, lost it completely and I hung up. I withheld the number.' He added quickly. 'She doesn't know where I am and won't be able to call back.'

'Do you want her to call?'

'No. I want to stay here and for her to leave me alone.'

Felix sat down as the group clapped and Adam held his arms out to his sides and addressed the group.

'Do you see, my beloved? This tale is a perfect example of what I teach and proves I speak the truth. Felix's mother should have been overjoyed to hear from her son after so long, don't you agree?'

Mumbled assent floated around the room.

'Yet within minutes she is shouting at him, trying to tell him what to do, trying to take control of his life again. You owe your parents nothing, remember that, nothing! It was they who wanted children and when they had some, what did they do?' He gazed around the room. 'Never forget, everything you do has consequences. You must be mindful and pay attention or you could miss the most important lessons of your life.' Adam sat on his cushion and held his right arm aloft. 'Now, I will lead you in guided meditation. Silent body, silent mind with only love and light in your hearts.'

Gradually the group settled and quietude descended on the room. Greta was sure she could hear everyone breathing. She felt strangely peaceful, even though she had just confessed to a room full of strangers she'd been in prison. She realised no one had judged her. Thanks to Adam she understood why she had been sent to jail, not for punishment but because incarceration was the start of her path. She knew she didn't need to feel ashamed or lie about her past. Prison was just one of the life lessons that had led her to this place, the church, and Adam.

* * *

Heidi and Erica slouched on either end of the long sofa in Heidi's basement flat, and massaged each other's feet, while a cello solo, performed by Jacqueline du Pré, floated from the speakers.

'Keep your feet still,' Erica complained. 'I can't rub your toes properly when I have to chase them about.'

'Sorry,' Heidi mumbled, 'but you must admit, she was bloody good.'

'Is she dead then?'

Heidi pinched Erica's little toe as the phone rang and reached behind her head to pick it up. 'Speak first, you're paying.'

'Heidi? Is that you?'

'Hi, Freddie. Sorry, I'm in a funny mood.'

'Aren't you always?' he grumbled. 'I've been expecting you to ring and tell me what you've found out about Greta.'

'Oh, yes. We've just finished supper and it slipped my mind.'

'Is Erica there? Do give her my best regards. Now, tell me, what have you discovered?'

'Depressingly little. I've been wading through reams of junk in cyberspace. One of the tactics cults use in this digital age is to fill the first internet search pages with stuff they sanction, any useful info gets pushed so far down the list people don't bother to look. This New Eden crowd have posted so much crap it's slowing the process down.'

'Have you found anything useful?'

'More background on Adam Inverdale; it seems he probably spent his missing year in an ashram in Southern India, Kerala way. There's a rumour he was there to dry out.'

'What?'

'Detoxify the Asian way. Some of these places specialise in cleaning up heroin addicts, but as I said, that's only a rumour.'

'Don't pass on gossip, that isn't useful. Tell me about Greta?' Freddie blustered. 'Where's your sister? Do you know?'

'I have an idea, might have tracked down the group's main commune site, but I want to be sure before we consider doing anything else. Has Greta contacted you?'

'No, she hasn't.' Freddie hesitated. 'Heidi, what if we can't find her? What will your mother say?'

'Who cares what she'll say?' Heidi growled. 'You? Got to go now, Pa, I'll be in touch.'

Heidi threw the phone away from her and rubbed her partner's feet furiously.

'Ow,' Erica yelped. 'Steady on, love, I need them for walking in the morning. What's up?'

'Nothing.'

Erica raised an eyebrow.

'Freddie gets on my nerves sometimes, that's all. Most of Whitehall jumps when he tells it to and he thinks I'll do the same.'

'He's probably just worried about your sister, bound to be. Aren't you?'

'Of course, just not as worried as he appears to be, and that's odd because Freddie doesn't really do worried. There's no need anyway, Greta has always been able to look after herself. I don't see her as being easy to brainwash, she's far too strong-minded and fairly intelligent, even if she hides it well.'

'Anyone can be brainwashed,' Erica said. 'I've been doing some reading in my spare time and it's frightening. Seems you're more of a target for a cult if you have a brain. So many people from all backgrounds get caught up in stuff like this. I was reading a blog written by a guy who'd been involved with a ghastly lot in America. You can tell by what he writes he's still not over his experience yet and that was fifteen years ago. Has Greta called home?'

Heidi shook her head and struggled out of the squashy sofa. 'Coffee?'

'Please.' Erica followed her to the kitchen. 'What are you planning to do when we find Greta, walk in and take her home? Cos if that's what you're thinking, it won't work, and the longer Greta is there, the more difficult her extraction will become.'

'I'll think of something. Anyway, I still reckon she'll see through any cult malarkey in no time and leave. Can't see Greta falling for anything like that – ever!'

Chapter five

'I've tracked down the girl who called the ambulance for the *Big Issue* seller on Saturday night,' Heidi suddenly announced from her corner of the squad room.

'How did you manage that?' Tegan asked. 'There wasn't a record of her name anywhere and her number wasn't captured during the 999 call – she withheld it.'

Heidi grinned, she loved astounding colleagues with her peculiar brain. 'Everything is captured somewhere,' she explained, 'no such thing as privacy anymore. We had the exact time of the call, so overnight I asked my system to track every call made at precisely that time to the emergency services, anywhere in the country. By various rounds of elimination, the system pared those calls down to one – a mobile contracted to Miss Geri Skinner, fifteen years old and out on the streets of Brecon way too late. My guess is her parents thought she was safely tucked up with a schoolmate somewhere and that's why she didn't leave her name.' Heidi tapped her keyboard and a school photo of a pretty girl with red hair, green eyes and freckles filled the screen. 'I've spoken to her headmistress and I'm popping over to the school for a chat, find out if Geri has any useful information.'

'We ought to interview her properly,' Erica said. 'Take a statement.'

'Let's wait and see what she has to say, if anything. Keep things friendly and try to leave angry, aggrieved parents out of it for now. Might be more useful.'

Erica nodded. 'OK. Worth a try. Ollie and I will speak with the other victims again and check in on Alex, just in case he's remembered anything more. Tegan, if you could…'

'Yeah, I know, "man the office", although if I'm honest, I prefer "woman the office".'

Heidi snorted with laughter, pushed past Erica and ran down the stairs. She discovered an unmarked car going begging in the yard and drove to Pantycelyn High School on the edge of town. She pulled up in a space at the rear of the car park and wandered towards the main entrance and reception. She was booked in, pointed in the direction of the headmistress' office, and set off through the maze of corridors.

A large man strode round the corner of the carpeted tunnel and stared at Heidi.

'Why are you out of class, girl?' he demanded. 'Where are you supposed to be?'

Heidi smirked, knew her distinctive appearance and small stature had confused him and held up her warrant card.

'DC Holtz. The headmistress is expecting me. Can you provide directions?' Her upper-class vowels bounced off the walls, the man spluttered and tried unsuccessfully to regain some composure.

'Ah, sorry. Miss Beech? Yes. Left at the end here, third door on the right.' He paused then asked, 'Have we, uh, got a problem, officer?'

'I haven't, sir, have you?' Heidi glared at the man until he strode quickly away. She didn't care much for teachers, never having come across many who seemed to have anything worthwhile to teach her. She cracked her knuckles and went in search of Beech's office.

She located the correct door, tapped and walked in.

'Miss Beech? Detective Constable Holtz, we spoke on the phone earlier. I'm here to have a word with Geri Skinner – with her permission of course.' Heidi flopped in a spare chair and looked expectantly at the older woman, recognised the shock on her face and as always, it amused her. She could never make up her mind whether it was her size that confused people, her short white hair or her clothes, usually black from top to bottom.

'Ah, Constable Holtz,' Miss Beech said. 'I wasn't expecting you so soon. I suppose I should really check your identity, I mean…'

Heidi waved her wallet under the head's nose and said, 'If you could arrange a meeting with Geri that would be marvellous. I am fairly busy.'

Miss Beech fiddled with her phone, nervous fingers not cooperating and finally managed to arrange for Geri to report to the office. After an uncomfortable wait, Geri knocked on the door. The headmistress introduced Heidi to the student and sat in a corner of the room, looking as though she wished she was somewhere else. The teenager sat nervously on the edge of a plastic chair.

'Hi, Geri. I'm Heidi.'

'Miss Beech said you are a copper. Are you really? You don't look anything like one.'

'Good!' Heidi said. 'Must be bloody awful being a copper and looking like one.'

Geri giggled.

'Are you happy to talk to me today?' Heidi asked.

'Fine. I guess you're here because of the other night.'

'Which other night?'

Geri hesitated. 'Look, I'm OK talking to you, like, but you mustn't say anything to me mam. She didn't know I was out, so I haven't told her about any of this. Please don't drop me in it. Trust me, she'll go mental and I didn't do anything really. Just, like, called the ambulance.'

'You quite possibly saved a young man's life,' Heidi said. 'He was in a bad way and if you hadn't helped him he might have died. I think your mam would be proud of you.'

'Nah, she'd still be mad. I was supposed to be somewhere else. Could he really have, like, died?'

'Maybe. Someone gave him a good going over.'

'I heard it before I saw it,' Geri said quietly, remembering. 'I was walking to me mate's, heard a right old row in Market Street and saw two blokes kicking someone on the ground.'

'Wait a minute, you saw the attack?'

'Some of it. I screamed at them to leave him alone and they legged it. I was shit scared when I saw all the blood and called 999. As soon as the ambulance turned up at the end of the street, I legged it too. How did you track me down? I didn't leave my name or anything.'

Heidi tapped her nose. 'I have ways. Why did you run?'

'I knew he'd be OK with the paramedics and like I said, I wasn't supposed to be there.'

Heidi nodded. 'I get it, but you did good. Now tell me, what did these scumbags look like? Did you recognise either of them?'

Geri giggled. 'You sound like a copper when you call people scumbags. Didn't see them properly, sorry, just two blokes picking on a smaller bloke. It was dark so I couldn't see much, but think they were wearing, like, camouflage trousers.'

'Any chance they were squaddies from Sennybridge Barracks?'

Geri shrugged. 'Dunno, just seemed like two pissed blokes looking for a punch-up. You know how men are sometimes. They didn't hang about when they knew someone was watching. Bloody cowards.'

'You got that right,' Heidi said. 'Thanks, Geri, you've been very helpful and well done. I can't see any reason why we need to mention this to your mam, but I think you should tell her. Once she gets over being pissed off because you were out late, she'll be proud of you.' Heidi took a card from her pocket and handed it over. 'My mobile number is on there, as well as the office. If you think of anything else, or just want a chat, call me, anytime. Take care, kid.'

* * *

Back at the station, Heidi typed up her notes before turning her attention to the small amount of CCTV footage relating to the mugging. The images had been gathered from the town centre four nights ago and covered the time of the attack. She began working through the tapes frame by frame, hunting for useful clues.

As she worked, she thought about Greta and wondered what was going on with her. Erica asked recently if the two of them were close and if Heidi was honest the answer was no, not since the trouble. Heidi pushed the thought from her head and concentrated on the why. Why had Greta been taken in so easily by an organisation like New Eden? The Holtz family had never been religious, she couldn't remember the last time she stood in a church, if not at a family funeral or a wedding. Same for Greta, so why had she joined an outfit like this now? It didn't make any sense.

Heidi checked the background programs running on her system, harvesting information about The Church of New Eden and uncovering Adam Inverdale's past. Everything she had discovered about the man so far was history, nothing recent or current and that was strange. Inverdale had one of the smallest digital footprints she had come across. There were countless Facebook pages for his church, and pages and pages of fairly meaningless information relating to the philosophy and beliefs of his 'religion', but Inverdale had left little of himself in cyberspace. After hours of work, Heidi hadn't been able to find out anything personal about the man, not even whether he had a family.

On the plus side, she had discovered the cult ran a small chain of herbalist shops in quaint market towns throughout the Cotswolds. Things were set up to look as though the shops provided the income for the church, but she was fairly certain the business was a front. No way could a smattering of tiny niche shops keep a group like New Eden going and the more she read about the cult, the more uneasy she grew. She needed to return to the Cotswolds soon, visit the shops, check out the possible location of New Eden's commune and talk to Freddie.

Chapter six

Oliver opened the driver's door, handed Erica a paper bag, wedged two steaming mugs of tea in cup holders and settled himself behind the steering wheel.

'Got you a burger with everything,' he said. 'Tea, two sugars.'

'Ta, Ollie.' Erica unwrapped her food and took a large bite. 'God, I needed this, I'm starving.'

'What do we do now, Sarge?'

'Not much we can do if we can't locate any victims. I wasn't overly surprised when we couldn't track down the first two. Brexit is stirring everything up big time and encouraging people to move.' She sipped her tea. 'But was very surprised when the ward sister told us Alex had left. I have no idea how he managed to get himself out of hospital though. Didn't look in a fit state to go anywhere when we saw him.'

'So we forget the whole thing and get on with other stuff?' Oliver asked. 'That means the muggers will get away with it and that's not right.'

'No, it isn't, but I can't think what else we can do. I'll have a word with DI James when we get back to the nick.'

A shout dragged their attention to a small group of men standing by the edge of the industrial estate's car park. Half a dozen hefty looking builder-types were squaring up and it wasn't long before the shoving began. Erica rested her half-eaten burger on the dashboard.

'Come on, Ollie, let's see what that's all about.'

They reached the group just before the first punch was thrown.

'Oi, Oi, lads! Pack it in!' Erica positioned herself between the groups, warrant card on display, Oliver at her shoulder. 'What's going on here? Speak up, someone, for God's sake. My lunch is getting cold.'

The men stared at their boots and shuffled dirt around. Erica moved closer to the smallest man.

'Well?' she demanded.

'Nothing's going on,' he mumbled.

'And you must think I'm blind!'

She glared at them until a tall man, with a strong South Walian accent, spoke up, 'Bit of a disagreement, officer, nothing serious.'

Erica turned to face him. 'You are?'

'Jon Williams, foreman for this lot. We're repointing the cathedral tower in town.'

'What are they scrapping about?'

Williams chuckled. 'Overtime, always the same thing.'

'Well, settle things like adults next time.' Erica turned on her heel and headed back to the car and her tepid burger.

'Bloody builders,' she grumbled. 'Why are men so quick with their fists?'

'Not just men, Sarge. I worked a nightshift in Cardiff a month or so ago. Squads of pissed up girls scratching each other like tigers at the slightest provocation. Bloody scary. Mind you, good for us they do. Means we'll always have a job.'

Erica stared at him. 'Are you for real?' She scrunched up her empty bag and lobbed it accurately into a rubbish bin. 'Get us back to the nick and we'll find out what the boss wants us to do with the case now.'

* * *

'You haven't been able to find a single victim?' Detective Inspector Ben James asked incredulously. 'Not even the poor sod in the hospital?'

'No, sir,' Erica answered. 'He checked out soon after we spoke to him, told us he was intending to return to Poland when he left hospital. Perhaps he's already gone.'

'What's the story with the others?'

'We think they've probably left for home as well. We checked at the magazine's offices and neither have been seen recently. One of the other sellers confirmed they were planning to go home.'

'We ought to be able to prove if they've left the country.'

'Yes, sir, we should, but… we never get very far with the Border Agency. Takes weeks to get anything useful out of them.'

'Ask Heidi if she can help. We have a duty to these lads and who's to say our local bully boys won't have another go?'

'Nothing,' Erica agreed.

'Do we have any idea who they are? Any witnesses or useful CCTV?'

Erica shook her head. 'Not so far.'

'We must at least try to tie up loose ends,' Ben said. 'Have a word with the uniforms, ask if anyone has heard anything on the street. The guilty parties might have been bragging – you know how stupid people can be – and keep me up to date.'

'I will, sir.' She paused. 'How's Stacey?'

'She's good, thanks. We ought to arrange a social, get the team together. Things have just been so mad lately.'

'I'm sure everyone would enjoy that.'

Ben groaned. 'I'm still bogged down with the internal inquiry surrounding the slavery case, so the get-together won't be any time soon. Feels like I'm bog snorkelling without a bloody snorkel.'

'How is the investigation going?'

Ben rubbed his face. 'Who can tell… OK I guess, but I am guessing. At least we're nearing the end now and a good result will mean I can get back to proper policing. Anything else going on? Did I hear something about Heidi?'

Erica nodded reluctantly. 'Yeah, her sister's got mixed up with a cult and gone missing.'

Ben chuckled. 'Are we talking about Greta? The one who whacked a copper? Sounds like she can look after herself.'

'Maybe, but I find it difficult to believe she'd just go off with a gang of people she'd only known a couple of hours. The Church of New Eden was allowed inside the prison where Greta was serving her sentence. They obviously spoke to her and a couple of days later they returned, paid the outstanding fine and the prison released her. She hasn't been in touch with her family since she left.'

'Surely there aren't any cults around anymore? That was all very late twentieth century.'

'The research I've been doing suggests they are more of a problem now with maybe 1,500 or so operating in the UK. Heidi has been collating information about this bunch – in her own time of course, sir. It all looks dodgy and no one's been able to satisfactorily prove how the commune finances itself. The church does run a few small herbalist shops in the Cotswolds, but no way do they bring in enough to keep the commune going.'

'Not on our patch though, is it? Not by a long way.'

'No, it isn't, but I can't see any harm in allowing Heidi to work on this, as long as the rest of her cases are kept up to date. You know how well she can multi-task.'

Ben nodded.

'I don't like the circumstances of Greta's disappearance – voluntary or not,' Erica said, 'and Heidi's pa, Frederick Holtz, is worried. Wouldn't hurt to look into this for him, would it? Never know when we might need a word in the right place, if you understand me, sir.'

Ben grinned. 'Perfectly. OK then, but keep me up to date. After my last little freelancing adventure the brass will go potty if we get involved in anything similar again.'

'Yes, sir. Meanwhile, I'll get out and about, see if I can learn anything about our muggers. Be good to take them off the streets.'

Erica walked upstairs to the squad room and helped herself to coffee from the machine.

'Right then, gang,' she said. 'DI James doesn't want us to pull stumps on the investigation yet. As he quite rightly points out, we may not have our victims to hand, but if we don't nick these bastards we could end up with more casualties. Heidi, try to confirm if any of the injured have left the area or the country, and keep on with the CCTV stuff. Ollie, get out on the streets and talk to the uniforms, ask if anyone has heard anything, knows anything or saw anything. Dig around a little. Tegan…'

'Yeah, I know.'

Erica grinned. 'You don't, actually. I'd like you to come with me to talk to the magazine sellers and we'll check with their office in case Alex has turned up. He may have been able to walk away from hospital, but I'm sure he wouldn't be able to make the journey home without more recuperation. Logic says he must be in town somewhere.'

Heidi hissed at Erica as the others left the room. 'Did you tell Ben about Greta?'

'Had to, he asked. Says it's OK to work on it, but definitely doesn't want you going off-piste, not after the mess earlier in the year. I don't either. You must keep me informed of what you're up to.'

'OK. I'm planning a visit to New Eden's shops in the next few days, Cotswolds way. Fancy coming along if you can get some time off? Thought I'd call in on Freddie at the same time.'

'Of course. We'll talk tonight.'

Chapter seven

Greta yawned as she weeded between rosemary bushes in the herb garden. Eleanor, who was cutting comfrey, noticed and giggled.

'You're not quite used to the early starts yet, are you?' she asked.

'It's not the early starts,' Greta said, 'it's the meditation sessions at two in the morning. I just get to sleep, then up again for an hour, then back to bed for another couple of hours snoozing before I have to wake up properly. Getting up early isn't a problem. I've been in jail for the last three months, don't forget.'

Eleanor frowned at her and said, 'You should.'

'What?'

'Forget you've been to jail.' Eleanor sounded cross. 'You should only carry memories about your life at New Eden, not anywhere else. Let it go, Greta. You know what Adam says, "breathe it away".'

'I know, but it's difficult to change my way of thinking overnight. This is all so new to me. I'm trying as hard as I can.'

Eleanor suddenly smiled. 'I know you are and you're doing really well. Don't worry, you'll soon get used to the timetable. Everyone finds it a bit of a struggle at the beginning, but it'll be worth it, you'll see.'

'I already see. Everyone here is happy, I've never seen so many smiling faces. I wondered for a while if you were all on drugs.' Greta chuckled and Eleanor joined in. 'Of course, I can see you're not. Everything works well here and we have all we need. I don't know why more people don't live like this.'

'Because they are all stuck in their old ways, the old systems. Anything new or radical frightens them. Adam has a vision and with his teachings and guidance we're making it work. Are you happy here?'

'Never been happier. I know I shouldn't talk about my old life, but it was difficult. I had a fairly privileged upbringing, didn't want for anything, but never felt like I fit in. I guess that's why I ended up where I did, a spoilt child playing up, wanting attention. I fit in here, I can feel it.'

'I'm so pleased for you. This is a great place and we're very lucky to be given the chance to live here.'

Greta dug out some deeply rooted dandelions, grunting with effort. 'I've never seen such an extensive herb garden. Looks like you got just about everything here.'

'We have, pretty much. The income the garden generates pays the running costs for the hall. We have a few shops scattered around and stock them with produce from the garden. Joe and Mack dry and pack the herbs, and Mala and Clover make hand creams, tinctures, salves, that sort of thing.'

'You have an herbalist called Clover?' Greta giggled.

'Yeah, great, isn't it? They live and work in one of the cottages. I'll take you over later so you can see how it all works.'

'Who lives in the other places?'

'Joe and Mack live in one and the other is rented out.'

'What, like a holiday cottage?'

'No, not quite.' Eleanor laughed. 'More of a hermitage for people who want to escape the rat race. We had one guy who stayed nearly a year and in all that time I only saw him once.'

'Don't the visitors attend Adam's meditations?'

'They can if they wish, but don't always. There's someone in there now I think, so I can't show you inside.'

Eleanor stripped off her gardening gloves and hauled herself upright.

'Gotta be tea-break time, so we'll deliver the comfrey to the boys and beg hot drinks from the girls.'

After tying string around bristly stems, Eleanor led the way through the garden to the courtyard behind the hall. The September morning was unseasonably warm and bees and butterflies clustered around the last summer flowers. Greta took deep breaths of the clean air. As each day passed she felt more relaxed and with the feeling came happiness. It was so easy to live here. Up until this point, her life had seemed so complex, so difficult. There was always someone – Pa mainly – nagging at her to do something, but whenever she did, no one liked what she did. She thought about her father and guessed she should call, not to tell him she was OK – he wouldn't care – but the call would prevent him sending out search parties. Greta didn't want anyone turning up at New Eden to drag her home. Could someone do that, she wondered, if she was here voluntarily? She made up her mind to talk to Pixie in the dorm later.

As they neared the open door of the largest cottage, Eleanor called, 'Mack, Joe! We've brought the comfrey for you.'

A short dumpy man in his early fifties appeared in the doorway, relieved Eleanor of her bundle and thanked her in a broad Scottish accent. The top of his head was completely bald, a thick fringe of hair surrounded the baldness. Greta thought if he dressed in a monk's habit, he'd pass for Friar Tuck any day of the week.

'Hi, both,' he said. 'Good to see you. Come in and say hi to Joe, he's busy with the drying racks.'

Greta ducked her head and entered a hot, gloomy room, so full of fragrance her eyes watered.

'Wow,' she spluttered. 'It's strong in here.' She blinked and spotted a man, who must be Joe, spreading layers of cut herbs on mesh racks hanging from chains attached to ceiling beams. He was very tall and incredibly thin, knobbly, with deep brown skin like the disgusting, biscuity-stick things people ate at Christmas. In his forties, he wore a vest and shorts, arms covered with tattoos of black Celtic designs, hair long and in dreadlocks. He stepped away from the rack, pulled on a chain and hauled it above his head.

'Hello, Greta.' He spoke with a northern accent. 'Eleanor giving you a guided tour at last?'

'We waited for it to stop raining,' Eleanor protested. 'No fun splashing around the place in the mud, not when Greta and I are out in it all day.'

'Fair point,' Joe admitted. 'So, Greta, do you like what you've seen of New Eden?'

'I don't like it, I love it. The place, the people, everything. I feel so relaxed here, even in the rain.'

'You're not alone, that's how we all feel. No one ever wants to leave.'

'Well, we're leaving you,' Eleanor said. 'Off to beg tea from the girls. See you later.'

Eleanor set off across the courtyard towards a twin of the cottage they'd just left. A young woman worked outside, stirring the contents of a large pot hanging over a fire in a stone pit. She was dressed in a pair of colourful dungarees, had short blonde hair, a shy smile and was heavily pregnant. She spotted the women when they were still halfway across the yard and waved.

'Hi, Clover,' Eleanor called. 'Is Mala in?'

Clover nodded. 'She's bottling up, go on in.'

Greta walked inside the cottage and found it very different from the hot dark cave on the opposite side of the yard. The large kitchen was light and airy, doors and windows propped open to allow the early autumn breeze to swirl through. Working at a stainless-steel sink was a slim woman, decanting straw-coloured liquid from a jug into small bottles. Her hair was long and candle-straight, ends stained henna-red. She wore a long, voluminous skirt and baggy tie-dyed top. Placing the jug on the drainer, she wiped her hands on her apron and turned to welcome the visitors, a quirky lopsided smile curled her full lips.

'Good morning. How are you both?' Mala asked. 'Glowing from the sunshine I see. Would you like some tea?'

'Yes please,' Eleanor said and settled herself at the large table.

'I'll make a pot of my special mix. Greta, do sit down, it's good to see you.'

'Thank you.'

Greta chose a spot near the door and watched as Mala spooned what looked like dried herbs from a tin into a large teapot. Clover walked in and joined them at the table.

Mala glanced at her. 'How are you getting on, my lovely?' she asked.

'OK I guess, but my ankles are swelling again.'

'You should sit down more often.'

'When's your baby due?' Greta asked.

'About three weeks,' Clover mumbled.

'You must be really excited. Are you going to hospital for the birth?'

'No, I'm staying here.'

Mala placed the teapot and a cluster of mugs on the table. 'Home births are the best way,' she said. 'Clover was born at home, so her baby should be.' Mala poured tea and handed out mugs.

'Are you mother and daughter?' Greta asked.

Mala smiled. 'Yes, we are.'

'Have you arranged a midwife?'

'No, we have our own, Winnie, it's what she did in her old life. She'll take care of Clover. We're a closed community and prefer to be self-sufficient.'

Mala almost sounded dismissive and Greta didn't feel she could ask anything about the baby's father, so sipped her tea and studied the room. She saw bottles and jars stacked on shelves, large cardboard boxes on the floor beneath, presumably filled with finished products. Several mounds of multicoloured labels covered a side table, a few spilled on the flagstone floor.

'This tea is gorgeous,' Greta said. 'What's in it?'

Mala smiled. 'Bit of this and that, secret recipe. I'm glad you like it.'

Greta drank some more, then asked, 'What do you make here?'

'Hand creams and skin lotions are our biggest sellers. We use wax from the beehives and lavender from the garden. We also make tinctures, herbal cures for just about everything.'

'Eleanor told me you sell the goods in your own shops. How many do you have?'

'Three now. We used to wholesale the herbs and did OK, but make more money retailing. It was Adam's idea, we opened the first outlet about eighteen months ago. It was so successful we opened the others soon after.' She glanced at her watch. 'Look at the time! If we don't get a scoot on, we'll miss the morning session. Clover, take the pot off the fire, quickly now or we'll be late. See you there, ladies.'

As Eleanor headed towards the hall, Greta asked, 'Is Clover's partner a member of New Eden?'

Eleanor frowned at her. 'Does it matter?'

'I suppose not,' Greta muttered and they walked the rest of the way in silence.

Chapter eight

Tegan parked the car in a space outside a block of shabby flats in a rundown area on the edge of Brecon.

'Do you really think we'll find Alex, Sarge?' she asked.

Erica peered at a crumpled scrap of paper. 'According to Ollie and his informant. Number six, I think. Christ, his handwriting is dreadful. Is that a six?'

Tegan nodded. 'Looks like it.'

'OK then, let's check it out.'

The main entrance door was propped open with a brick and the officers set off upstairs to find the flat. Erica rang the bell and the door was opened almost immediately by a small, dark woman, dressed in jeans and a black knitted jumper. Overly long sleeves obscured her hands.

'Yes? Can I help you?' she asked in a foreign accent.

'I'm DS Bevan from Brecon station,' – Erica held out her wallet so the woman could read her credentials – 'and this is DC Hedges. We're looking for a man called Alex. We've been told he may be staying here.'

'Why you want him? He in trouble?'

'No, not at all. Is he here?'

The woman nodded reluctantly and stepped to one side of the door. Erica and Tegan squeezed past and walked through the hall to a small living room. Alex was lying on a lumpy looking sofa, propped up with pillows and covered by a blanket. He peered at the officers from between bruised, swollen eyelids. He recognised Erica and groaned.

'Why you here? I tell you in hospital I have nothing to say.'

Erica perched on the corner of the coffee table and faced Alex. 'We've come to check on you, make sure you're OK, that's all.' She nodded towards the woman standing in the doorway. 'Is she your partner?'

'No. Just friend. Sally. She take care of me.'

'You should tell them,' Sally said. 'Then they help.'

Alex shook his head. 'No, they can't help.'

'They are police. They must know.'

'Make things worse. I not say.'

'Other people get hurt.'

Alex grunted and sank deeper under the blanket.

Sally stomped into the room. 'Then I tell if you won't. The Nazis beat him.'

Erica stared at Sally. 'Nazis?'

'Yes. They beat others too. Threaten, say to go home. They tell Alex go home, he stay and they beat him.'

Erica glanced back at Alex's damaged face. 'Why didn't you tell us? If we don't know what happened, how do we stand a chance of making any arrests to take these thugs off the street?'

'I was threatened,' Alex admitted, 'but didn't see men who beat me.'

Sally snorted, blowing air loudly from her nose and berated Alex in loud, rapid Polish.

'Hang on, love.' Erica held up her hands to stem the flow. 'Can you yell at him in English so we know why you're pissed off?'

'He should have said!' Sally snapped. 'I told him. He must report, but he doesn't listen. He never listen.'

'These Nazis you mentioned, can you describe any of them?'

Sally shrugged. 'Maybe.'

'You make things worse,' Alex protested. 'I go home soon, better to forget.'

'No,' Sally yelled. 'Forgetting not make things better, make things worse. Men should not beat other men because they come from different place.' She turned to Erica. 'I will try to help, even if he won't.'

'Thank you. Any chance you can come to the station now? We have photographs of local bad boys we can show you. Be a good place to look for these Nazis.'

'No problem. I come. Alex can manage alone. Soon he well enough and can run away home like little boy.'

* * *

Tegan took Sally down to one of the interview rooms to show her mugshots, while Erica went upstairs to check on the team. Oliver was shuffling paper at his desk, Heidi hidden behind her screens. She looked up when Erica walked in.

'Did you find Alex?' she asked.

'Yes, just where Ollie said he would be. Any luck with the CCTV footage?'

Heidi shook her head. 'No, it's useless, crap quality and not nearly enough of it. Why doesn't the council invest more in surveillance? Make our job a lot easier if we had something decent to work with.' She lowered her voice and asked, 'Did you manage to get some time off?'

'Yeah, slightly early finish tonight and tomorrow off, but only tomorrow. How about we drive over this evening?'

'Good plan. I'll let Freddie know.'

'Any news from Greta?'

'Not so far. Found lots of crap about New Eden, but nothing useful. The doctrine is a right old mishmash of outrageous mumbo-jumbo, why does anyone fall for it? Most of what this Inverdale character spouts is utter garbage, nonsensical rubbish. He's pinched great chunks from the Christians, Muslims, Hindus – you name it – and inserted them in his text.'

'Anything further on Inverdale himself?'

'Not yet, work in progress. I'm not sure his name is Adam Inverdale and that may be why I'm struggling to uncover much, but I'm running search programs. I'll let you know.'

* * *

Heidi leaned back from the large kitchen table and groaned contentedly. 'That was wonderful, Freddie, thank Cook for us.'

'I will. Now, come to the library, the fire's lit and we can catch up in comfort.'

They settled themselves in front of the large fireplace and Freddie passed Heidi a brandy bottle.

'Help yourselves,' he said. 'Don't be shy.'

Heidi poured measures for herself and Erica, sank into a wing-backed chair, draped her legs over one arm and took a sip. 'Yum, this is good stuff, Pa. Just what I needed.'

'So tell me,' Freddie said, 'how are you getting on with the search for your sister?'

'That's part of the reason we're here,' Heidi said. 'I've been able to discover New Eden run three herbalist shops not far away. Things are set up to look as though the shops finance the running costs of a large hall which they run as a commune. I reckon the business is a front for something else. Not sure what yet.'

'A commune? In the Cotswolds?' Freddie sounded surprised.

Heidi laughed. 'Probably not what you're thinking… hippies, muddy kids and three-legged dogs. The place is registered as a church and New Eden is classed as a religion. You'd be amazed the tax breaks these set-ups can claim if they make a good enough case with the authorities – being holy and all that.'

'Really?'

'Yes, really,' Erica said. 'Makes it very difficult for the police to raid somewhere like that.'

'I don't see why?' Freddie muttered. 'You're looking for a missing person.'

‘It could be seen akin to storming a monastery and we wouldn’t do that without a bloody good reason. Think of the headlines, “British police conduct dawn raid on monks”.’

‘I see your point.’

‘The other problem we have is Greta is an adult. If she has joined the group of her own free will, there’s nothing we can do to make her come home if she doesn’t want to and no laws have been broken.’

‘She was kidnapped from HMP Heatherlea,’ Freddie snapped. ‘That must be illegal.’

‘If we could call it kidnapping,’ Heidi said, ‘then yes that’s illegal, but we can’t. Greta went willingly.’ She poured more brandy. ‘We have a plan though. Erica and I will make visits to the shops tomorrow, and on the way back to Wales, we’ll try to track down the location of the commune. I have a rough idea where it is.’

‘When you find it,’ Freddie grouched, ‘just knock on the door and if Greta is there, bring her home.’

‘Did you read any of that stuff I printed for you?’ Heidi asked and glared at her father.

‘Skimmed through it.’

‘Well, read it properly. Family members turning up at communes is always a bad idea. We’ll never get to see Greta – even if she is there – and our visit won’t be viewed favourably by cult members. No, we’ll stay away for now. I want to find out more about their leader before we formulate a plan to remove Greta. I don’t think she’s in any immediate danger and fairly convinced she’ll work out what a pile of shite the whole thing is and come home.’

‘I don’t understand why she hasn’t been in touch,’ Freddie said. ‘You’d think she’d call, send a postcard or something. I’m going to have to say something to your mother soon.’

Heidi’s face turned dark. ‘Do what you like. Come on, Erica, we’ve a lot to accomplish tomorrow so we’ll need an early start. Night, Pa.’

Heidi strode from the room and Erica had to trot to catch up.

'Hey, wait for me. What's up?'

'Nothing.'

'Something is. Or is "nothing" Heidi-speak for don't be nosey?'

Heidi shrugged, cracked her knuckles and pushed open the door to their bedroom. Firelight flickered on the walls and Erica squeaked with delight.

'Oh, wow. A real fire and a bearskin rug, every girl's dream. Thank you for this, what a treat. Let's sleep on the floor tonight and I won't ask any more questions. You'll tell me when you're ready.'

Chapter nine

Greta leant against the headboard and sipped camomile tea. She didn't like it much even with a spoonful of honey, but caffeine was banned. The dormitory door opened and Pixie slipped in.

'Greta, you're still up. Can't you sleep?'

'I've been waiting for you. I could do with a chat.'

'Is something wrong?'

'Yeah, sort of.'

Pixie sat on the bed and peered at Greta. 'So, tell me. What's on your mind?'

'I think I need to speak to my father to let him know I'm OK. If I don't he might come to take me home and I really don't want that.'

'I doubt he'll find you,' Pixie said. 'Adam doesn't advertise this place, so your dad couldn't just look up the address and arrive on the doorstep.'

'I'm not so sure, he can be very resourceful. If I tell him I'm fine, I'm sure he won't bother and I'll be able to stay.' Greta sighed. 'I love living here and if Pa causes a scene Adam might make me leave.'

Pixie giggled. 'There's no danger of that,' she said. 'You're a member of the church now and members don't leave.'

'What, never?'

'I've never known anyone who has. You should speak with Adam after the early meditation and ask his advice. That's what he's there for, so don't worry. Now, get some sleep. God bless, beloved.'

Greta snuggled under her blankets, but sleep evaded her. She couldn't settle and her mind churned constantly, worrying about what Adam would say. When the alarm sounded at quarter to two, she hauled herself out of bed, dragged on her clothes and headed for the great hall. She was the last to arrive and was aware of the others watching her as she took her place.

Adam raised his arms and began the session but Greta wasn't paying attention. Her brain bubbled with worries. What could she say to Adam? She wasn't used to feeling so unsettled and remembered Felix, how he'd confessed to speaking with his mother and the reception he'd received. Come to think of it, she hadn't seen Felix recently and made up her mind to ask Eleanor where he was.

An hour later the assembly broke up and the faithful shambled back to their beds, yawning and rubbing their eyes. Greta walked towards Adam and he smiled a welcome.

'Do you have something to say?' he asked.

Greta nodded. 'Yes, I had a chat with Pixie and she said I should speak with you.'

'Of course, come to my room.'

Adam stood, led the way to the rear of the low stage, opened a narrow door and ushered Greta inside. She'd expected an office, but the room was more like a bedroom, dominated by a large bed. Hangings covered the walls, coloured glass candle lamps glowed, and the air was saturated with the sweet scent of incense. Adam directed her to a seating area by the fireplace.

'Greta, please sit and tell me what's on your mind.'

'I need to ring home,' she mumbled. 'My father is bound to be worried about where I am and may look for me. If I phone and tell him I'm OK he won't bother.'

Adam pushed a mobile phone across the low table between the chairs. 'Go ahead, call your dad.'

Greta wasn't expecting the response and didn't move.

'Go on, phone him,' Adam said. 'Tell your father you're fine and you've chosen to be here, but don't tell him where here is.'

'It's just after three in the morning,' Greta stammered. 'I can't ring him now.'

'Why not? You should always be able to speak to your family, regardless of the time of day.'

'Yes… but… it'll worry him.'

Adam sighed. 'You've just told me you want to contact him so he doesn't worry. Which is it, Greta? You're not making sense.'

'I don't want him causing a fuss because he thinks I'm missing, that's all. He might send someone here to drag me home and I really don't want that to happen.'

'He can't remove you.' Adam steepled his fingers. 'You are here by choice and don't forget, your family didn't serve you. They are part of the reason you found your way to us.' He pushed the phone closer. 'Call him… then you can forget him.'

Adam smiled for the first time, stretched across the low table and laid a gentle hand on Greta's cheek. 'You are not alone, beloved, I am with you.'

Greta reached for the phone and noticed her fingers were trembling. She didn't know whether it was fear she felt or some sort of nervous excitement. After a couple of false starts she tapped in her father's number.

'Put the speaker on,' Adam said. 'If I hear both sides of the conversation, I can support you more ably.'

Greta pushed a button and a ringing tone filled the room.

Eventually, a gruff, sleep-soaked voice answered. 'Holtz. Who's ringing at this time of the morning?'

Greta hesitated, voice cracking as she spoke, 'Pa?'

'Greta! Is that you?'

'Yes, it's me.'

'Where the hell are you? Is something wrong?'

'No, everything's fine.'

'It's after three and I asked where you are. Your sister says you've joined a cult, New Eden or something. What's that all about?'

'It's not a cult, it's a church and yes, I am a member.'

'You still haven't told me where you are?'

'All you need to know is I'm fine, happy and healthy. You don't need to know where I am.'

'When are you coming home?'

'I'm not,' she stammered. 'I'm happy here and going to stay. I just wanted to tell you so you wouldn't look for me.'

'This is not good enough, Greta. You can't just vanish like this. It's not on, you should…'

Greta cut the call and handed the phone back to Adam. 'Thank you.'

'Do you feel better?' he asked.

'Not much if I'm honest, but I won't worry about him looking for me anymore.'

'He didn't sound very pleased to hear from you,' Adam said. 'If anything, he sounded angry.'

'He usually does. Always seemed to be shouting at me when I was little.'

'Have you a mother?'

'Yes.' Greta hesitated. 'But I didn't think we were supposed to talk about our past lives.'

Adam smiled. 'You're right of course. Now, if that's all, you better get back to bed. Eleanor will want you in the garden tomorrow ready for work.' Adam stood and embraced Greta warmly, wrapped her in his arms and stroked her hair with one hand.

Greta gently tried to pull away, unsure of how to behave, but he held on and spoke quietly.

'Never be afraid to bring me your worries,' he said. 'I am here to guide you, to soothe you and show you the way to God. Newness is always difficult in the beginning, but I can feel you're one of us. I am thankful we met you, Greta, the church is thankful you are here and you will grow. This night is passed, you will never have to live it again. Tomorrow is always waiting, God willing.'

He finally released her and Greta escaped gratefully. Her head was thumping, stress probably from talking to Pa. Why couldn't he just be happy for her? Why did he always try to order her about? She ran upstairs to the dormitory and snuck into bed, anxious not to wake the others, and was soon asleep.

* * *

A knock on the door roused Erica from sleep. She crept out from beneath the quilt, slipped on a robe and shivered. The logs in the grate had burned to embers and the room had cooled. Padding to the door, she pulled it open and discovered Freddie standing outside.

'Are you OK?' she asked. 'It's early. Have we got burglars or something?'

'I'm so sorry to disturb, but Greta's been on the phone. Is Heidi awake?'

'She is now,' Heidi mumbled and disentangled herself from crumpled bedding. 'Did you say Greta rang?'

'Yes. A few moments ago.'

'Is she OK?'

‘Said she was, but why ring in the middle of the night unless something’s wrong?’

Heidi pulled on a baggy jumper, crawled closer to the fire, stirred the embers and threw on a couple of logs.

‘Come and sit by the fire, Pa, and tell us what Greta said.’

Freddie perched on a leather pouffe and stared at the growing flames. ‘Not much really, said she was – how did she put it – happy and healthy. Told me she’d joined The New Eden Church, had no intention of coming home and wouldn’t tell me where she was.’

Heidi picked up the house phone and dialled 1471.

‘Withheld number,’ she said. ‘Not that I’m surprised. Call made at 03.36. I’ll see if I can trace it.’ She sat at the desk and woke up her laptop. ‘What did you say to Greta, Freddie? I hope you didn’t give her a hard time after all I’ve said.’

‘Didn’t have time to say anything much. I told her she should come home and she hung up on me. I asked a couple of times where she was, but she wouldn’t say, told me I didn’t need to know.’

‘Bloody crappy system,’ Heidi grumbled. ‘It’s no good, I’ll need access to my kit in Brecon if I’m to achieve anything.’

‘So what are we going to do?’ Freddie asked.

‘I’m planning more sleep,’ Heidi said. ‘Followed by breakfast. You should do the same and we’ll talk then. Don’t worry, at least you know Greta’s OK. How did she sound?’

‘No different, less to say than usual perhaps, uncommunicative, but alright I suppose.’

‘Go to bed, Freddie,’ Erica said. ‘Heidi’s right, this can wait until daylight.’

Freddie wandered back to his room. Heidi slipped under the quilt and patted the space beside her.

‘Come on, E, bed for you too, we’ve a busy day tomorrow.’

Chapter ten

New Eden Herbs was situated in a prime site on the High Street of Upper Yanworth. The small market town was busy as early customers bustled in and out of the shops. Erica parked opposite the small establishment and the women watched the foot traffic.

The shop appeared well organised. A few wooden tea chests stood on the pavement beneath the window, filled with multicoloured squash, green apples and bunches of organically grown carrots. A brightly painted sign advertising the herbalists hung above the window and the door stood open welcomingly.

'Let's go and take a look,' Erica said and opened the car door.

Heidi tapped on her phone and didn't look up. 'You go. I'm busy.'

'Are you sulking?'

'Why would I be sulking? I'm working and don't want any of that lot in there to see me.'

'Why not?'

'Because of my distinctive look. People remember me. If I have to go inside the commune to fetch Greta, I don't want anyone recognising me.'

Erica shut the door and stared at her partner. 'What do you mean when you say "go inside"?'

'What do you think I mean?' Heidi fiddled with her phone and Erica snatched it from her hands.

'Hey!'

'Talk to me and you'll get it back.'

Heidi huffed and cracked her knuckles. 'OK. I give up. You've read the same stuff I have about cults and the various ways of getting people out, and none of them are easy. I'm still hoping Greta will be a walkaway.'

'A what?'

'A "walkaway". That she'll see something she doesn't like which reactivates her critical mind and she walks away. Otherwise it could take months, years even to bring her home.'

'Why not leave her there if she's happy?' Erica asked. 'You haven't discovered this lot are a suicide cult, have you? There are lots of communes scattered around the country that have existed for years without any problems. There's one not far from Brecon, tepees and hobbit houses.'

'I haven't discovered much,' Heidi snapped and grabbed back her phone, 'but something's definitely off with this lot. I want Greta out, so does Freddie, and if it comes to it, I'll go in and get her.'

'Everything I've read says not to do that.'

'Can we talk about this another time?' Heidi begged. 'Go and check out the shop and let me concentrate.'

Erica gave up, stepped out of the car and ran across the road, dodging a speeding cyclist. She walked inside the shop and quickly took stock of her surroundings. The walls were lined with shelves, crammed with jars and packets, bundles of freshly dried herbs and boxes of specialist teas. The air smelt sweet, dusty. A handful of customers milled around, picking goods from the displays and placing them in wire shopping baskets. A couple in their late fifties served at the counter, bagging purchases and working the cash register. They chatted away cheerfully with their clients and the queue moved slowly.

Erica helped herself to a basket and began browsing, listening to the conversations flowing around her.

'Mrs Fletcher, how are you today?' the man behind the counter asked. 'Has the nettle-rub helped with your rheumatism?'

'Yes, it has, Bruce, made a huge difference. Emma said you have nettle soap too and I wondered if that would be a good idea.'

'Certainly won't do any harm,' Bruce said, reached behind his head and lifted down a box of handmade soap.

'I'll take two,' Mrs Fletcher said. 'How is Emma?'

'Fine, just nipped out the back. I'll give her a shout and you can ask her yourself.'

Erica moved closer to the counter. She spotted a pile of leaflets and dropped one in the basket with a couple of jars of hand cream she'd chosen from the display by the door, two butternut squash and a large bunch of carrots.

'Can I help you?' Bruce asked.

'Yes, please.' Erica put the basket on the serving area. 'You have a lovely shop,' she said. 'I don't think I've ever seen such a well-stocked herbalist.'

Bruce smiled. 'Thank you, we try.'

'The labels say you grow and make everything yourselves. That's a lot of work and you must have a huge garden.'

Bruce chuckled. 'Fairly big, but we don't do everything on our own. We work as part of a cooperative, there's a few of us.'

'I'd love to visit one day. Is that possible?'

Bruce ignored the question and packed the goods in a brown paper bag.

'That'll be £16.98 please.'

Erica tried again, 'Do you have open days or anything?'

'No, we don't, but it's not a bad idea. I'll mention it when I get back. Here you go, £3.02 change. Anything else I can help you with?'

'No, thank you, but I'm sure I'll be back.'

Erica walked to the car, handed the bag to Heidi and installed herself behind the steering wheel.

'What's this?' Heidi asked and opened the bag.

'Hand cream for you, veggies for soup and a leaflet promoting the benefits of New Eden.' She started the engine. 'Where to now?'

'I can't see the point of visiting each shop, they're bound to be much the same, so let's see if we can find the commune. I think I've managed to pinpoint the location of the mobile Greta used this morning to about ten miles west of here. Might as well go take a look, so turn around.'

Erica executed a neat U-turn and headed towards Cheltenham, passing through small villages of chocolate-box cottages, roses growing over more than one porch.

'What are we looking for?' Erica asked.

'A large Victorian pile, not far from a place called South Hatherop.'

'The countryside is really beautiful here, softer than Wales,' Erica said, negotiating a small roundabout. 'The place names are easier to pronounce than at home.'

Heidi giggled. 'You should try harder – seeing you were born in Wales. Now take the next left and keep your eyes open. If my calculations are correct, the house should be somewhere to the right. I don't want to get too close, just take a gander at the layout of the place.'

They travelled in silence for a few miles before Erica jumped on the brakes and reversed. Through a gap in a tall hedge Heidi glimpsed a large property tucked behind a straggly copse.

'Is that it?' Erica asked.

'I reckon. Let's hide the car somewhere and try to get closer.'

A couple of hundred yards further on Erica pulled into a wide gateway and turned off the engine. 'Now what?'

'Cross-country walking,' Heidi said. 'You want to come or stay here?'

'I'll come, make sure you don't do anything daft.'

Heidi cracked her knuckles. 'Do I ever?' She opened the door, slipped out and using a hedge as cover, made her way closer to the house.

After ten minutes spent avoiding thick stands of nettles and large patches of mud, they reached a drystone wall, crouched behind it and peered over the top. Heidi dug a small pair of binoculars from her pocket and focused them on the building.

'God, what an awful carbuncle,' she muttered quietly. 'What were the Victorians thinking when they built places like this? There's even a crenulated tower – truly ghastly.'

'Can you see anyone about?' Erica asked.

'Not so far. There's what looks like a walled garden, or courtyard at the back. Window shutters on the upper floors are closed and I can't see anyone moving around downstairs. Let's see if we can sneak around to the other side.'

Erica's phone chirped and Heidi glared at her.

'DS Bevan.'

'Sarge, where are you?' Oliver Langdon asked.

'Cotswolds,' Erica hissed.

'You better get back over the bridge. There's been another mugging – a bad one – young Hungarian girl beaten to a pulp and the brass are proper agitated.'

'Another magazine seller?'

'No, barmaid from one of the city centre pubs, attacked on her way home after work, but it sounds like the same thing. Two blokes, unprovoked attack.'

'Any witnesses?'

'One of the customers from the pub. Chased the muggers away and called the ambulance.'

'You said "bad",' Erica mumbled. 'How bad?'

'Intensive care in a coma. Terrible head injuries and facial damage.'

'OK, Ollie. We'll get there as soon as we can.' She cut the connection. 'We've gotta go, young girl mugged in

Brecon last night. We'll either have to come back to this or knock on the door and ask for Greta. Your decision.'

Heidi groaned. 'No point in a house call, so we'll go home. At least I know where the commune is and having a definite location will help with my searches. As you say, we'll come back to this. How's the victim?'

'Bad.'

* * *

Greta and Eleanor pushed loaded wheelbarrows along brick paths laid between raised beds in the vegetable garden. The weather had remained warm and dry, perfect for spreading manure on empty beds. Mack and Joe stood ready with forks and as soon as the barrows had been tipped, worked the natural fertiliser into the soil. The women wheeled back to the muck heap for refills.

'I haven't seen Felix for a while,' Greta said. 'Is he OK? He seemed a bit upset the other evening, that business about him ringing his mum.'

'He's on a five-day retreat,' Eleanor said. 'Adam thought a period of personal meditation would help Felix.'

'Where's he gone?'

'There are some rooms at the top of the house, old servants' quarters with views over the grounds. Great place to work out issues on your own in silence. He's in one of those.'

'Like solitary confinement?' Greta was surprised.

'What awful words! No, nothing like that, more a cloistered period, a quiet time for reflection, to be with God.'

'What are the rooms like?'

Eleanor chuckled. 'They're nice, little bathroom attached to each one. Someone takes his meals up and as I said, there's a fantastic view. A perfect space for contemplation. When Felix is back with us, I'll take you up and show you.' She laughed again. 'If only you could see your face. I don't think it did you any good talking to your dad, you look so worried. Don't be, everything about this is new for you. Hang in there, Greta, the longer you live with us, the more you will understand and accept the change in your life. It won't take long, honest.'

Chapter eleven

Heidi winced as Erica slid a set of colour photographs across the desk. The pictures recorded an utterly ruined face, criss-crossed with numerous stitches, black against purple and crimson. The nose was obscured by a large piece of gauze, eyes invisible, scalp shaved and also stitched, breathing tubes snaked out of the mouth. If Heidi hadn't known the victim was female, she would never have been able to make up her mind.

'Filthy beasts,' she muttered darkly. 'We've got to catch these bastards, this can't go on a minute longer. Any CCTV?'

'Not yet,' Oliver admitted. 'The manager at the pub – The King's Head – said he'd get someone to bring in what he has, but we haven't received anything yet.'

Heidi exploded. 'Then go and bloody get it, or are you welded to your chair? Move about a bit more and you wouldn't have weight problems.'

Oliver looked hurt and muttered, 'I haven't got weight problems.'

'Yes, you have. You're a useless lump.'

'Shut up, both of you,' Erica said. 'You're not producing anything useful.' She glared at them. 'That's better, this is not a bloody playground. Ollie, go into town, collect the tape from the pub, check if there are any other privately owned cameras in the area and, if there are, we want those tapes too.'

'I'm knocking off in a couple of hours,' he grumbled.

'Then you'd better get a move on, because until we have the tapes you stay on duty.' Erica turned away from him. 'Tegan, bring us up to date.'

Oliver banged out of the room as Tegan stood in front of the incident board.

'Attack took place about 12.35am, ambulance in attendance at 12.53. The victim is Daniela Stoica, twenty-two-year-old student, ID in pocket.' She pointed to an enlarged photo of a pretty young girl with long wavy hair, grey eyes and a wide, friendly smile. 'She left The King's Head, where she works as a barmaid, and turned down New Road where she was set on by two blokes. Our witness – Jon Williams – entered the street a few minutes later and disturbed the attackers, but not before they had inflicted serious damage. He yelled at them, they legged it and he gave chase. Managed to grab the jacket of one, kid wriggled out and left it behind. Williams called 999 and waited until we got there.'

'Jon Williams?' Erica said. 'I know that name… where? Is this guy a builder?'

'Yeah, how did you know? He's working on the cathedral tower in town.'

'Had occasion to speak to him recently, bit of a rumpus on the industrial estate with a few of his men. What's happened to the jacket?'

Tegan opened a file and removed a set of photos which she passed to Heidi. 'I took pictures then sent it to forensics.'

'Did our witness look through the mugshots downstairs, in case he could recognise anyone?'

'Not yet, he's coming in at ten tomorrow. Didn't have the time today, council building inspection.'

'How about Sally? Alex's friend. Did she pick anyone out?'

'A couple of possibles, nothing definite. Neither victims nor witnesses managed to get much of a look at these individuals and all the attacks have been at night. Sally thinks she recognised a guy who sometimes shouts abuse at her on the street, usual thing along the lines of, "go home". She's coming in again tomorrow so you can speak to her.'

Erica sighed. 'Anything else to tell me?'

'Not really. DI James has requested an update, but said it can wait until the morning. He's probably already left. There isn't much any of us can do until then. I asked forensics to get a move on, but we'll be lucky to have anything by tomorrow and Daniela Stoica won't be talking to anyone for a while.' Tegan flinched and glanced at Erica. 'This is supposed to be your day off, Sarge, so why not go home and look at all this tomorrow? I'll wait for Ollie to get back with the CCTV and take a quick look through. If there's anything you need to know, I'll call you.'

'I'm staying,' Heidi said. 'When Ollie eventually returns with the footage, I can get to work on it. You know I like an empty office. You get off, E. I'll be home later.'

Erica nodded and said, 'On the condition you don't bite Ollie's head off when he does return… and you're not to stay here all night.'

'I'll be home by one,' Heidi promised. 'Go on, see you later.'

Tegan tactfully turned away as Erica brushed a kiss on Heidi's cheek.

***

The tapes Oliver collected from cameras in the pub, and others close to the town centre, had mostly been useless, although Heidi was sure she had a couple of frames of one of the attackers, captured inside the pub.

After an hour of eye-straining work with the recordings, she was certain she had been able to match a hoodie on a customer with the one Williams had torn from the back of one of the muggers. Frustratingly the footage did not show the wearer's face, but it was a start. There was a badge of some sort on the left breast of the jacket but she couldn't see what it was, just the colour and the shape – a small, black fuzz on a red background, a blob really. Removing the pictures of the jacket from the file, she examined them. Annoyingly, Tegan hadn't taken a decent shot of the embroidered patch – which was partially obscured by a fold in the fleece – but Heidi was sure she knew what it was. It looked like a swastika.

* * *

The silence of the session in the great hall was suddenly shattered by a piercing scream. All heads turned to the back of the room where Clover was groaning and holding her stomach. Mala leapt to her feet and ran to her daughter's side, an elderly woman from the far side of the hall also stood. Adam sent a visual question to the women and Mala nodded.

'It's time,' she said. 'Winnie and I will take her to the medical centre.'

Adam smiled and clapped his hands to settle his congregation as the women helped Clover from the hall. Greta watched as they left and felt uneasy, hoped everything would go well. The commune was pretty isolated and if help was needed it would take a while to arrive.

Adam clapped his hands again. 'Come now, everyone, we must focus. New life is a cause for celebration, so join me as we contemplate God's powerful magic.'

The room fell silent and Adam continued the session. Greta couldn't wait for it to be over and as soon as they were released, sought out Pixie who was heading for the dormitories.

'Hey, wait for me.'

Pixie looked behind, spotted Greta and leaned against the wall of the corridor to wait for her to catch up.

'Do you think she'll be OK?' Greta asked.

'Clover? Yeah, she'll be fine. Winnie's good, worked for the NHS before she came to us.'

'Mala said she was a midwife.'

'Certainly a nurse for over thirty years. There isn't much she can't cope with.'

They began to climb the stairs.

'It'll be lovely to have a baby around the place,' Greta said.

Pixie stopped and caught hold of Greta's hand. 'Of course, you don't know.'

'Don't know what?'

'The baby won't be staying. Clover is a Host.'

'A Host? Who for?'

'Friends of her mother. Members of New Eden who have been unable to conceive.'

'There are more church members then? Not just us?'

Pixie laughed. 'No, not just us. There are two other communes and many of our members live in their own homes.'

'I didn't know.' Greta paused. 'When will they come for the baby?'

'Soon. I expect Adam is ringing them now. They wanted to be here for the birth, but the baby's coming early.'

'And Clover is OK with this? Giving up a newborn must be really difficult.'

'She's fine, agreed to act as a host mother as soon as she was asked.'

'And this is legal?'

Pixie ignored the question and pushed open the door of the dorm.

'Clover's very brave,' Greta said. 'I don't think I could carry a baby for nine months then just hand it over, and she's so young. Do you think she realises the possible implications?'

'Clover has a generous spirit. The gift of a child is the ultimate gift.'

Greta undressed and slipped into bed. 'Where is the medical centre?'

'Down on the ground floor at the back of the building.'

'Maybe we could visit when the baby's been born.'

'Maybe,' Pixie muttered. 'Sleep now.' She turned off the bedside light and snuggled under her quilt. 'See you in the morning, God willing.'

Pixie was soon asleep and the sound of her breathing filled the room, but Greta couldn't relax. She worried about Clover. The girl was only seventeen and had made a huge decision which was bound to affect the rest of her life. Had she received any counselling before she embarked on this path? Was the arrangement official, or something New Eden members had cooked up themselves? Was it legal? Greta wasn't sure, the whole situation seemed crazy to her.

An hour passed and sleep still evaded her, so she crept out of bed, left the room and headed towards the kitchen in search of a milky drink. On her way back to the dorms she wondered again where the medical centre was and paused in the corridor. The halls were empty, so she wandered towards the back of the house, padding quietly on wooden floors in her bed socks.

Greta hadn't been to the back of the building before and wondered why the medical centre hadn't been included on Eleanor's tour. The silent house smelt musty and the passageways were even shabbier than the main hall. She was glad she'd brought a torch and felt like a thief in the night as she crept along in the dark.

She'd just decided to go back to bed when she heard a cry of pain somewhere off to her left. She quickened her pace and was startled when a nearby door suddenly opened. Mala stepped out.

'What are you doing here?' she demanded. 'You should be in bed.'

'I couldn't stop worrying about Clover,' Greta said. 'Is she OK?'

'She's fine.'

'Can I see her?'

Mala stared at her. 'No, of course you can't! She's in the middle of giving birth. Now return to your dorm, we're busy and you're in the way.'

Chapter twelve

Erica glanced up from the table as Tegan showed Jon Williams into interview room number two.

'Good morning, Mr Williams,' Erica said. 'Good of you to come in. I hope we won't take up too much of your time.'

'It's OK. The lads will be fine for a couple of hours.' He grinned. 'I've warned them not to thump each other. How can I help?'

Erica dumped a stack of heavy folders on the table in front of him. 'We'd like you to take a look at these mugshots to find out if either of the men you chased off are here. We're pretty sure the same two guys are responsible for attacking four individuals in town, including the girl you helped two nights ago. None of the victims got much of a look at their attackers and so far you're our best witness.'

'How is she?' Jon asked.

'Bad,' Tegan answered. 'Still in hospital in an induced coma. Suffered dreadful facial injuries and a fractured skull. The doctors say she's lucky to be alive… good job you were there.'

'Would have been better if I could have hung on to the rat who did this,' Jon grouched. 'He wriggled out of his jacket as easy as a dog slipping its collar. I couldn't run after him and leave the girl.'

'You did the right thing,' Erica said reassuringly. 'Now, take a look at these photos, see if you can pick anyone out. Would you like a cuppa?'

'Please, milk, two sugars.'

Erica nodded at Tegan who left the room. Jon flipped pages and scrutinised the photographs.

'Have you remembered anything else from the night of the attack?' Erica asked.

'No, sorry, only what I've already told you. Will the girl be OK, do you think?'

'Too soon to tell, but the doctors are hopeful. She's being well cared for.'

'Tragic,' Jon said. 'Came here for a better life and look what happened. Her poor parents. I've got a girl and if anyone did that to her I'd want to kill them.'

Erica chuckled. 'Probably not the kind of remark you want to make in a police station, sir.'

'No,' he agreed, 'probably not.'

Jon turned another page and hesitated. He tapped his finger on the picture of a young man in his twenties, thin, pasty-looking with an aggressive skinhead haircut. Tegan returned with tea and Jon smiled his thanks.

'He looks familiar,' he said. 'I reckon he was in the pub before closing time with another kid, very similar looking, same haircut and almost identical clothes, dark hooded jackets and camouflage trousers.' He sipped his tea thoughtfully and peered closely at the picture. 'Yes, I'm sure he was in the pub, but can't say for certain he was the bloke I chased, only really saw his back. The other one was bigger, tubby and taller, not runty like this one. They were in the pub together but I can't see a photo of tubs here.'

Erica checked the records. 'The one you recognise is Jonesy Francombe,' she said. 'Does the name ring a bell?'

'No, sorry, never heard of him, but I'll keep an eye out. You'd be surprised how much we can see from the top of the scaffolding in town. If I spot him, I'll call you.'

'Thanks, but there's no need, we know where he lives and will pay him a visit.' Erica stood and held out her hand. 'Thank you for taking the time, sir, and if you think of anything which might help, please give us a call.'

'No problem and thanks for the tea.' He winked at Tegan. 'You make a better cup than the wife, I could do with you at home.'

She grinned and said, 'I'll walk you out, sir.'

Tegan escorted him to the main entrance and Erica walked upstairs to the squad room where she found Heidi hammering the keys of her computer.

'We may have caught a break,' Erica said and dropped the photo of Jonesy Francombe on the desk in front of her partner. 'Jon Williams reckons this guy was in the pub just before the attack, with another guy, taller, heavier, but dressed the same. See if you can find either of them on the footage and check the stuff captured during the other attacks. You never know, we might get lucky.'

Heidi picked up the picture and stared at it. 'Wasn't he pulled last year?' she asked. 'I'm sure we picked him up during the military's, "Freedom of Brecon Parade" in April, when the Gurkhas marched with the Small Arms School Corps. Him and a few of his mates were shouting abuse at the squaddies.'

'Yeah, that's him. Obnoxious little shit. Good job he was nicked or the Gurkhas would have probably done for him. What happened when he went to court?'

'Let off with a caution for causing a disturbance. I'd have thrown him to the squaddies, save us having to deal with him.'

Erica flopped in an empty chair. 'Have you had any luck?'

'Some. Sally came in, Alex's friend, and took another look at the mugshots, but couldn't pick anyone out. She did say she's heard the "Nazis" – as she calls them, and I don't think she's wrong – meet in one of the pubs on the A40, not far from Carmarthen. Thought it might be worth a trip over, discover what we can winkle out of the landlord.'

'Where did she hear this?'

'There's a social club in town for Eastern European migrants. They meet every other week, and she picked up the information there.'

'OK, so we need to visit the pub and the social club. Any idea when the migrant's group meet next?'

Heidi shook her head. 'No, but Sally has given us the name and address of the woman who organises it, Lottie, followed by something unpronounceable. The details are on your desk.'

'Any good news regarding Greta?'

'Not really, no. The more I dig into the cult, the more convinced I am the only way to get her out is to go inside the place and remove her. I'm thinking I could pose as a convert; that would be the easiest way. As soon as I gain entry to the commune, I can find my sister and bloody carry her out if I have to.'

'No, Heidi! We've discussed this, you can't. I know you want to, but it's not the way to solve the problem. You are not to try anything like that, especially without talking to me first.'

'Is that a work directive or a personal one?' Heidi muttered.

'Both! We'll chat later. Carry on trying to track down our muggers and I'll take Ollie with me to talk to the landlord of the pub on the A40. Also, try to get hold of this Lottie who runs the social club.' She stood and glared at Heidi. 'Promise me you won't do anything daft, let's explore the options first.'

Heidi waved a hand and retreated into cyberspace and Erica, knowing she wouldn't get anything more out of her partner, went in search of Oliver Langdon and a car.

* * *

Greta and Eleanor were working side by side in the vegetable garden covering the newly mulched beds ready for winter, when Adam appeared by their side with Mala. Eleanor looked up from her work and smiled.

'Hello, Adam, Mala,' she said. 'How's Clover?'

'She's fine,' Adam said, 'resting. We've come for Greta.'

'Me?' Greta asked nervously. 'Why do you want me?'

'Just a chat up at the house,' Mala said.

Adam smiled and held out his hand. Greta allowed herself to be helped upright and followed them towards the residence. They led her through the main entrance and headed up the stairs.

'Where are we going?' Greta asked.

Adam took hold of her arm and guided her firmly towards the upper floors.

'Mala told me you were out of bed last night,' he said, 'wandering the corridors, asking questions, but not the right ones.'

'Right ones?'

'The questions you've been asking are the wrong ones. Answers will come to you without the need to ask, if you are granted the wisdom. Three days of quiet meditation will help, away from the rest of the church members.'

'I don't want to,' Greta said. 'I'll stop asking. I don't want to spend three days alone. Eleanor needs help in the garden, I'm more use here.'

'We can't always do what we want to,' Adam said. 'You need to trust me, Greta, things will be clearer after your brief sequestration.'

Reaching the top of the stairs, Mala led the way along a narrow corridor to the end, opened a small door under the eaves and beckoned Greta forward.

'I really don't think this is necessary,' Greta protested. 'I'm just getting used to my new life.'

Adam took her by the shoulders and gazed deeply into her eyes.

'Greta, listen to me. This is very necessary. Everyone here has to fit in and everyone has an effect on everybody else. You won't be alone. God will be with you. I will be with you, guiding you, showing the way. This time of reflection is a gift, so accept it.'

He pushed Greta gently towards the open door and not wanting to cause a scene, she shuffled inside the small room and Mala shut the door behind her. Greta heard them walk away along the corridor. Trying the door handle she was horrified to discover it was locked. Why had they locked her in? She yanked and rattled the handle with no result and panicking, launched a hefty kick at the door with no effect.

She gazed around the room. A metal framed, single bed rested against the side wall, identical to her prison bunk and she shivered. Folded bedding balanced on the end and two towels rested on top of the pile. The floorboards were bare apart from a fraying rag rug that appeared as old as the house, faded and thin. She peered through a narrow doorway and discovered a tiny bathroom. A small window opposite the door faced over the front grounds and the gravelled drive leading away from the commune. Greta peered through murky glass, but couldn't see anyone moving about. She tried to open the sash window. It was stuck and she gave it a few good thumps before realising with dread it was nailed shut. She was a prisoner again and wasn't sure how that had happened.

She turned back to the room. Apart from the bed, a small wooden table, a chair and the rug, it was empty. No books, nothing. A single frame hung on one of the bare plaster walls, not a picture but a script, 'Seek and you will find'. She knew the quote had been taken from the Bible and shuddered. She had hated all that rubbish as a child.

When she was young her father enrolled her in the choir at the local church and for years she had been bullied by the choir master because of her lacklustre voice. She'd thought New Eden was different, but maybe all religions were the same. She turned the quotation to the wall, placed the chair to face the window and sat.

The manor house was quiet. With the window shut she couldn't even hear any sounds from outside and felt lonely and isolated. Perhaps coming to this place hadn't been such a good idea after all. A noise behind her made her leap up from the chair in time to see a plate of food slide through the wide gap at the bottom of the door. Lunch.

She dashed to the door and called, 'Hello. Is anyone there?'

She listened but heard nothing. The door was still locked so she carried the plate to the bed and picked at lettuce leaves, her appetite having deserted her. She wasn't sure she'd be able to stand being here on her own for three days, belatedly realising she didn't have a choice. There was no way out.

* * *

Oliver Langdon held the door of The Prince Llewelyn Inn open for his boss. Erica marched into the public bar and wasn't surprised to find the place nearly empty. Most of the pubs around here were struggling and it was too late in the season to attract many holidaymakers; not that they'd choose this place, Erica thought. Too grubby and rundown, definitely a pub for locals who weren't as fussy as tourists.

A couple of ancient farmer types sat either side of the fire, nursing half-drunk pints, an equally ancient sheep dog at their feet. A middle-aged man stood behind the bar polishing glasses and glanced up as the officers walked in.

'Can I speak to the landlord?' Erica asked.

'That's me,' the man growled. 'What do coppers want with me?'

'How do you know we're coppers?'

'Bloody obvious.' He laughed humourlessly. 'You two don't go together at all. So… what do you want?'

Oliver pulled a photograph from his inside pocket and placed it on the bar.

'Do you know this man, sir?'

The landlord barely glanced at the picture before shaking his head. 'No, never seen him.'

'Perhaps a second look,' Erica said and held the photo in front of the man's nose. 'We've been told he drinks in here.'

'Well, you've been told wrong. Like I said, never seen him. What's he done anyway?'

Oliver removed a second picture of Daniela Stoica in her hospital bed and held it up.

'We want to talk to him in relation to an attack on this young girl. Now, do you know who he is?'

'That's a girl, is it?' the landlord asked. 'Christ, what a mess. Hope you catch this bloke whoever he is, but like I say, I don't know him. Now, can I get you anything or are you leaving?'

'Two coffees, please,' Erica said. 'Bring them over, will you? Thanks.'

She settled in a window seat at the front of the building ignoring hostile glances from the landlord. He brought the mugs over, plonked them on the table, and then vanished into the kitchen.

'He's not helpful,' Oliver said. 'Waste of time coming out here.'

'Maybe not.' Erica sipped her drink before adding, 'Make sure you use the loo before we leave.'

Oliver looked surprised. 'What are you, Sarge, me mam?'

She laughed. 'I want you to check out the graffiti. Very enlightening bog graffiti – according to DC Holtz. She says you can get an idea about the kind of people who write on the walls by what they write, so go and check it out and make a note of anything you think is relevant, then we'll go and find this Lottie. As you say, Mr Helpful behind the bar isn't going to tell us anything. I'll have a chat with Carmarthen nick later, find out what they know about this place.'

Chapter thirteen

Heidi and Erica were working side by side in the squad room, reviewing the statement from Jon Williams. They glanced up when the door opened and DI Ben James walked in.

'Evening, sir,' Erica said. 'Can we help you with something?'

'I've just heard from the hospital. Daniela Stoica has died.'

'Shit! What happened?' Heidi asked. 'Last time I checked, the doc told me she was stable.'

'Suffered a massive bleed on the brain and couldn't be saved, so now you're hunting a murderer. How is the investigation going? Any progress?'

'We have a possible identification, Jonesy Francombe,' Erica said. 'Local bad boy, been in trouble before, minor stuff – nothing like this. Ollie and I went to his address, but no sign of him. He lives with his grandmother in a place just outside town. She told us he was staying with a friend of his, Peter Leech, another bad boy. Both were arrested during the Freedom of Brecon march back in April, both released with a caution.'

'If you know all this, why aren't they in custody?' Ben asked.

'We went to Leech's flat, but no sign of either of them. I've arranged to have them picked up first thing tomorrow. Heidi has managed to discover some CCTV footage from town on the night of the attack. We can prove the pair were in The King's Head where Daniela works… worked. We have the hoodie Jon Williams snatched during the attack. Link it to either lad and we can begin to make a case against them.'

'Any ideas regarding motive?'

'Not really,' Erica said. 'Worryingly, we've heard whispers about a far-right group operating out of a pub on the A40 not far from Carmarthen. Ollie and I went out this afternoon but the landlord wasn't very forthcoming. I'm planning to send in a couple of incognito officers to check the place out this evening.'

'If we have got a far-right group operating locally, we'll need to inform the Counter Terrorism Unit,' Ben said.

'Not yet,' Heidi muttered. 'Too soon to know what we're dealing with. Give us a couple more days so we don't look foolish if we're wrong.'

'OK, I agree. How is the search for your sister going?'

'I know where she is now, sir, a commune near South Hatherop in the Cotswolds. The place is run by a group calling themselves "The Church of New Eden". A bloke called Adam Inverdale is the leader, a shady character with rumbles of an even shadier past. I'm struggling to find out much about him. Getting Greta out if she doesn't want to leave is going to be problematic.'

'Have you heard anything from her?'

Heidi nodded. 'She's been in touch – sort of. Pa took a call from her in the middle of the night. He told her to come home and she hung up.' Heidi sighed. 'I was hoping she'd be a walkaway, but from what she said to Pa, it doesn't look like that's going to happen and we can't just go in and snatch her. Although… if it was left to me…'

'Have you been in touch with the Gloucestershire force? Maybe they know something about this group?'

'On my list for tomorrow' – Heidi turned off her computer and shrugged into her jacket – 'together with everything else.'

'Make sure you don't tread on any toes, DC Holtz,' Ben warned, 'this is well outside our jurisdiction.'

Heidi nodded. 'Of course. Any news on the internal investigation regarding the slavery case?'

Several months previously, the team had discovered a gang trafficking individuals from Eastern Europe. The gang brought them into the UK from Ireland by boat and landing on the West coast of Wales in a cove close to the Harold Stone.

'Drawing to a close now,' Ben said. 'It was a bit touch and go at the start, but it looks as though me and Nettle will be OK. Dylan Hunter's future doesn't look good. Got too cosy with the other side. The large number of arrests we made certainly helped. It's difficult to sack coppers who catch bad guys. Still, it means I can assist with the murder investigation. I'll review the papers tonight to get up to speed and with a bit of luck we'll have two suspects in custody tomorrow. Make sure you round them up, we don't want to have to launch a manhunt.'

'We'll do our best, sir,' Erica said.

'Good. Get off now then, both of you, we'll reconvene tomorrow.'

* * *

Greta fidgeted on the wooden chair. She had been sitting facing the window since her imprisonment in the austere room. The sun had set but she didn't know what the time was. There was no clock in the room and she didn't wear a watch so could only guess how long she had been there. Knowing time was passing, but not how quickly, was disorientating, unsettling.

She stared through the glass but saw nothing. No lights shone anywhere and the sky was covered by thick cloud so even the moon was obscured. It seemed as though she had left one prison cell for another and this was worse because she didn't understand why she had to be here. Adam told her it was because she asked too many questions, but that was normal, surely? She'd only wanted to know if Clover and her baby were OK. Greta wondered if she would see the baby when she was released, or whether it would already have been taken by the couple Clover was acting as surrogate for. Was the child a boy or a girl?

A tawny owl shrieked close by and startled her out of the dark brooding. She strained her ears and heard the bird's mate return the call, but nothing else. No sounds from the house or the grounds. She stood, yawned, made up her bed and slipped under the sheets fully clothed. The bed felt like prison, the same thin mattress, wiry springs poking her ribs uncomfortably and pillows which refused to be plumped. With a surge of anger and frustration she hurled them across the room, pulled the covers over her head and tried not to cry.

The solitude was difficult to bear after the last few days working, eating and praying with the converts. She enjoyed the buzzing busyness of the commune, people always around. She missed Pixie and the others, longed for the open space of the garden. A worrying notion nudged the back of her skull. Maybe coming here had been a mistake. Maybe when she was released, she'd leave, go home to Freddie, endure the shouting that was bound to follow, then get back on with her life. Maybe New Eden wasn't for her.

* * *

The desk sergeant looked up from his paperwork as the main door was shouldered open by Oliver Langdon who grappled with an unwilling prisoner.

'Stop being a mug,' Oliver snarled. 'You keep this up and someone will get hurt and I'll tell you one thing – it won't be me.'

The sergeant summoned a couple of uniforms who joined the fray and took the squirming man to the cells.

'Are the others back yet?' Oliver asked, adjusting his jacket.

The sergeant said, 'You're the first. Who's that?' he asked and nodded towards the custody suite.

'One Jonesy Francombe. Not best pleased being yanked from his bed before cock-crow. Mouthy little sod, don't know how his gran puts up with him.' Oliver headed for the stairs. 'I need a coffee, give me a call when Peter Leech arrives. Is the sarge in?'

'Yeah, DS Bevan and DC Holtz clocked on early. DI James is up there too.'

The squad room was busy as the investigation changed gear and direction. Erica and Heidi were preparing to interview Francombe and taking another look through the CCTV footage. Ben James gazed at the incident board, while a pair of uniforms set up extra workstations at the back of the room, as the case morphed into a fully-fledged murder inquiry.

Oliver carried in a box full of plastic evidence bags and dumped it on a desk before heading to the coffee machine in the corner.

Erica looked up. 'Everything go OK?'

'Yeah, pretty much. Francombe is being booked and I believe Leech is on his way, haven't heard otherwise. This stuff came from Francombe's room.'

'What is it?' Heidi asked.

'Mainly paperwork,' Ollie said, 'including some nasty far-right magazines, couple of knives – one appears to be a copy of a Nazi Youth dagger – one tear gas canister and a taser.'

'Nice!' Heidi muttered ironically. 'With that little haul the bottom feeder downstairs won't be going anywhere soon. Does he have anything to say?'

Oliver laughed. 'Plenty, none of it repeatable.'

Ben moved closer, began removing bags from the box and lined them up on nearby desks. At the bottom he found a small book, similar in size to a passport and peered at it through the plastic before holding it up.

'Anyone ever heard of a group called "Cenedl Cymru"?' he asked.

Heads shook all around the room while Heidi attacked her keyboard.

'Yes, sir,' she said, 'internet says it's a far-right group promoting amongst other things, "Wales for the Welsh". The literal translation of the logo is "Nation Wales".' She scrolled screens. 'None of this stuff is good, mostly XRW material.'

'What?' Ben asked.

'Extreme Right Wing.' Heidi stood. 'Let's get downstairs, see what Francombe has to say for himself.'

'You and DS Bevan handle the interview,' Ben said. 'I'll be up here wading through the evidence.'

Chapter fourteen

Downstairs in the custody suite the sergeant asked, 'DS Bevan. Do you have a minute? I think it'll be worth you taking a quick look at something before you interview Francombe.'

'What have you got to show me, sergeant?'

'CCTV images captured when we booked him in.' He tapped his keyboard. The custody suite appeared on a computer screen and he advanced the footage slowly. 'I was asking him about any distinguishing marks or tattoos he had, for the sheet, you know, and he… there… just peeled off his shirt. Look at that lot.'

Erica and Heidi peered at the screen as the sergeant froze the image.

'Bloody hell,' Heidi said. 'He's got more ink than skin, what an appalling jumble.' She traced the images with a finger. 'What is all this? I recognise the swastikas and the stylised SS symbols, but what are all these numbers? 1488, 14, 5, 28 – they're everywhere.'

'Let's ask the boy himself,' Erica said and strode along the corridor to the interview rooms. Heidi trotted to catch up.

Erica barged into the small room, bounced the door off the wall and nearly gave the prisoner a heart attack.

'Bloody hell!' he yelped. 'Frightened me half to death.'

'Really?' Heidi asked quietly. 'Only half to death?'

Francombe stared at her. 'What did you say?'

Heidi ignored him, started the recording equipment, the officers sat and Erica opened a file as the machine whirred quietly.

'So… Jonesy Francombe. Is that you?' Erica asked.

'Yeah.'

'You live at 93 Church Street on the edge of Brecon with your gran, correct?'

'Yeah, it is.' He leaned back in his chair. 'So is one of you girls gonna tell me what this is about? You can't drag people out of bed at sparrow's-fart and not say why.'

'We obviously can,' Heidi muttered.

Francombe looked away and his face lost its smirk.

Erica asked, 'Where were you on the evening of the twenty-fifth of September from eleven onwards?'

'I'm not talking if you don't tell me what's going on.' Francombe grinned. 'Maybe I should have a solicitor?'

'Maybe you should,' Heidi muttered. 'Want one?'

Francombe stared at her again and blinked as though he couldn't believe what he was seeing.

'Is she a copper?' he asked Erica. 'Looks like a five-foot, skinhead Barbie. Cute.'

'Yes, she is a police officer. Now, answer my question. Where were you on the twenty-fifth?'

'I told you, unless you give me a clue why I'm here, I have nothing to say.' He pointed to a tattoo on the back of his middle finger, a blue-black, stylised number five, spiky and aggressive looking.

Heidi peered at it. 'What's that mean?'

'What I told you, "I have nothing to say". Five words, it's code.' Francombe grinned again. 'Alex Curtis said it, he's a big man in the States. It's a code of silence.'

'Who's Alex Curtis?' Erica asked.

'Someone who wants to protect white people from being overrun. Keep white people pure.'

'Are you talking about a white supremacist?'

Francombe shrugged and leaned back in his chair, balancing on two legs. He folded his arms and glared at Heidi.

'You better start talking,' Erica warned. 'There's big trouble coming down the line for someone… could be you. Talk to us and it might not be.'

'Then tell me why we're here!' Francombe snapped. 'We're going round in circles, this is bloody mental. You've got nothing and I have somewhere to be.' He rocked back and forth on the chair.

Heidi was sorely tempted to push him over, but instead lifted a box from the floor and held up evidence bags containing items removed from the prisoner's room.

'Let's talk about your toys,' she sneered. 'Little boy with some big knives. What's that all about, Jonesy? Can't afford a Porsche?'

He chuckled uneasily. 'Come on, copper, you can do better than fling insults around and if you can't, get on and nick me for my toys. I'm not bothered.'

'You could get ten for this haul,' Heidi hissed, 'and I'll make bloody sure that's what you do get.'

Francombe snorted. 'Ten years? Yeah right, dream on. First offence? Not a chance. Probation more than likely. Anyway, everyone knows the jails are full.'

Heidi reached into the box again and this time removed the small passport-like notebook. She flapped it under the prisoner's nose.

'We're considering charging you under the Terrorism Act,' she said, 'and being a member of a group like Cenedl Cymru won't help your case. Cenedl means nation, doesn't it? Nation Wales? What's that all about?'

'Still not bothered. Terrorism? Yeah, right.' He lifted his middle finger again and waved it under Heidi's nose. 'Not another word, bitch, until I get a solicitor.'

'Have it your way.' Heidi shot out a hand, snatched hold of the finger, dragged Francombe closer and slapped off the recording machine with her free hand.

'Hey!' Francombe yelped. 'Let go of my finger, you mad cow, that hurts. You'll break it!'

Heidi dropped his hand as Erica stormed angrily from the room, knowing her partner had blown any further attempt at interview. Heidi bent to pick up the box of evidence and leaned in close to Francombe.

'You think ten years is unlikely?' she whispered nastily. 'I'm betting on you getting life, scumbag. How'd you think you'll cope with that? Oh, and shame there's no room for any jail tattoos on your scuzzy hide, you'll just have to start collecting scars.'

* * *

Greta woke, splashed her face with cold water in the small bathroom and gazed through the window. The sun was still low in the sky so she knew it was early, but not how early.

A plate of muesli, soggy and disgusting rested on the floor behind the door. Surprisingly, Greta was hungry and bad as the cereal was – like sawdust and Polyfilla – she forced it down and drank water from the sink. She slipped the empty plate back under the door and went to the window. Spotting a movement at the far end of the drive, she watched as a dark grey people carrier drove towards the hall. It parked close to the front entrance and, by standing on the chair and peering towards the ground, Greta saw a middle-aged couple step out onto the gravel, watched as they entered the building. She didn't recognise them and wondered if they had come to collect Clover's baby.

Was that really possible? Surely the days when babies could be handed over to someone other than the parents were long gone. Maybe that was why no midwives were involved, no one in authority even knew the child existed. She thought again about Clover, how young she was and whether she was really OK. Then wondered how much longer she would have to stay in the room. Was it two nights and three days? In which case she only had to be here for one more night. Or three nights and four days? Questions zipped inside her brain, jumbled together. Confused and frustrated, she got into bed, curled into a ball and faced the wall.

With her eyes closed, she slipped easily into the space between waking and sleeping, an odd kind of gravity-defying state, where nothing seemed to matter. Thoughts spun webs of silk through her mind, twisting and sparking, but none were real and moved too fast to pin down. The room was still, silent. Greta heard no sounds from the house, had no external distractions, only internal ones. She knew she should wait by the window to see if she could get a glimpse of the baby – if that was why the couple had come to New Eden – but her half-conscious limbs were heavy and uncooperative. She remained on the bed, floating, listening to blood swish in her ears and the faint thump of her heart.

* * *

In interview room two, Peter Leech slumped in the chair, chin resting on his chest. A damp sheen covered his scalp which shone beneath the aggressively short haircut. In his early twenties, he could easily have passed as the older, fatter brother of Jonesy Francombe. He wore a dark shirt with short sleeves from which heavily inked arms protruded. More tattoos snaked across the backs of his hands and fingers, his arms wrapped protectively around his torso.

'If you don't speak up, Peter,' Heidi warned, 'you'll cop the lot for this. Jonesy has told us everything that occurred on the twenty-fifth, said it was your idea. Told us you used a lump of wood on Daniela, beat her so hard you flattened her face. You know she's dead, don't you?'

Leech swung his head from side to side. 'No, no, no. That's not what happened. I wasn't even there.'

'Which is it?' Erica cut in. 'You weren't there, or you know things didn't happen that way because you were there?'

Heidi leaned across the table. 'You snivelling bully boy. Look at the size of you. You should be ashamed, picking on a woman half your size. Like to tell us why?'

'Why what?' Leech mumbled.

'Why you attacked and killed Daniela? What had she ever done to you?'

'I didn't kill her,' Peter said. 'It wasn't me.'

'Jonesy said it was,' Heidi said, bending the truth even further. 'Been describing events in great detail, how you picked her out, waited for her outside the pub in a side street, pushed her to the ground, smashed the wood in her face… all you.'

Peter rested his head on his arms and groaned. 'He's lying. He chose the barmaid, said to wait for her to leave. Told me she was foreign and should go back home, not be over here taking our jobs.'

'So you're admitting you were there?'

Leech nodded.

'What do you do for work?' Erica asked.

'Unemployed,' Peter muttered reluctantly.

'Not taking your job then?' Heidi growled sarcastically.

Leech wouldn't meet her gaze and stared at the tabletop.

Erica opened the file, removed photographs of the victim's ruined face and spread them on the table in front of the prisoner. He winced and looked away.

'Horrible, aren't they?' Heidi snarled. She held a large picture in front of his nose. 'Don't you dare look away, you repulsive bastard.'

'So,' Erica said. 'Now we've established you were there, give us your version. If you're going to salvage anything from the rest of your life, here's your chance. Help us sort this out and who knows, we may be able to help you when this mess reaches court.'

'I'd bring back the death penalty for rats like you,' Heidi said. 'As it is, you'll get life and that's way too good for you. Your victim can't be given life, can she?'

Erica frowned at her partner, willed her to stay quiet, knew the prisoner was right for cracking.

'Tell us, Peter,' Erica implored. 'What happened?'

Minutes ticked by before he eventually spoke, 'We didn't mean to kill her.'

Erica waited, allowed the silence to stretch, knew Peter would feel under pressure to fill it.

'It was Jonesy's idea,' he muttered eventually. 'It always is. He said we should teach her a lesson, give her a bit of a smack, but he lost it, went mental, swinging the wood about. I tried to get it off him, honest I did, but he wouldn't let go, on autopilot or something. Then this massive bloke came charging down the street and we legged it. He grabbed hold of Jonesy, but he got away and the bloke gave up.'

Heidi glared at Leech across the tabletop and he looked away.

'Why did Jonesy want to attack Daniela?' Erica asked.

'Cos she wasn't from round here,' he mumbled.

'Is that it?' Heidi snapped. 'You killed a young woman because she "wasn't from round here"? You utter moron. Are you a member of this Cenedl Cymru lot?'

Peter nodded.

'Tell us about it.'

'I can't. My life won't be worth living.'

Heidi sniggered. 'And you think it is now? Do yourself a favour, stupid, provide a full statement and maybe, just maybe, you can improve your luck... a little.'

Chapter fifteen

Greta was hungry and snatched the plate of rice and lentils as soon as it appeared under the door. She ate quickly with her fingers, sitting on the chair in front of the window. The sun was sinking rapidly and she watched it drop towards the treetops, night would arrive soon.

Surprisingly quickly she had slipped into a natural sort of time, one which didn't need clocks. Mealtimes, the sun and shadows on the walls had become her markers. She finished her food and put the plate beneath the chair, eyes fixed on the window, anxious not to miss a second of the sunset. Pale orange and salmon pink stained the sky and set fire to low clouds. She smiled, felt the last warmth of the sun on her face. After the last shard of light had vanished, Greta stood, pushed the empty plate back into the hallway and curled up on the bed.

She allowed herself to slip into the tranquillity of almost-sleep. Having discovered the trance-like state she now craved it, sought it out; the floating sensation and the twisting, dreamy thoughts were addictive.

She tried to remember how long she had been in the room, two nights? Three? Did it really matter? She couldn't even be sure why she was here, couldn't remember what Adam had told her. Questions swamped her tired brain. Why did she feel so exhausted? She hadn't done anything but sit on the chair or lie on the bed. How could doing nothing make her so tired? What would happen when she was released? Would she be allowed to stay at New Eden? Greta realised she didn't want to leave, wanted to stay more than anything, and how could she possibly go home? Back to all the rubbishy shenanigans of her utterly dysfunctional family? She couldn't do that. When Adam opened the door she'd tell him she was committed, a true acolyte and would do whatever it took to be allowed to stay.

* * *

Heidi pulled up in the parking space at the front of her building, turned off the engine and yawned.

'God, that was a hard day,' she grouched. 'Always wears me out, being stuck in interview rooms with uncooperative bottom feeders.'

Erica smiled at her partner. 'You do look done in. Hot bath for you, I'll cook supper.'

'I was hoping you'd offer.' Heidi giggled, slipped out of the car and headed down stone steps to the basement flat. Erica was left to round up a spill of files on the back seat, squirming fingers beneath the front seats to snag stragglers. She locked the car, entered the flat and heard bath water running. She dumped the mound of cardboard and paper on the sofa, followed a discarded trail of clothing and peered around the bathroom door. Heidi was just lowering herself under a hillock of bubbles, the room full of steam and neroli.

'Anything special you fancy?' Erica asked.

'You,' Heidi said, stirring foam suggestively.

Erica chuckled. 'For supper.'

'Anything that's food. Fridge is full, help yourself.'

A while later, Erica served plates of spiced king prawns nestling on beds of wild rice, green salad in a large bowl. Heidi poured wine and toasted her partner.

'This looks fab, thanks, E. All I have to do now is stay awake long enough to eat it.'

'We made good progress today,' Erica said, spearing a prawn with her fork, 'even if your interview technique stinks and winds me up something terrible. Why did you antagonise Francombe?'

'Cos I could!' Heidi chuckled. 'Oh, don't look like that, he was never gonna talk to us and as Leech came up with the goods it doesn't matter.'

Erica huffed, 'It matters.'

'Not much,' Heidi said and changed the subject. 'How did the cops you sent to The Prince Llewelyn last night get on? Return with any useful info?'

Erica poured more wine. 'Some. Identifications of a few known-to-police types and descriptions of another ten, all of whom appear to be members of this Cenedl Cymru group. Our guys managed to snap a few furtive shots on their phones. Can you believe it? The suspects were all wearing printed T-shirts, bold as brass, skin covered in swastikas and Klu Klux Klan crosses.'

'The XRW are not known for their shy and retiring nature.'

'Ollie and Tegan are busy putting names to these characters and Ben James has been talking with the Counter Terrorism Unit in Bristol. Seems they're coming in tomorrow morning to meet the team.'

'I don't know when racism morphed into terrorism,' Heidi said. 'That isn't what we need, a bunch of out-of-town plods telling us what to do. We ought to just round up the bad guys, lock them up and chuck away the key. Job done.' Heidi sighed. 'I can't stop thinking about that poor woman.'

They ate the rest of the meal in silence, immersed in their own thoughts. Erica cleared away the plates, placed a dish of ice cream in front of Heidi and asked, 'Any more contact from Greta?'

Heidi shook her head and mumbled through a mouthful of chocolate chip, 'No, but I have uncovered more of Inverdale's past. His birth name is Adrian Ingham, born and bred on the outskirts of Bath in Twerton, a tough council estate. Patchy record, minor stuff, shoplifting, nicking cars, drugs. No jail time, but a short spell in rehab after he got involved with class A's.' She spooned in more ice cream. 'Then a long gap in his CV until he turns up running self-improvement seminars – ironically! Another shorter gap – I'm certain he went to dry out at an ashram in Kerala. Then just over three years ago, The Church of New Eden arrives on the scene and Adrian is now Adam.' Heidi laughed. 'Sounds like a story from the Bible, local ne'er-do-well has a moment of enlightenment in a strange land and bingo – a new religion is born.'

'Have you been able to discover how the group is financed?'

'No, but what I can tell you is there's way too much money involved. Three small niche shops cannot possibly support the commune or stuff Inverdale's private coffers, and trust me when I say his coffers are well and truly stuffed.'

'You got into his personal bank accounts?'

Heidi grinned. 'Of course! Easy once I knew who I was looking for. He's worth a mint. There was a large deposit just a week ago, £125,000. Haven't been able to trace where the cash came from yet, but I will. I did wonder if he's fleecing his converts, but I've checked Greta's accounts too and there haven't been any withdrawals since before she was sent down.'

Much to Erica's amusement, Heidi picked up the empty dessert dish and licked it clean. She plonked the dish back on the table, wiped her mouth with the back of her hand and stared at her partner across the tablecloth.

'I have to rescue Greta,' she said. 'Everything about New Eden reeks. The place is a cover for something, I know it is. The converts are being used like human shields, a distraction to keep us from looking where Adam doesn't want us to.'

'OK, honey, I get it, really I do. If Greta was my sister I'd want to bring her home, but what if she doesn't want to be rescued? What then? And how are we going to get to her?'

'I've given the matter a lot of thought,' Heidi said. 'I'll sign up. If I'm a card carrying member I'll have access to everything and will be able to check out what's really going on at the hall at the same time as I remove Greta. I'll take a week off, pull a sickie if I have to, but don't think I can leave it much longer. Apart from anything else, Freddie's getting antsy and that could spell trouble.'

Heidi's mobile tinkled and she answered without checking the number.

'Yep. Holtz.'

'Heidi? Is that you?'

Heidi froze. She hadn't heard the voice for years, but recognised it instantly and shuddered.

'What do you want?' Heidi asked coldly.

'I've been speaking with Freddie, and I…'

'Get to the point, Mother. I'm busy.'

The woman spluttered on the other end of the line. 'It's just… he says Greta is missing. Gone off with a cult or something.'

'If you know that, why are you ringing me? We don't have anything to say to each other and you know that too.'

'Well… because, you're police. You ought to be able to do something to help.'

'Only ring when you want something, is that it? Where are you?'

'At the house in Northumberland.'

'Thank God. I'd hate to think you were making Freddie's life a misery. Don't ring me again.' Heidi hung up and dropped the phone in her pocket.

'That was your mum?' Erica asked. 'You hung up on your mum?'

Heidi cracked her knuckles and got up from the table. 'I don't want to talk about this, really I don't. I'm tired and off to bed. You coming?'

Erica waved at the pile of folders on the sofa. 'I'll have a look through the case first.'

'Please yourself.'

Heidi disappeared into the bedroom and with a sigh Erica collected the paperwork, spread it on the table and wondered whether she should find some spare bedding and sleep on the sofa.

Chapter sixteen

Oliver Langdon crept in at the back of the squad room as DI Ben James introduced his team to the officers from Counter Terrorism. He stood in front of the incident board to speak.

'I'd like you all to meet DI Lizzie Wild and DS Connor Haskins.' The newcomers nodded and offered friendly smiles. 'They've been sent from Bristol CTU to help us with the murder case. They have much more experience of XRW groups than we do and, having established there is such a group operating in the area, their expertise will be invaluable. The group calls itself "Cenedl Cymru" – Nation Wales – and we believe two of their members, Francombe and Leech – both in custody – are responsible for the murder of Daniela Stoica on the twenty-fifth and maybe three earlier muggings in town.' He took a sip of coffee before continuing. 'They have been detained under the Terrorism Act so we have longer to question them, but need to ensure we use that time efficiently, hence the seconded officers. DI Wild will head the team from now on and I expect you to show her how well Dyfed Powys can perform. Don't let me down. Now, DI Wild, would you like a few words?'

Ben perched on the edge of a desk and Lizzie Wild took his place. She was in her fifties with shoulder length, silver-grey hair. Tall and muscular, she wore a well-tailored, dark trouser suit and spoke in a broad Bristolian accent. Connor Haskins stood by her side. He was younger, ginger with watery blue eyes nestling in a mass of freckles. A thin man, scruffy, suit shiny, shoes unpolished, chin unshaven.

'Morning everyone, good to meet you,' DI Wild said.

Heidi zoned out. She had more pressing things on her mind than meeting new coppers and listening to their spiel. Speaking to her mother had left a nasty taste she couldn't get rid of, and the call had angered her beyond what was reasonable. The woman had obviously called Freddie after Heidi hung up on her, because he'd phoned to have a moan. He couldn't understand why Heidi hadn't brought Greta home yet, even though she told him over and over again that wasn't going to happen. It couldn't, not just like that. He was becoming a pest and was now threatening to go to the commune himself and cause a scene. Heidi knew if she didn't show him some positive results soon, he'd do just that, probably with a SWAT team in tow. She smiled, it took one to know one.

Erica was also a problem for the first time since the start of their relationship. Heidi knew her partner was curious about the past and also knew she didn't want to tell her about it – not yet, maybe never. Erica was special, different and Heidi adored her company, and was fascinated by her quick mind, but felt as though her partner was not on side. She constantly repeated that Heidi shouldn't go in and rescue Greta, but didn't make any sensible suggestions about how to get her out – and Greta couldn't stay. Heidi was sure of that. It was time she took some positive action and if Erica didn't want to be part of it, so be it. She heard her name called and mentally rejoined the group.

DI Wild was speaking to her, 'Will that be OK with you, Constable?'

'Will what be OK?'

'If you spend time with DS Haskins this morning, walk him through the case?'

'No problem,' Heidi said and dragged an extra chair towards her desk.

Wild nodded. 'On with it then the rest of you. Bad guys only get caught when we're out on the streets, maybe you can bring me one each.' She winked and Heidi cringed, pretty certain she wasn't going to get on with the new boss.

* * *

Greta heard a rattle at the door and jumped to her feet. The sound was startling after the hours of silence and the hairs on the back of her neck prickled uncomfortably. She faced the door and waited for it to be opened. When the barrier swung wide she saw Adam standing outside, arms outstretched, a broad smile on his face.

'Greta. Beloved,' he intoned. 'It is time to leave this place. Come to me.'

Greta dashed across the room and Adam wrapped her in his arms. This time she felt the love he offered and didn't pull away, relaxed into his embrace, and held him to her.

He opened his arms. 'Did you find answers to your questions?' he asked, studying her face, hands resting on her shoulders.

'Yes, I did,' she breathed. 'I know what I want.'

'And what is that?'

'To be here with you, a member of The Church of New Eden. I want to make my new life work and want you to show me how. Show me the way to God.'

'Bravo, Greta! A true disciple. Come, take my hand and we'll share your enlightenment with the others at early meditation. A good way to ease you back into the community.'

Greta took his hand willingly and allowed him to lead her from the room, along the narrow corridor and down to the great hall. He pushed open the heavy door, the congregation rose as one and burst into spontaneous applause. After the silence of the last few days, the noise sounded like a football crowd and Greta flinched.

Adam squeezed her hand. 'Don't be afraid, beloved, they are happy to see you. Open your heart and allow God's righteousness in. Allow the community to cradle your spirit, be assured, we won't drop you. Now, take your place and we'll begin. Deep breaths, Greta.' Adam released her hand and gave her a gentle push towards the devotees.

Pixie leapt up and hugged Greta, helped her to the cushions. Eleanor kissed her, others waved and smiled encouragingly. Greta looked for Clover, but her place was empty. Mala was present but wouldn't catch Greta's eye. Adam walked through his followers, brushing heads with his fingers and took his place on the low stage. The hall quietened, Adam raised his face and arms to heaven and the session began.

Later, Greta was aware of a hand on her shoulder and opening her eyes, she looked up at Adam. The hall was empty and she struggled to her feet.

'Oh, Adam, I'm sorry…'

'Shush, beloved.' Adam embraced her, held her tight, then led her gently through the red cushions to the back of the stage. He opened the door to his private chambers and ushered her inside.

'You will spend the rest of this night with me and God,' he said and pushed the door closed.

* * *

Erica leant on a council rubbish bin at the rear of the police station, trying to shelter from sticky drizzle which floated down in sheets. She turned up her collar, tapped a number on her phone and willed the call to be answered quickly.

'Hello, Milebrook Manor.'

'Morning, Freddie, it's Erica.'

'Good morning, my dear. Everything OK?'

'As well as can be expected, thank you. If you have a moment I wanted a word about Heidi.'

'What's she done now?' he asked.

'Nothing, it's what she's going to do that bothers me. She's planning to masquerade as a convert of The Church of New Eden so she can gain entry and remove Greta.'

'That's a good thing surely?' Freddie asked. 'It's about time something was done. My daughter has effectively been kidnapped and no one seems to want to do anything about it. Utterly outrageous!'

Erica sighed. 'We've been through this. You know why nothing's been done, and let's be honest, I'm sure you'll have been talking to your Whitehall buddies. I'll bet none of them have suggested raiding the place. If they had, you'd have made it happen.'

Freddie chuckled. 'Didn't take you long to get to know me, did it?'

'I'm a good judge of character, that's why I'm a copper. We must stop Heidi trying to do this. She's too close and I think she'll be in danger. She's not the most discreet individual and upsets people, even when she's trying to be pleasant, so the cult members won't like her infiltrating their numbers. She's not invincible, merely thinks she is.'

'So, what do you suggest?'

'I'll go in. I'm not so emotionally attached and well aware of the techniques cults use so I'm not worried about being brainwashed. I'll go back to the shop in Upper Yanworth and convince the members who work there that I'm serious about joining. Maybe they'll just take me home with them.'

'I'm sure it won't be as easy as that,' Freddie said. 'Surely they don't just pick random people from the street.'

'How do you know? They obviously pick random prisoners from jail or Greta would have been home a week or more ago.'

'A fair point.'

'I agree with Heidi that someone has to go in and not only to rescue Greta. There's far too much money involved with this group and the cult leader isn't who he says he is. Something dodgy is going on which the police may be able to get involved with, but not without any proof something is going on, if you understand me.'

Freddie said, 'I see that, yes.'

'So, my plan is to book a week off, get myself inside, find out what's going on and get back out again, hopefully with Greta. If I can't persuade her to leave, I might be able to discover a reason the police can use to raid the place. It's a bit ifs, buts and maybes, but the best I can come up with.'

'What does Heidi say?'

Erica hesitated. 'We haven't talked about it,' she admitted. 'I've tried, believe me, but she's not being very receptive. She received a call from her mother yesterday and it's really rattled her.'

'Yes,' Freddie muttered, 'it would. She hasn't spoken to her mother since she was six years old.'

Erica was hoping he'd say more, but he didn't elaborate.

‘I’m planning to leave Heidi a note,’ Erica said, ‘tell her what I’m doing and why. Hopefully she’ll do as I ask and stay put. She can be a bit like a firework in a hay barn sometimes, whizzes around in all directions starting fires.’

‘You’re not wrong.’ Freddie laughed. ‘Probably picked that up from me, that and her brains.’

‘I’m sorry, Freddie, but I have to go. We’re in the middle of a murder investigation on top of all this. The brass aren’t going to like me taking time off, but I must do this to keep Heidi safe.’

‘Make sure you update me regularly and if you do get into any sort of trouble, there’s bound to be something I can do from my end.’

‘OK, will do. I’m planning the operation for as soon as I can get away but I’ll phone when I get a chance. Please, do not mention this to Heidi.’

‘I won’t, you have my word and thank you for trying to help my family. I shall always be grateful never mind the outcome.’

Chapter seventeen

The drizzle had finally lifted, autumn sunshine bathed the kitchen garden in sparkles and leaves dripped diamonds. Greta and Eleanor were harvesting potatoes. Greta was humming.

‘You’re happy this morning,’ Eleanor said. ‘Glad to be back with us?’

‘You have no idea. Being here, in this place, with you,’ Greta planted a sudden kiss on Eleanor’s cheek, ‘is just sensational.’

'Your seclusion brought you peace and closer to God, I can see it on your face. You've let go, Greta. Seeing you so happy is like watching magic.'

'It's not just that, it's everything!' Greta leapt to her feet, flung her arms wide and whirled like a top between the vegetable beds. She hadn't covered much ground before she cannoned into Mala who had entered the garden unnoticed.

'Bloody hell,' the woman snapped. 'What do you think you're doing?'

'Being happy, being alive,' Greta sang.

Mala shot out a hand and dragged Greta closer. 'Well don't! Do your work.' She shoved Greta away from her.

'Hey!' Greta protested. 'Don't push me around. You can't do that.'

'Don't think you're special, Greta. There's nothing special about you.' Mala laughed nastily. 'Think you can share Adam's life because you've shared his bed? Wrong. We all share his bed eventually.'

'What?'

Mala ignored her and turned to Eleanor. 'Clover still isn't fit for work and things are backing up. Can I have one of the kitchen girls? Everyone else is too busy and Felix is missing.'

'Where's he gone?' Eleanor asked.

Mala sighed. 'If I knew, he wouldn't be missing. When you take the veg up, send Pixie to the cottage, the other two are useless.' She turned on her heel and marched away.

'What did she mean?' Greta asked. 'About everyone sharing Adam's bed.'

Eleanor shrugged. 'What she said. He sleeps with all the women. You obviously can't have a problem with that or you wouldn't have spent the night with him.'

'But… I thought…'

'Greta, enough with this negativity. Look how happy you were just minutes ago. Be that! Don't let Mala upset you. She's worried about Clover and stressed with work.

Take the spuds up to the kitchen and tell Pixie she's wanted at the cottage. Forget the rest, it's just noise.'

Greta loaded a trug with tubers and set off towards the house. She realised she was crying and wiped a muddy hand across her face, angry with herself. She was confused, disorientated. Just when she thought things were settling down, sorting themselves out, something else had happened and now nothing made sense. Adam had been so tender last night, cradled her in his arms, she had felt his love. She couldn't believe he was like that with all the women. A sudden thought hit her, was Clover's baby his? Maybe Pixie knew.

Greta pushed in through the kitchen door and dumped the trug in the sink. Pixie was stirring a huge pot of stew, the others chopping vegetables and grating cheese.

'I've brought you some potatoes,' Greta said. 'Hope that's enough.'

Pixie glanced up from the pot and giggled. 'You have mud all over your face. Here.' She wiped Greta's face with a tea towel and peered into the sink. 'That should be plenty, thanks.'

'Mala wants you to help her at the cottage,' Greta said. 'Everything's getting behind because Clover isn't back at work and no one knows where Felix is. Do you?'

Pixie coloured, caught off guard. 'No, I don't… not really.'

'Do you or don't you?' Greta was getting fed up with people who didn't speak plainly.

Pixie glanced at the other girls and whispered urgently, 'He's left. Gone. We aren't supposed to talk about it.'

'Why not?'

Pixie shrugged. 'Adam says not to.'

'Why did he leave?'

'Who knows? Not like he left a note or anything, just walked away during the night.'

'You're sure he's gone and not still somewhere around?'

'I haven't seen him, not since he came out of seclusion, so he must have.' Pixie retied her hair. 'When does Mala want me?'

'Now, I think. She seemed stressed.'

'I'll be in for a fun day then. See you at supper.'

Pixie dashed out. Greta picked up the empty trug, smiled at Suzy and Cassie and left the kitchen, head full of worries. She wanted to talk to Adam, ask him what was going on, but no one bothered Adam, other than at mealtimes and after meditation sessions, and she couldn't speak to him in front of the others.

Instead of returning to the garden, Greta turned into the main part of the house and wandered the corridors. She was miserable, wanted to see Clover and guessed she was still in the medical centre. She walked down the passageway at the back of the house and found the door Mala had burst out of a few nights ago. Greta pressed her ear against the wood, held her breath and listened. She couldn't hear any sounds from inside, so cracked open the door and peered in.

Four metal framed beds lined one wall, all empty apart from the last one in the row. A shape was curled beneath the quilt and Greta moved closer, trying not to make any noise. Walking to the side of the bed she recognised Clover, fast asleep, bedclothes clasped beneath her chin. The young girl was pale, skin the colour of milk, apart from her eyelids which were hideously swollen and bright crimson as though she had been crying for days.

Greta stretched out her hand, then hesitated. Clover didn't look peaceful, but she was asleep and while she was sleeping, she wasn't crying. Greta knelt on the floor by the bed and watched the girl as waves of sorrow washed over her. She tried to imagine what giving away a baby must have been like – and couldn't. Reluctantly she struggled to her feet and crept from the room. She shut the door quietly behind her and headed back out to the garden.

* * *

Lizzie Wild stood at the front of the squad room and called the officers to order.

'I won't take much of your time,' she said, 'but we've had some luck identifying members of Cenedl Cymru using photos taken at The Prince Llewelyn earlier in the week.'

She turned to the incident board and pinned up an enlarged photograph of a handsome man in his early thirties with dark, curly hair, strong chin and a wide smile.

'Let me introduce you to Daffydd Owen, thirty-four years old, moved here from a small settlement on the edge of Porthmadog in the north. He is known to the CTU and Clwyd Police, mainly due to the exploits of his family. His grandfather and father' – she pinned two more photos to the board – 'were both suspected of being involved with the holiday cottage fires in the eighties and members of Meibion Glyndŵr, a far-right group. Dad did some time, couldn't get anything to stick to Granddad. Daffydd doesn't have a record himself, but has shown excessive interest in XRW groups. Constable Holtz has uncovered some useful details regarding this individual's internet use and his radical views.' Lizzie nodded and smiled at Heidi. 'Thank you, Heidi.'

Heidi didn't look up, not interested in praise. She waved a limp hand and continued to work the keyboard, immersed in her own world.

Lizzie continued, 'I've spoken with DI James and we've agreed to put a tail on Daffydd, find out who he meets, where he goes, usual drill. Heidi will monitor his internet use twenty-four seven and report anything that causes concern. The more information we can gather about Daffydd Owen, the better. Francombe and Leech have both been denied bail – unsurprisingly – and Connor and I will be reinterviewing both again later today.' She took a gulp of lukewarm coffee and grimaced. 'So, I need three teams of two for the tail. Oliver Langdon and Tegan Hughes will take the first shift, team two take over at 1am, team three at 9am. Daffydd Owen is living in a bed and breakfast in Brecon, so we'll stake the place out and begin the tail when he leaves. Langdon and Hughes, get a scoot on and make sure you don't lose him.'

Oliver and Tegan left the room to begin the surveillance.

'DS Bevan and DC Holtz will run the office; the rest of you, get some sleep. I have a feeling we're going to need it over the next few days.'

The office emptied quickly leaving Erica and Heidi with the phones and the paperwork. Erica yawned.

'Why don't you go home?' Heidi asked. 'You look shattered. I can handle the office on my own, so sneak off and have a rest. If we're lumbered with any tailing duties tomorrow you'll need to be awake.'

'No, I should stay, there's so much to do.'

Heidi shook her head. 'No, you should get some rest. I'll cover for you. Go on, I'll be home before midnight and try not to wake you.'

Chapter eighteen

Oliver pulled up in the car park outside The Prince Llewelyn Inn and struggled to find a space.

'Blimey, it's busy,' he grumbled. 'Still, should make it easier for us to keep an eye on our man.'

'Let's hope the landlord doesn't recognise you,' Tegan said. 'Don't forget you came here recently with DS Bevan.'

'Good point,' Oliver said. 'You buy the drinks and I'll tuck myself away.'

They walked across the yard, slipped in through a side door and found a small table in a dark nook. Oliver sat with his back to the room and Tegan pushed through the drinkers to the bar.

A young woman was simultaneously serving and fending off a group of male customers who were trying to chat her up.

'Yes,' she said. 'What can I get you?'

'Two halves of best please.'

The barmaid pulled the drinks and placed condensation covered glasses on the bar.

'Anything else?'

'No, that's fine for now, thanks.' Tegan paid for the beer, carried the glasses over to the nook and glanced at the customers as she passed.

'Daffydd Owen is on the far side of the bar,' she hissed, 'at a table near the back door with two men. Should we get closer? Maybe we can hear what they're talking about.'

Oliver shook his head. 'No. We're only here to watch. I'll try to grab a photo of his buddies if I can, but no – we sit tight.'

Daffydd was deep in conversation with his friends, animated, and every now and again laughter broke out.

'How's Granddad?' Daffydd asked. 'I should have got up to see him before now, but things are gaining momentum here.'

'He's fine.' Rhys chuckled. 'Still hates the English. Lobbed his Zimmer frame at a tourist's car last week, put a bloody great dent in the door. Got away with it, the driver was too scared to get out and face him, just drove off.'

Daffydd laughed. 'Christ, the old fella is ninety-one! Some people haven't got any balls at all.'

'Lily-livered lot, the English,' Geraint muttered. He drank deeply and wiped damp lips on his sleeve. 'How's it going down here for you, boy?' he asked.

'Can't get work,' Daffydd grumbled. 'Qualified stonemason and I can't get work. The cathedral in Brecon is undergoing major refurbishment, but the foreman said he couldn't take me on, couldn't afford my rates.'

'Bloody immigrants,' Rhys mumbled, 'undercut the rest of us so we go without.'

'I even tried looking for labouring jobs,' Daffydd said. 'Not a chance. The building sites are all fully staffed and not a Welsh accent to be heard on any of them. I can't believe how many foreigners have found their way here, they're everywhere. Haven't even been able to find a decent place to live yet, making do with a scuzzy Bed and Breakfast in town. Granddad would hate it.'

Geraint went to the bar to refresh their drinks and returned with three pints and three whisky chasers balanced on a tray.

'How's it going with Cenedl Cymru,' Geraint asked. 'I heard you had a bit of trouble.'

Daffydd sighed heavily. 'Two stupid lads have been wandering around town beating up immigrants. Took it too far the other night and smacked a Romanian girl so hard she died. Both are in jail on remand.' He drank from his glass. 'At least I don't have to put up with them any longer. Idiots, both. I told everyone in the group we need to change our image, tone things down and look respectable. Everyone understood, except those two.'

'Will they cause trouble for you?'

'Doubt it. The coppers haven't got anything on me. I'm clean and what could these kids say? That I'm running a far-right group? Cenedl Cymru isn't on any banned list, so we're not breaking any laws. All we're doing is trying to stand up for the white man, the Welsh.' Daffydd drained his whisky. 'Look around you, boys,' he said. 'This place is packed with like-minded folk. None of the men in here want foreigners taking our jobs and our homes and we are all entitled to an opinion. You can't be arrested for an opinion.'

'Not yet,' Rhys mumbled darkly. 'Give the bastards time.'

'Until then,' Daffydd said, 'we spread the word. Are you planning to stay down here to help the cause?'

They nodded.

'Good. We've a rally planned for Brecon city centre in a couple of days. I'm hoping for a good show, but our protest must be peaceful. No running battles or anything daft, but we can make as much noise as we like. We'll frighten the shit out of the incomers.'

* * *

Greta and Pixie sat side by side on Greta's bed. Pixie was crying and Greta was trying to stem her tears.

'Hush now, sweetie,' she said and handed her friend a wad of tissues. 'Talk to me, tell me what's wrong?'

Pixie snuffled, wiped her eyes and began to cry again.

'Come on, tell me what's up,' Greta begged. 'I can't help if you don't. This isn't like you, Pixie, you're always so happy.'

'Everything's wrong,' the young girl sobbed, 'bloody everything. It's all going wrong.'

'What is?'

'I told you… everything. Mala has been a bitch all day ordering me about, keeping me at it. I don't know how Clover puts up with her, even if Mala is her mother. I never want to work in the cottage again. If they try to make me, I'll do a Felix and get the hell out.'

Greta handed the distressed girl more tissues and a glass of water.

'You must calm down,' she said. 'You'll make yourself ill. Drink some water.'

Pixie slurped noisily and put the empty glass on the bedside table.

'I miss Felix,' she sniffed. 'Me and him were – well, you know – but he's gone. We came here together and he's just walked away, didn't even tell me he was going. I can't believe it.' Pixie sobbed some more and Greta hugged her tight. 'And there's Clover…'

'I saw her today,' Greta said quietly. 'After you went to the cottage, I snuck to the back of the house and found her in the medical centre.'

'How is she? What did she say?'

'Nothing. She was fast asleep and I didn't want to wake her. Looked like she'd been crying.'

'She didn't want to give her baby away,' Pixie whispered, 'but Adam insisted. Told her she had to, that it was God's will her child was brought up by others.'

'Why didn't she leave before her baby was born?'

'Couldn't. Nowhere to go and no money, so she stayed and hoped Adam would change his mind, but he didn't. Her baby was taken as soon as the new parents arrived. I think it was a little girl.'

'Who is the father?'

'Adam of course. He's had three since I've been here and they've all been taken away. Adam says New Eden is no place for children and that by fathering children for childless couples he is doing God's work.'

'Adam slept with Clover and made her pregnant?' Greta was appalled. 'Clover's little more than a child. How does he get away with it?'

'No one outside New Eden knows what goes on. Adam can pretty much do what he likes and the others go along with it, but it's not right, is it?'

'No, it isn't.' Greta stood and began pacing the room. 'Why did Felix leave?' she asked.

'I don't really know. Missing his mum maybe, that's why he called her, but he hated being shut away from the rest of us. I didn't see him after Adam let him out, he got away as soon as he could. I've tried to talk to the others, but they won't speak about it – Adam has ordered us not to.'

'Do you want to leave?'

'Oh, I don't know, can't get my brain to work properly. I'm so tired all the time, but love the people here – not Mala – but most of the others, and if I leave, where do I go? It's not like I have a family to go home to.'

'You don't have a family? No one?'

Pixie shook her head. 'They disowned me three years ago. I was caught with cannabis and fined. Dad told me to leave and never come back home, said I'd brought disgrace on the family.'

'That sounds harsh.'

'He was a bully my dad, always laying down the law and made my life miserable. That's why I joined New Eden, thought things would be different here. Adam convinced me he knew the path to God, told me he'd care for me, show me the way and I believed him.' Tears began to trickle down her cheeks.

'Get into bed, Pixie,' Greta said and pulled the quilt aside so the girl could slip underneath. 'Sleep on it. We'll talk again in the morning, but you need some rest.'

'What about you?' Pixie asked. 'Are you happy here?'

'I was – very – now I'm not so sure. Get your head down now, early meditation will roll round quickly and you look exhausted.'

Greta climbed into her own bed and tucked the covers tightly around her shoulders, but she didn't sleep, couldn't, mind fizzing with worries and questions.

Chapter nineteen

Heidi unlocked the front door of her basement flat, and crept inside, anxious not to wake Erica whom she was sure would be in bed. The flat was dark, no lights on anywhere and after checking the bedroom door was shut, Heidi flicked on a lamp in the bay window where her cello rested on a stand. Immediately she noticed a scrap of folded paper tucked beneath the strings on the finger board, slipped it out and found a note from Erica.

My Darling Girl,
Please read this before you start breathing fire, and then read it twice more!
With a bit of luck by the time you find this, I'll be inside the New Eden commune hunting for Greta – obviously – but also trying to get a handle on what else is going on. Might as well have a sniff around if I get the chance, eh?
I made this decision because I know you were planning to go in yourself and I didn't want that. You're much too close to the situation to be effective, something you'll realise if you take a moment to think about it.
If I can phone I will, but don't expect a call. No news is always good news. Keep that in mind and DON'T – whatever you do – come steaming over to the Cotswolds, you're more use where you are. Freddie knows what's going on and has promised to stay close to the phone in case I encounter trouble. I'm pretty sure I won't need him, but good to know backup is available.
I plan to stay no longer than a week. DI James was not best pleased when I demanded time off, not that he had a choice. Watch your back, honey, cos he's going to be a grumpy bear tomorrow and I don't want you to be my whipping girl.

'A week?' Heidi asked the empty room. 'Why stay so long?' She read on.

Seven days should give me enough time to find out about all the money sloshing around. As you said, there has to be something criminal going on so I plan to find out what it is, bring Greta home and then we can take down The Church of New Eden. Who knows, everything may go so well I'll be back tomorrow.

Heidi screwed the paper into a tight ball, lobbed it at the chandelier hanging from the ceiling, grinned when the scrap snagged on glass droplets like a mini snowball trapped in an icicle cage. She went to the drinks cabinet, poured a large brandy into a crystal glass and took a hefty swig. She swirled the spirit round her mouth before swallowing and closed her eyes as fire blossomed in her throat.

She placed the glass on a side table, lifted her cello from its stand, tuned the strings, cracked her knuckles, then stroked the catgut with the rosined bow. A deep mellow note sounded and filled the room with a bass vibration. Heidi held the note, bowing slowly back and forth across the strings. Her thin, spidery fingers twitched suddenly, wrapped themselves around the neck of the instrument and she began to play, an Elgar cello concerto so loved by her icon, Jacqueline du Pré.

The moment the first note floated into the room Heidi was transported elsewhere, hands and fingers on remote control as notes flew wildly above her head. She drowned in the music. Racing to the end of the piece, she held the final note as long as possible, then placed her cello back on the stand, poured another large brandy and carried it to her desk.

She switched on the computer, sipped her drink and waited for her system to wake up. The screen saver flashed up and Heidi typed a command. Another short wait until a detailed map of South Hatherop appeared. More tapping to enlarge the area surrounding the commune and the layout of the building itself. Heidi peered at the screen. A small red blob suddenly appeared inside the boundaries of the building and she breathed a sigh of relief. Erica was wearing her necklace, the one Heidi had given her soon after they had become an item. The pendant contained a tiny GPS device and allowed Heidi to keep track of her lover's movements. She'd never checked it before and was sure if Erica knew what the locket contained she'd be furious, but Heidi didn't care. She'd never become attached to anyone before and was determined not to lose her lover.

She glanced at the paper ball snagged in the chandelier and used a mop handle to knock it back to earth. She flattened out the paper and finally read the rest of the note.

> *You should know by now I am perfectly capable of looking after myself, so please, my love, stay where you are. Let me do this for you and don't worry. Everything will be fine, I promise. If it isn't I'll shout for help.*
> *Don't forget, darling girl, that I love you.*
> *E xxxx*

* * *

The team assembled in the squad room to listen to an update from Lizzie Wild. She wasn't in the best of moods.

'OK, gang, it's like this. DS Bevan has gone AWOL,' she snapped. 'DI James informed me this morning your sergeant has taken a week's unplanned leave. Obviously this will leave us understaffed so you're all going to have to put more hours in.' She lifted her head and glared at Heidi who was working at her computer. 'DC Holtz, I'm guessing you know what she's up to. Care to enlighten the rest of us? What is so important that DS Bevan can't do her job?'

'My understanding is she's been granted compassionate leave,' Heidi said, without looking up, 'for a personal matter. I have absolutely no intention of discussing with you, or anyone else, the sergeant's private business.'

'I beg your pardon?' Lizzie snapped.

'You heard,' Heidi snapped back.

'You need to moderate how you speak to me,' Lizzie said. 'Insubordination will not be tolerated.'

Heidi ignored her and concentrated on the red blip on her screen, indicating Erica's location.

'Have you anything useful to tell me?' Lizzie said. 'Have you been productive in your corner?'

'On the board,' Heidi muttered, before shutting down her system and heading towards the door.

Lizzie grabbed her arm as she passed. Heidi forcefully removed the woman's hand and dug sharp fingertips painfully between wrist bones.

'Don't touch me!' she hissed. 'Don't ever touch me.' She stormed out and slammed the door behind her.

Lizzie blushed pink, knew everyone in the room had witnessed the exchange and were staring at her. She turned her back and looked at the board. Heidi had pinned a sheet of paper in the middle. Lizzie ripped it from the board and read the contents. Her mood dropped further. Connor Haskins peered over her shoulder.

'A rally?' he exclaimed. 'Cenedl Cymru are holding a rally in Brecon?'

'Looks like it,' Lizzie growled. 'This weekend, and DS Bevan decides she needs time off. Bloody woman!'

Tegan frowned and thought it was a good job Heidi had walked out. She wouldn't like hearing her partner described in such a way and there would have been an almighty row. She tried to calm the situation.

'We're still tailing Daffydd, boss,' she said. 'He can't pick his nose without one of us seeing him and DC Holtz is monitoring his internet use. Surely all we have to do is make sure we have enough personnel on the street to keep things under control on the day. I can't see they're going to goosestep down Brecon High Street en masse. It'll be a bit of ranting and raving from a podium, then everyone will go home, especially if we turn out in force.'

'Not bloody good enough,' Lizzie said, grouching. 'You lot don't seem to understand how serious a group like this is, or how much trouble they can cause. If we don't get this right, there will be ructions.' She turned to face the room. 'Get on with your assignments, all of you, and do them right. I'm not in the mood for crappy policing. I need to go upstairs to run this by the bosses. We only have a couple of days to prepare and events like this can turn nasty in a heartbeat, so we must be ready. And someone find DC Holtz for me. I need a word.'

Chapter twenty

Greta and Pixie worked together in the kitchen, filling serving dishes with food ready to be delivered to the dining room.

'I'm so glad Mala didn't want me in the cottage today,' Pixie said. 'She was bloody unbearable yesterday. Honestly, Greta, I'm not sure how long I can put up with her.'

'Is Clover back at work?'

'No, but I'm staying away and keeping my head down.' Pixie scooped mounds of mashed potato into large bowls and they were carried out of the steamy kitchen.

'Do you want to leave New Eden?' Greta asked.

'Oh, God, I don't know.' Pixie sighed. 'I've loved living here, but like I said, things don't feel right now. Anyway if I left, I don't know where I would go.'

Mala burst through the door, eyes searching the room.

'Pixie! There you are. You should have been with me this morning. Why are you in here?'

'Sorry,' Pixie mumbled. 'I'm sure you said you didn't need me.'

'Report to the cottage immediately after lunch. Don't be tardy.'

She swept back out and as Greta watched, a single tear slid down Pixie's cheek. Greta gave the girl a quick hug.

'You'll be OK. Hang in there and we'll think of something.'

Greta didn't like to see Pixie so distressed, she kept an arm around her waist and they headed towards the dining room and took their places at the long table.

A few minutes later, Adam walked in with a woman they didn't recognise.

'Everyone,' Adam called. 'Here… is… Erica.'

'Hello, Erica,' the group chanted.

Adam led Erica to the head of the table and raised his glass in the customary toast. 'To Erica – you are welcome at New Eden.'

Everyone sat, Adam said grace and they began to eat.

Erica took her place next to Adam and helped herself to food from the dishes. She gazed around the room, surprised to find so many people involved with the cult. Nearly thirty individuals surrounded the table, young and old. She spotted Greta immediately and was heartened to see she looked well – if not particularly happy – and also recognised the couple from the herbalist's shop.

Adam had welcomed Erica with open arms when she'd arrived at the front door begging admission. She had constructed a believable cover story that she was unloved and unwanted by her family, there was a rift that couldn't be healed and felt she needed to get away. She told Adam she'd heard about the commune at the shop in Upper Yanworth, and how she'd decided her life needed to change. Adam had lapped up her story, offered her a place, and allocated her a bed in one of the female dormitories.

She would work in the kitchen until a job which suited her better could be found. Adam believed she used to work in a bank and Erica hoped he might find her something to do in administration – the right place to look for secrets. So far so good, she thought. All she had to do was discover exactly what was going on at New Eden, then convince Greta to leave with her.

Erica planned to watch and wait for a day or so. Greta didn't know who she was and that suited Erica perfectly. No one in the commune knew who she was. The thought comforted her, made her feel safe. She'd only been at New Eden a few hours and already the place had unsettled her. The atmosphere was all wrong and the wide, permanent smiles worn by the converts looked utterly false.

She ate her meal in silence. A woman sitting next to her introduced herself as Mala. Erica wasn't keen. Her first impressions were nearly always correct and she didn't like Mala. It was as though she could smell something was off with the woman and didn't engage in conversation. Adam didn't notice and rabbited on about how Erica had made a wise choice joining the church, how wonderful her future life would be, and how he would guide her along the spiritual path to God. Erica thought he sounded mad, wondered if he believed the crap he was spouting, or if the whole thing was a massive con.

What really surprised her was the age range of the converts. She had thought they would be young, impressionable kids, but at least four of the residents looked well over fifty and one woman was obviously the wrong side of seventy. What were these people doing here? Did they believe Adam's rubbish? She finished her meal and wished she could ring Heidi, tell her Greta was OK, but knew instinctively it was a bad idea so headed to the kitchen for her first shift. Maybe the girls there would talk to her about what was really going on.

* * *

Daffydd sat in a back room of The Prince nursing a pint, deep in conversation with Rhys and Geraint.

'Is everything set for tomorrow?' he asked. 'We can't afford any mistakes. It's time we are recognised by the powers that be as a serious political force… and not in a negative way. The boys know they mustn't let things get out of hand, don't they?'

'I've drummed it into them,' Rhys said, 'but they're a volatile bunch, so we'll have to keep an eye out. Where did you find them?'

'Wasn't difficult,' Daffydd snorted. 'Welshmen aren't keen on incomers, especially if they are losing their jobs and homes because of them. People are angry and I don't blame them. Da and Granda have been trying to drive the English out for years. Da did time don't forget, and things are much worse now. It isn't just the English we need to worry about, but all the bloody immigrants. Wales for the Welsh I say.'

The other two raised their glasses and toasted the sentiment.

'We'll meet in town at 10.30 tomorrow morning,' Daffydd said. 'Pass the word and reinforce the "no trouble" message. Our sole purpose is to convert others to our way of thinking, recruiting if you like, spreading the word. The more of us who make our voices heard, the more likely we are to be listened to. If we deliver our message in a professional manner, we will be taken seriously.' He drained his glass. 'Bloody good job Leech and Francombe are locked up. Couldn't trust those two buggers further than I could throw them. We're lucky their stupidity didn't bring any shit down on our heads.'

'Did you inform the local authority we're holding a rally?' Geraint asked.

Daffydd chuckled. 'No. Haven't told anyone, so we shouldn't have any problems with the police. Can't wait to see the looks on the faces of the locals when they spot us at the war memorial.'

The others laughed, looking forward to the forthcoming event.

'We'll meet up again afterwards,' Daffydd said. 'I need to talk to you both. I have a bigger plan, something which will shake everyone up, better than rallies, but we need to move carefully. No room for error, this is too big and too important. We must reclaim our country before it's too late.'

* * *

Heidi glanced up from her screens as DI Ben James entered the squad room.

'Heidi, you still here?'

'Obviously,' she said. 'Can I help you with something, sir?'

Ben pulled up a chair, squatted on the edge and peered over his constable's shoulder.

'What are you working on?'

'This and that,' Heidi said. 'Trying to plan for this bloody rally Cenedl Cymru have arranged for tomorrow.' She hesitated. 'I'm also keeping an eye on Erica. Did she tell you why she wanted leave?'

'Yes, she did,' Ben admitted. 'Said not to mention it to you until she'd been able to tell you herself. How are you keeping an eye on her?'

Heidi pointed at one of her screens. 'This is a blueprint of New Eden's commune. See that tiny red dot?'

Ben nodded.

'That's Erica. When we got together I gave her a locket, luckily for me she liked it and wears it all the time. There's a miniature GPS device inside so I can track her. She's inside the commune, has been all day, but of course I don't know what's happening.' She sighed. 'We didn't actually talk. She left me a note.'

'What did it say?'

'That I was to stay here and trust her. She also said she'd spoken with Pa and I'm reasonably sure if things go to worms, she'll call him. Thankfully he's like me – doesn't always stick to the rules. What I don't understand is why we can't go in ourselves.'

'You know why. The group is classed as an NRM – new religious movement – registered as a charity and more or less untouchable. Can you imagine the backlash we'd get in the press if we raided a religious group?'

'It's a front, sir, I know it is. Erica is planning to find some dirt on this bunch of loons while she's inside. If she finds good stuff, presumably we can go in then?'

'I'd have to see the material, but yes, if there's evidence of law-breaking we can become involved.' He placed a hand on Heidi's arm. 'I'm sorry I can't help you with this, but you do see why I can't, don't you?'

'Sort of,' Heidi grumbled, 'but I'm not happy.'

Ben chuckled. 'I can see that, but I must ask you to give me your word you won't do anything without talking to me first. If you act rashly, it could be the end of your career with the force, so be smart, Heidi. Be smart.'

Chapter twenty-one

Members of Cenedl Cymru had turned out in force and nearly forty men, hats pulled low over their eyes, hoodies and sunglasses concealing their identities, swarmed around Brecon's war memorial. Daffydd, Rhys and Geraint wore smart suits, faces uncovered and took their places in the middle of the group.

A small crowd of locals, interested to find out what was going on, gathered on the wide pavement beneath the roll of honour – a mix of teenagers, the retired and nosey shoppers. At exactly ten thirty, as the town clock finished its chime, Daffydd held a megaphone to his mouth.

'People of Brecon,' he began. 'We are Cenedl Cymru and are fighting to keep Wales for the Welsh. Fighting to keep jobs, homes, schools and hospital services for taxpayers who have lived here all their lives, not incomers who have contributed nothing to our society.'

The crowd grew as others stopped to listen and Daffydd was encouraged.

'Wales is losing its culture,' he proclaimed. 'Our proud nation is sleepwalking, while migrants from all over the world flood into our towns and swamp our green valleys. There shouldn't be mosques in Wales, or burkha-clad women on our streets. On our Welsh streets. Multiculturalism is a failed experiment, foisted on us by a government in London which clings tightly to the plan, forcing its will on citizens who don't want it… or need it.'

There was a ripple of agreement through the bystanders. Rhys tapped Daffydd's arm.

'The police are here,' he muttered and pointed across the street where a squad of uniformed officers climbed out of a transit van.

'No problem,' Daffydd said. 'As long as our boys behave themselves, the coppers will leave us alone. Peaceful protest hasn't been banned – yet.' He held the megaphone to his lips.

'There's a war coming, ladies and gentlemen,' he announced. 'The white man is a threatened species and needs protection before he vanishes beneath the murk the incomers bring with them. We need foot soldiers, committed individuals who support and will fight for the cause. The Welsh demand their country back!'

The motley crew surrounding Daffydd and his sergeants cheered, chanted slogans and unfurled red and white flags with swastikas printed on them. Nazi flags. The police squad spread out as DI Wild scanned the crowd for any signs of trouble. A group of four young Asian men pushed through the mass of people, heads down, moving quickly, anxious not to become involved. A particularly vocal member of Cenedl Cymru spotted them and began hurling abuse. The obscene chant was quickly taken up by other members.

The men stopped in their tracks and turned to glare at the group surrounding the war memorial. The youth who initiated the chant leapt off the steps and with three of his comrades, marched determinedly towards the four who stood their ground.

Daffydd spotted what was going on. 'Rhys, Geraint – stop them!' he ordered, but the situation was already out of control.

A Cenedl Cymru member suddenly took a swing at the Asians who didn't take kindly to being attacked and defended themselves vigorously. In seconds they were all involved and a vicious brawl kicked off. The watching crowd encircled the fight like children in a playground, and DI Wild ordered her officers to advance as more people joined the ruckus. Bystanders scattered. One woman climbed on a bench and began taking photographs.

Daffydd watched in horror as the planned event disintegrated in front of his eyes. Lizzie Wild appeared by his side with another plain-clothes officer who grabbed his arm.

'Hey,' Daffydd protested. 'Get your hands off me.'

'You're under arrest, sir,' DI Wild said.

'On what charge?'

'Inciting a riot. You'll have to come with us,' DS Haskins ordered and dragged him in the direction of the van.

Other members of Cenedl Cymru scattered, weaving through the mass of fighting people to vanish in the side streets. Lizzie sent officers after them, anxious to round up as many as possible. The main scuffle between the Asians and the protestors showed no sign of cooling down and battens drawn, a contingent of six officers waded in to pull the fighters apart. The Asians regained their feet first, one aimed a particularly vicious kick at one of the men on the floor and cracked a rib.

'Now then, sir,' the nearest officer warned and snagged him by the arm. 'That's enough.'

'No,' the man said, 'it is not enough. We are from the Gurkha regiment. We come here to fight for your country and this is how you welcome us. You should be ashamed!'

'I agree, and I am. Are any of you injured?'

'No… only them.'

The officer chuckled. 'Give your names to DS Haskins, the redheaded bloke over there, then get back to barracks. We'll clear up here and if we can keep you boys out of it, we will. You have my word.'

The remaining protesters were finally rounded up and stuffed in the van, ready for transportation to the station. Two needed medical attention and were driven to hospital under guard. The crowd dispersed slowly and the woman on the bench with the camera jumped down and marched up to DI Wild.

'Good morning,' she said. 'My name is Stacey Logan, reporter for *The Mid Wales Times*, I wondered if you'd like to comment on the events of this morning.'

'No, I bloody wouldn't,' Lizzie snapped and turned her back.

Stacey circled with her, refusing to be ignored.

'Were the police notified of the rally in advance?'

Lizzie glared at the reporter. 'We're here, aren't we? Defused the situation, pinched the bad guys and now we'll interview and charge those we can. Happy now?'

'What's your name?' Stacey asked. 'For the article. I know most of the coppers round here, my partner is a local inspector, DI Ben James, but haven't met you before.'

'DI Wild,' Lizzie growled. 'Now, if you'll excuse me, I'm busy.'

Stacey took a few shots of the woman's retreating back before heading towards the car park, anxious to return home and write up her story.

* * *

Erica was washing dishes at an enormous white sink while Cassie and Suzy dried and put away. Erica was frustrated. She'd been in the place over twenty-four hours and was struggling to find anyone willing to talk to her.

Although, that wasn't strictly true. Plenty of people spoke to her, but almost everything that left their mouths was utter garbage. They all wandered around the place grinning like they were demented, or on drugs, and seemed totally incapable of independent thought. They spouted Adam's doctrine without thinking about what they were saying, like children repeating their lessons. Erica wanted to shake the lot of them vigorously and drag them out the front door.

The kitchen door swung open and Erica glanced up from her work as Pixie and Greta pushed in, arms full of freshly cut rainbow chard. Erica rushed to give them a hand.

'Wow, what a lot of greens,' she said. 'Surely we'll never eat all that?'

'You'll be surprised,' Greta said. 'Eat like horses, all of us.' She wiped her hands and gave Erica a hug. 'Welcome to New Eden, Erica.'

Erica stepped back, uncomfortable with the contact. 'Thanks,' she mumbled.

'You're with me this afternoon, Erica,' Pixie said. 'Adam has asked me to show you around, introduce you to the others. Greta can wash the chard, come on.' Pixie left the kitchen without waiting to see if Erica was following or not. 'We'll go to the cottages and the garden first – while it's not raining.'

Erica trotted to catch up. 'Hey, wait a minute.'

Pixie leaned on a section of damp wall and smiled. 'You'll need to speed up here, there's always so much to do.'

'Like what?'

'Well, duh. Running the place and the business – the shops. You know we grow and process all the herbs, it's a lot of work.'

Pixie set off across the courtyard towards the cottages, threading her way through a motley selection of ducks and chickens.

'How long have you been here?' Erica asked.

'Three years, there about, since the commune opened.'

'You must love it… I mean, if you didn't, you wouldn't have stayed so long. Where did you come from?'

'Erica, you've heard what Adam says, "live for the now, not for the then".'

She walked up to one of the cottages, tapped on the door and called, 'Joe, Mack, you've got visitors.'

* * *

Adam was in his quarters gazing out across the courtyard and spotted Pixie shepherding Erica around. He liked the new girl, was drawn to her as soon as he saw her at the door, begging entrance to New Eden. Tall, dark and slim, a perfect match for him, and she had gorgeous green eyes. He'd noticed she didn't wear make-up and he liked that too. She was good looking enough without adding anything.

There was something different about her, he wasn't sure what, but she appeared intelligent, educated and sincere. He wondered idly if she might eventually become his second-in-command. Mala was beginning to irritate him. She had bored him for the last few months, but now she wound him up and he needed to move her. She used to be a worthy lieutenant, dependable, but hadn't been the same since Clover fell pregnant and more difficult since the baby was born. She had even asked, no, pleaded with him, to let the child stay. Why did she do that? She knew the rules and had helped with two other births before Clover's.

He saw Erica and Pixie leave the drier's cottage and cross the yard towards Mala's place. He followed Erica with his eyes and liked what he saw. She was so graceful, as though she floated a few inches off the ground, back straight, head held high and Adam knew he wanted her. He also knew that getting her wouldn't be difficult. He could do anything, have anyone. Never mind dragging these needy people along the path to God, as far as they were concerned, he was God.

Chapter twenty-two

Heidi and DI James made themselves comfortable in the observation room adjacent to interview room two, as Daffydd Owen was escorted in by the custody sergeant. Interviews were not Heidi's forte, but she missed nothing and was more useful behind the scenes than out front upsetting prisoners. Daffydd's handcuffs were removed and he sat at the desk opposite DI Wild and DS Haskins.

He rubbed his wrists and grinned. 'Let's get on with it then,' he said. 'I have better things to do than this.'

Lizzie Wild switched on the recording machine, stated time and date, who was present and the interview began.

'That was a bit of a rumpus earlier,' Lizzie said. 'Care to tell me what it was all about?'

'A legitimate protest which unfortunately got out of hand when a group of passers-by attacked some of my men.'

Lizzie raised her eyebrows. 'Your men? What makes them your men?'

'They're all members of Cenedl Cymru and were protesting about the numbers of immigrants in our country. Perfectly legal.'

'If we overlook the fact that you didn't inform us of the rally in advance, and as you say, things got out of hand. I'm not sure the Gurkhas attacked your men, more the other way around from what I saw of it.'

Daffydd shrugged, studied his fingernails and picked at a wick of skin.

Lizzie chuckled. 'Did your men know they were taking on army personnel?'

Daffydd said nothing.

Lizzie continued, 'I guess not. Two of them took a right old pounding, still at the hospital as we speak.'

Daffydd sighed. 'Then charge them with ABH or GBH or whatever, I don't care. I'm prepared to accept a caution for not notifying you in advance of the rally, but as far as I can see, there's not much else you can do.'

Connor Haskins rested his elbows on the desk and glared at Daffydd; he tried and failed to look menacing. 'You don't think?' he said.

Daffydd threw his head back and laughed. 'I'm so scared I can hear my ribs rattling.' He looked at Lizzie. 'Is this the best you can do? This baby copper?' He got to his feet and Connor flinched, encouraging more laughter. 'Inspector, you know this is a waste of time. No way can you charge me with inciting riot, you'd be laughed out of court. Cenedl Cymru is not a banned organisation…'

'Not yet,' Connor muttered.

'… and peaceful protest is allowed, as you well know. So, how about it? Where do we go from here?'

'Sit down,' Lizzie ordered. 'You're a cocky sod, aren't you? Stirring up the locals, spreading fear among newcomers. Two of your men are banged up in Cardiff awaiting trial for murder. Do you have anything to say about that?'

'Like what?' Daffydd said. 'I didn't have anything to do with it. You caught those who did and as you say, you'll try them and no doubt lock them away for a long time. I don't see what it has to do with me.'

'If you incited them to commit violence, you'd be just as guilty.'

'*If* I did, something you'll never be able to prove or disprove.'

'Everything you say incites violence,' Connor said. 'You sound like Hitler – raving, bloody bonkers.'

'If you'd listened to what I actually said, officer, you'd know I sound nothing like Hitler. I don't advocate murder. I'm not planning mass genocide. All I'm asking is we stop outsiders flooding our country. What will happen to the Welsh if this keeps on? We'll be bred out if we're not careful, not that I expect you to understand, being that you're English,' Daffydd sneered.

'We need a full list of your members,' Lizzie said.

'Do you? Where are you going to get one of those?'

'From you, while you're here.'

'No chance,' Daffydd said, 'and unless you bring an end to this farce immediately, I shall have no option but to call my solicitor. I'm sure he will advise me to keep my mouth shut and we'll all waste some more of each other's valuable time. What about that, Inspector?'

Lizzie knew he was right. There was very little she could charge him with, even less she could make stick. She'd leave the tail on him and ask Heidi to work her magic with the computers, look into his background and those of Geraint and Rhys Jones, the brothers from the north, and continue to monitor their internet usage.

'OK.' She sighed. 'DS Haskins, take Mr Owen back to the custody suite, caution him, together with those who weren't involved in the fight, then release them. The others get the book thrown at them. Now lose him, I'm fed up of having to look at his grinning mug.'

* * *

When Lizzie entered the squad room, Heidi was at her workstation, eyes flipping from screen to screen as she trawled cyberspace for useful information. The top right-hand screen displayed the outline of New Eden and Heidi kept an eye on the small red dot crawling slowly around the house and gardens.

'DC Holtz, at last. I need you to do some researching, quick as you like.'

Heidi barely raised her eyes as she took the file Lizzie offered.

'Details of a few more Cenedl Cymru members,' Lizzie explained. 'I could do with in-depth backgrounds. Any idea when they'll be ready?'

'When I've finished. I'll let you know.'

'That's not what I asked.'

'Best I can do. Busy here.'

Lizzie pointed at the top right screen and the red dot. 'What's that?'

Heidi tapped the keyboard and the image vanished.

'Nothing. Stuff I'm working on.'

'Can you be more specific?' Lizzie was beginning to lose patience with this odd little woman.

'No.' Heidi put on a set of earphones, worked the keyboard and hummed quietly to herself. Eventually Lizzie took the hint and got lost.

Heidi recalled the location screen, checked Erica's whereabouts then began to dig into Cenedl Cymru's background and finances. A relatively new group, it seemed as though Daffydd had been given a large donation from a group in Porthmadog, started years ago by Granddad Owen and his son, Daffydd's father. Both long ago members of Meibion Glyndŵr – the cottage burners.

The further she dug the dirtier she felt, it was like swimming through excrement, the views expressed vile and extreme. It was obvious the websites she was viewing were basically tools used to radicalise the young. Disturbingly, records indicated over 70,000 individuals were regular visitors, with thousands posting nastiness. When Heidi discovered photographs of small children at a beauty spot being encouraged to hold up swastika flags she had enough, slapped off her system, dumped a thick file of researched documents on DI Wild's desk and left the office.

She went in search of DI James for a chat, but his office was empty and no one had seen him, so fed up with looking at the inside of the police station she went home.

* * *

Erica hung back as the congregation filed out of the hall and back to their dormitories. She peeped round the door to check the hall was empty then set off through the maze of corridors on the ground floor of the house.

She pulled her woolly cardigan tightly around her shoulders. The building was cold, damp walls made it feel as though she was taking a stroll inside an industrial fridge. Using a torch with a dim bulb, she quietly opened doors and peered inside. Most of the downstairs rooms were unused, semi-derelict. One obviously used to be an impressive library, but the damp had penetrated there as well and soggy stacks of books gently mildewed away, unloved and undisturbed. Further along the hall, Erica discovered a locked door and nothing intrigued her more. People locked doors to keep the stuff behind them safe, or to keep someone prisoner.

Erica knelt on the frayed carpet, peered through the keyhole and discovered the door was not locked from the inside, no key sat in the lock. Checking the corridor was still empty and hearing nothing from the house, Erica removed a bent piece of metal from her boot and fiddled it inside the keyhole. She fussed at the lock for a few minutes, but the mechanism was old. She required something more than bent metal to gain entry and decided to leave it for another day. She wondered if there was an office behind the door, and if that was where she'd find New Eden's secrets.

She padded towards the back of the house, paused at the corner of the corridor and squinted round carefully. Seeing no one, she began the same process of quietly opening doors and looking inside, but found nothing until she reached the last door. There was a light shining beneath and Erica could hear voices inside the room. She flattened herself in an alcove and strained her ears to hear what was being said.

Two women were speaking, an older voice and a much younger one, childlike.

'It's no good carrying on like this,' the older voice said. 'It's not like we can change the past, so buck up, for God's sake. I can't stand seeing you mope about, it's pathetic.'

The younger voice mumbled something, but Erica couldn't hear what.

'Yes, I know you're miserable, but I don't have a magic wand. Winnie gave you something, didn't she?'

Another muffled response.

'Well then, what else do you expect me to do? You're due back at work tomorrow. The rest of us can't keep carrying you, so sort yourself out and I'll see you at the cottage first thing.'

Erica heard footsteps on bare boards, squashed herself closer to the wall and froze when the door swung open. Mala strode out and away down the corridor without glancing back. After a few minutes, Erica crept to the door and silently cracked it open.

There were four metal beds resting on the boards. The last of the four, next to the window, had a lump on it and as Erica watched, the lump turned over and a young woman's face appeared, a pale unhappy face, eyes swollen from crying. Erica had to stop herself from rushing in to comfort the girl but couldn't risk causing waves, not yet. Rash reactions could spark trouble before she was prepared for it. Unseen she quietly closed the door and headed back upstairs to the dormitories. Maybe she could discover what this was all about in the morning and felt sure if she could befriend Pixie she'd learn something. Although Pixie spouted the same rubbishy doctrine as the others, Erica didn't think she was as committed as the rest. Maybe Pixie could tell her about the girl in the room.

Erica paused outside her dormitory, removed a tiny mobile from a money belt next to her skin and sent Heidi a text:

All is well. Greta is fine. Don't worry. Love you. E x

The chirp of her phone shook Heidi awake. She reached out from under the duvet and fished around on the bedside table. Snagging the device, she pulled it under the quilt, read the message and smiled, comforted. She had been worrying about Erica since she'd gone inside the commune and still felt hurt they hadn't been able to talk about the plan. Heidi wasn't entirely sure she was cut out for this partner stuff if she had to deal with the anxiety which came with it, an emotion new to her. She knew sending a text in return was a bad idea and wondered why Erica hadn't said more while she had the chance.

Heidi tossed and turned, mind full of questions, none of which she could answer. She missed Erica and wanted her home, together with Greta, and enough dirt on the cult to bury it. She wondered briefly if Freddie had heard anything but decided to ring him in the morning. Two sleepless nights wouldn't solve anything.

Chapter twenty-three

Daffydd and Geraint sat at a corner table in the Cwtch Café in Brecon, backs to the room. Rhys brought over three mugs of tea and plonked them on the table.

'Breakfast on its way,' he said and pulled up a chair. 'Take the taste of the police station out of our mouths.'

'Bit of a result though,' Geraint said. 'Three cautions, no charges.'

'Won't always be like that,' Daffydd muttered. 'We'll have to be more careful in future and weed out the idiots.'

A waitress approached, balancing three plates covered in food. She took three sets of cutlery wrapped in napkins from her pocket, placed them on the table and returned to the counter. The men tucked in enthusiastically.

'Are you busy tomorrow?' Daffydd asked.

'Nothing on,' Geraint said. 'Why?'

'I told you I had something planned, something to wake up the Welsh and frighten the shit out of the English… and all the other incomers. I need to take a trip up north and I'd like you boys to come with me.'

'Always up for a road trip,' Rhys said. 'Where are we going?'

'Need to call in on Granda,' Daffydd said, 'to collect some stuff. Up and back in a day.'

'What sort of stuff?' Geraint asked.

Daffydd lowered his voice. 'From his time in the quarries. You know he was an explosives man, a shot-firer?'

The others nodded.

'Seems he has some dynamite left over and if we're going to war, we could do with some, don't you agree?'

'Yes,' Rhys said, 'but what are we going to do with it?'

'All will become clear,' Daffydd said. 'Let's go and find out what he's got first before we make too many plans. He says he has a few boxes, but he is in his nineties and could be talking rubbish.'

'Not him,' Rhys said. 'Still the sharpest knife in the drawer. If he says the stuff is viable it will be. Ask him nicely and he'll probably travel back down with us and show you how to use it.'

Daffydd wiped his greasy plate with a scrap of bread and crammed it in his mouth.

'How many of our lads were released?' he asked.

'All but four, the two in hospital and two others charged with affray.'

'Daft buggers. Fancy taking on the Gurkhas!' Daffydd laughed. 'That was always going to end in tears. Still, we won't miss them, we have enough troops. Pass the word, tell the boys we'll meet up at The Prince in a couple of days and don't mention our trip to anyone. Keep this strictly between the three of us.' Daffydd stood and threw his paper napkin on the table. 'I'll pick you up from your digs at eight in the morning. Be ready, we've a lot to do.'

* * *

The afternoon meditation was due to begin. Members filed into the great hall and squatted on their cushions. Erica watched, studied their faces, the sleepy eyes and forced smiles. Adam emerged from a door at the rear of the low stage and Erica made a mental note to get through the door to see what was on the other side. He took his place at the head of the room and held his hands high for silence.

'Welcome, all of you,' Adam said. 'You are here to find God and with my help you will all achieve your goal. Here is love, here is peace and here is contentment. Everything else must be left outside the door or shared in the room.'

Adam turned his gaze on Pixie who immediately looked uncomfortable.

'Pixie, please stand.'

The girl struggled to her feet.

'Mala tells me you have been unhappy lately. Please, share your feelings with the group. Tell us why you're unhappy and we can help you heal.'

Pixie stared at the floor. Her face glowed pink and she shifted her feet on the boards.

'Come now, beloved,' Adam implored. 'We are all friends here. Tell us why you're troubled. Share with us.'

Erica felt the tension in the air. It distressed and angered her to see Pixie singled out and how uncomfortable the girl was.

'Pixie!' Adam snapped. 'Tell us what is wrong, nothing can be done if you don't. Mala tells me you've been upset for a few days.'

'I… I'm fine, Adam. Nothing's wrong.'

'Are you telling untruths now?' he asked. 'Do you think lying will help? Why are you concealing your feelings? Be honest with us. We all love you, so trust us with the truth.'

'It's Clover,' Pixie blurted out. 'She isn't well and misses her baby.'

Erica's brain snapped to attention. What was this about a baby?

'That's natural,' Adam said. 'Of course Clover misses the baby, but not her baby, the child was never hers. She understood that when she became pregnant, knew she was a Host and she wouldn't be able to keep the child.'

Pixie began to cry. 'It was taken away the day after it was born,' she sobbed. 'Clover is really ill, must be or she'd be back with us in the community and I haven't seen her. She's still here, is she?'

'Of course,' Adam said, 'and she'll be returning to work soon. You've upset yourself with needless worry. Clover is being well cared for and is loved, so there's no need to be concerned.' Adam nodded at Mala and Winnie who moved to stand each side of Pixie and took hold of her arms. 'I think you will benefit from some quiet reflection, time with God and your spirit. We'll talk again when your mind is settled.'

'No!' Pixie wailed. 'I don't need it. I'm fine here, just worried about my friend, that's all.'

'And I've told you there's no need,' Adam said. 'We will talk again, I promise.'

The older women began leading Pixie from the hall and Erica struggled to stay seated, appalled by what was happening. The bullying of an unhappy young woman was almost too much to bear, but Erica knew she had to remain quiet for now. Her mind buzzed with questions. Was Clover the girl she'd discovered in the room last night? Had she really given birth to a child she wasn't allowed to keep? What had happened to it, and where were the witches taking Pixie? The longer Erica was in the commune, the angrier she became. Heidi was right, there was something really off with the place and Erica struggled to understand why members put up with the madness. The answer was obvious, they had all been brainwashed by the charismatic Adam. He had welded them to him and it made Erica feel ill.

Pixie was finally removed and the meditation continued. As soon as it was over, Erica dashed to the kitchen in search of Greta. She found her scrubbing roasting dishes in the scullery and was shocked to see she was crying.

'Hey, sweetheart,' Erica said. 'What's up?'

'Nothing.' Greta wiped her face angrily and attacked the burnt tins with renewed vigour.

Erica grabbed her arms and turned her away from the sink.

'Something is very wrong,' she said. 'I'm not daft. Tell me what's bothering you. Where did they take Pixie?'

Greta sighed and slumped against Erica who wrapped her arms around her, squeezed tightly and felt deep sobs shake Greta's body.

'They've taken her to the meditation rooms at the top of the house. I don't know how long she'll be there. I spent three days in one.'

'I don't understand.'

'If Adam thinks you need it, you are locked upstairs, all on your own, in a tiny room. It's awful, so quiet you can hear the blood in your ears. I hated it.'

'Why were you sent there?'

'I asked questions about Clover and her baby. Adam and Mala took me there and locked me in. When I was released I was so… exultant. Adam came to fetch me, we went to early meditation and afterwards… afterwards…' She broke down and sobbed loudly.

Erica glanced toward the kitchen, anxious they weren't overheard.

'What happened afterwards?' she asked.

'Adam took me to his room and… and…' she gulped back sobs. 'He slept with me and I let him. Mala says he sleeps with everyone, and Pixie said he's the father of Clover's baby.'

'Where is the baby?'

'I don't know. Clover was a host mother for a couple of church members who couldn't have kids. They came for the baby while I was in the room upstairs. I'm sure I saw their car arrive, but didn't see the baby. I was in a bad space.'

'Why don't you leave? Come away with me now.'

'I can't. I'm not leaving Pixie and haven't anywhere to go… anyway, Adam wouldn't allow it.'

Erica opened her mouth to answer when Eleanor bustled in.

'Haven't you finished those pans yet?' she asked. 'You should have been back out in the garden with me ages ago.' She turned to glare at Erica. 'Why are you in here? Aren't you supposed to be working with the kitchen girls?'

'I was just talking to Greta,' Erica said. 'Learning more about your way of life.'

'Not our way of life, but yours too, your new life. It takes a while to fit in, but you will and you'll be happy, I can tell. Now, both of you, chop, chop. Lots to do.'

Eleanor swept out of the room and Erica squeezed Greta's arm.

'We're not done,' she whispered. 'I'll find you later after supper. Hang in there, everything will be OK, I promise.'

Chapter twenty-four

Oliver put the car in gear and pulled away from the kerb in the centre of Brecon to follow Daffydd's car, careful to leave a decent gap so he didn't tip off their quarry.

'That's all three Stooges together,' he said. 'I wonder where they're going?'

Tegan giggled. 'If you don't lose them – like yesterday – we'll find out.'

'God, don't remind me,' Oliver grumbled. 'Loopy Lizzie gave me a right old roasting. She doesn't like me.'

'She doesn't like anyone and has made it plain she doesn't want to be here.'

Daffydd's car headed out of town and turned onto the A470 towards Builth Wells. It was easier to maintain the tail on busier roads and Oliver sped up.

'Don't get too close,' Tegan warned, 'and drive smoothly, I want to read this stuff Heidi gave me.'

'What is it?'

'Records of what The Stooges look at online, browsing history, emails, that sort of stuff. If you wibble about too much, I'll get car sick.'

'I don't wibble.'

'Just drive.'

Oliver stayed on Daffydd's tail to Llangurig where his target turned towards Aberystwyth on the A44.

Tegan glanced up from the paperwork. 'Maybe he's going home?'

'Yeah, maybe. Anything useful in the file?'

'More or less what I expected. All three are regular viewers of nasty far-right material, lots of it from America, but there are plenty of groups locally to keep them online half the night.'

'Anything we can nick them for?'

'Probably not and if we try, they'll probably tell us they're writers and conducting research for a book.'

Oliver laughed. 'You reckon they can read?'

Daffydd made another turn at Aberystwyth and onto the coast road.

'Porthmadog here we come,' Oliver said and rapped his fingers on the steering wheel. 'Give Heidi a ring, let her know where we are and ask if she can work out where these blokes are likely to end up, just in case they suss us.'

Tegan tapped in Heidi's number.

'Holtz.'

'Hi, it's Tegan. We're heading towards Porthmadog. Daffydd and his cronies are all together. We wondered if they are going back home, giving up on Powys.'

'I doubt it,' Heidi said. 'I'm sure they'll be back. I have a feeling they've planned something down here, but haven't been able to find out what as yet. Just make sure you don't lose them.'

The connection cut.

'Heidi says to keep following them, thinks they're up to something.'

* * *

Daffydd led the way through the farmyard to the back door of Trefor Farm just outside Porthmadog, and hammered loudly on the black oak. A group of dogs barked and clamoured inside and the door was eventually opened by an old man leaning on a Zimmer frame. Lively blue eyes peered out of a pale face covered with stubble.

He smiled. 'Daffydd, *bach! Croeso*. Come in, you look like you could do with a cuppa.'

The man shuffled back from the door. His visitors squeezed past his walking frame and filed into the kitchen.

'You're looking well, Granda,' Daffydd said. 'I heard about your ruck with the English tourists. Any comebacks?'

'No, as if there would be. The local cops are on our side – even though they can't admit it – and the English never have the balls to report anything.'

The old man slowly made his way to the sink, filled the kettle and put it on the ancient Rayburn to boil. Daffydd watched him. Granda Owen was looking much older, frail even, never a word he would have applied to him in the past, but he was doing well for his age and had lost none of his spirit.

'Where's Da?' Daffydd asked.

'In the pub, where did you expect?'

'Still a pisshead then?'

'No chance he'll grow out of it after all this time. Never the same after he'd been banged up, and losing your mam soon after didn't help.'

Geraint finished making the tea. Granda Owen sat at the table and shoved the walking frame away from him.

'Bloody thing!' he snapped. 'I hate it. Now, tell me what you've been doing in the south.'

'Got a good group going,' Daffydd said. 'We meet regularly, great bunch of boys. Held a rally in Brecon couple of days ago.'

Geraint snorted. 'That didn't go according to plan, a few of our lads took on some off duty Gurkhas. Two are still in hospital.'

The old man laughed, a wheezy, creaky sound which set off a coughing fit. Rhys pounded him on the back while Daffydd topped up his mug.

'I'm surprised they're still breathing!' Granda Owen gasped. 'Bloody idiots. Couldn't they tell the difference between a Gurkha and a Paki?' He laughed some more. 'Any trouble from the police?'

'Not for us,' Daffydd said. 'The lads involved in the fight have been arrested and two youngsters were nicked earlier on when they went freelance beating up foreigners. They killed a young woman.'

'*Duw duw*. What were they thinking?'

'Haven't got a bloody clue, but I'm sure they won't cause us any more problems. They're banged up awaiting trial and I've been able to distance Cenedl Cymru. Rhys and Geraint are keeping an eye on the rest. We can't have any more mistakes.'

'No, you can't. Don't want to end up like your Da.' The old man drained his mug. 'I guess you're here to pick up the stuff from the shed.'

'Yeah, that's right, if you're still offering it.'

'No bloody good to me. I might be able to shout at tourists, but blowing things up is beyond me now. Help me up and we'll go and see what's out there.'

The trio followed the pensioner out of the kitchen and across the yard to an old stone shed. They pulled open the door and dragged out three crates from under the workbench.

Daffydd ripped open the lids and whistled. 'Bloody hell, there's a lot in here.'

'Should be enough for your purposes,' Granda Owen said. 'The detonators are in a box on the windowsill, you'll need those too.'

'You're sure this stuff is stable, are you?' Rhys asked. 'We don't want any accidents on the way back.'

'Safe as houses – best not to smoke in the car though.' He chuckled. 'Bring it inside and I'll show you what's what.'

* * *

Oliver peered through his binoculars. 'They're taking boxes out of the shed at the back,' he whispered.

'Can you see what's in them?' Tegan asked.

'Like I've got X-ray vision! How the hell can I see what's inside?'

'Might be something written on the sides.'

'No, nothing. They look like wooden tea chests, three of them, heavy, by the way The Stooges are struggling.'

The crates were carried inside the house and the door firmly shut.

'Now what?' Tegan asked.

'Wait is all we can do. Shame we're so far away from base and someone can't take over. We'll be off shift long before we get back to Brecon.'

'Stop moaning, Ollie, overtime is always useful and I'd rather be on the road than stuck in the office with Loopy Lizzie and her sidekick. Connor hardly ever speaks and when he does I can't understand him, that awful Bristol accent.'

'I reckon DI James jumped the gun calling in the CTU. We can manage our own rubbish, don't need people coming from England to tell us what to do.'

'Careful, Ollie, you're beginning to sound like a member of Cenedl Cymru.'

'They're coming out.' Oliver peered through the field glasses. 'Loading the boxes in their car, looks like they're getting ready to leave. Do you fancy taking the wheel? I've done enough driving for today.'

Chapter twenty-five

Erica had been looking for Greta all day and so far hadn't bumped into her. She hadn't seen Eleanor either and guessed maybe they were working somewhere together. Not having an excuse to wander around the garden, Erica stayed where she was, worrying about Pixie and desperate to talk to Clover.

As soon as she had the chance, Erica slipped out of the kitchen and set off through mouldy corridors towards the back of the house. She met no one, reached the door at the end of the long hall and pressed her ear against the wood. Hearing nothing, she cracked open the door and peered inside. The bed beneath the window was empty and stripped of bedding. Erica walked to the window, the view of the grounds was dingy. Drizzle fell from grey skies in thick clumps and she saw no one. A last quick look around and Erica left, closing the door quietly behind her.

She changed direction and headed back to the locked door she had discovered on her previous night-time wander. She was about to tackle the lock when the door opened and Mala walked out.

'Erica! What are you doing?'

'I'm looking for Greta. We need some help in the kitchen.' It sounded lame but Mala seemed distracted.

'She'll be in the garden with Eleanor, not back here. You shouldn't be wandering around on your own.'

'Why not?' Erica asked.

Mala stared at her. 'You have work to do and don't have time for aimless wandering. New Eden isn't a holiday camp.'

'Yes, I'd worked that out.'

'What do you mean by that?'

Erica smiled innocently. 'We're here for a purpose, aren't we? Adam is showing us the way to God, a new way of living. Doesn't sound like a holiday.'

'Just get back to the kitchen! I haven't got time for this.'

Mala stomped away down the hall and Erica headed back towards the main entrance and the sweeping staircase. She glanced around and sure no one was watching, began the climb to the upper floors. She passed the dormitory levels and carried on to the top of the house. The stairs became narrower, tattier if that were possible, and she watched her feet, anxious not to take a tumble.

Reaching the top floor, she padded along a narrow hall lined with doors, a faint mushroom-like scent pricked her nostrils. She opened doors and each room was empty apart from a bed, a chair and a small wooden table. The floors were bare, walls gungy plaster, damp and cracked. Each room had a small window which looked out over the drive, and a tiny alcove containing a toilet and basin.

The door at the end of the hall was locked. Erica knelt to peer through the keyhole and was sure she saw movement.

She tapped the door gently. 'Hello? Is anyone in there?'

The shadow moved closer to the door and a face appeared beneath the four-inch gap.

'Erica? Is that you?'

'Pixie! Yes, it's me. Are you OK?' Erica slipped her fingers under the door and Pixie grasped them tightly.

'I guess.' Pixie sniffed. 'Have you come to let me out?'

'No, sorry, I haven't.'

'Don't get caught talking to me. Adam won't like it.'

‘I don’t care what Adam likes,’ Erica snapped. ‘He shouldn’t be locking people up. Do they feed you?’

‘Oh, yes, three meals a day. They push it under the door. Lentils and muesli usually, not very nice, but it stops me being hungry.’

‘I’m going to see if I can get you out,’ Erica said.

‘No, you can’t do that. You’ll get into trouble.’

‘Like I said, I don’t care. This isn’t right.’

‘What isn’t right?’ a voice behind Erica growled. ‘And why do you think you are qualified to make that judgement?’

Erica struggled upright and found herself toe-to-toe with Adam who was accompanied by Mala and Eleanor.

‘What are you doing up here?’ Adam asked.

‘I wanted to find Pixie, make sure she’s alright.’

‘She obviously is, so come away. Pixie won’t benefit from her period of seclusion if we don’t leave her alone.’ He caught hold of Erica’s arm and began to lead her gently, but firmly away.

Mala blocked the corridor and opened one of the doors. As Erica drew level, Eleanor and Adam gave her a shove which sent her stumbling inside. Mala slammed the door and locked it. Erica leapt to her feet and pounded on the door.

‘Open up, you bastards! Let me out, you can’t do this!’

Adam’s voice filtered through the barrier. ‘Calm down, beloved. There’s no need to distress yourself. You came to New Eden to find God and we are showing you the way.’

‘This is bunkum,’ Erica shouted. ‘Open the bloody door and let me out. You can’t keep me prisoner.’

‘You came here willingly,’ Adam said, ‘by choice. We love you, Erica, and want you to be part of our new life, you just need time to adjust. Accept it, let God inside your heart, trust him – and me. I won’t let you down.’

Erica kicked the door. It was solidly built and her boots made no impression. She kicked again, but heard nothing more from the other side. She peered under the door and saw the corridor was empty, the others had left.

'Pixie,' she called. 'Can you hear me?'

Erica heard a muffled response.

'Have you tried to get out?' she asked.

'No point,' Pixie said. 'The window is nailed shut and the door is too thick to smash open. We'll have to wait until Adam comes for us.'

'We could break the glass.'

'Then what? Have you seen how high up we are?' Pixie asked. 'We'd never get down in one piece.'

Erica felt at her waist for her money belt and the tiny phone, horrified to discover the device was missing. She checked her clothes, it wasn't there. She peered under the door but couldn't see it in the hallway. She smacked her forehead, angry with herself. Why hadn't she checked for the phone before she really needed it? She wondered if she had dropped it in the dormitory, or maybe in the kitchen or garden, and hoped no one else found it.

* * *

Heidi was sitting at the desk in her flat, gaze fixed on the red dot representing Erica's location. She dialled Freddie's number, impatient when he didn't pick up immediately.

'Milebrook Manor.'

'Evening, Freddie. How's tricks, you OK?'

'Heidi! Very well thanks. You?'

Heidi giggled. 'Listen to us small talking, can't keep it up, sorry. What's going on your end, has Erica been in touch?'

'Not a peep since she told me what she was planning. Why?'

'I put a tracker on her and the bloody thing hasn't moved for hours.'

'Probably having a nap or something.'

'That's not it. I've only received one brief text from her since she went inside the commune and can't call her for obvious reasons.'

'You sound worried. I've never known you to worry about anything.'

'I didn't… until Erica. I want to keep her safe and can't do that while I'm not with her.'

'Capable woman, Erica,' Freddie mumbled, surprised by his daughter's candour. 'She can look after herself. I've offered my assistance should she need it, but I'm sure she'll be home soon, dragging Greta with her. Why on earth your sister got involved with this crazy bunch, I have no idea. Stupid girl!'

Heidi let the comment go, knew there was no point in becoming involved in an argument. Everyone needed to be on the same side until Greta was back home.

'How's the job?' Freddie asked. 'I heard a whisper Bristol CTU is over your way.'

'The whisper was correct. A particularly vile group of far-right racists have reared their ugly heads in Powys. The brass called in CTU, but I'm not sure how much use they're being and can't stand the woman in charge.'

'There's a surprise.' Freddie chuckled.

'All she's achieved is to put the leader of the group under close surveillance and has me tracking him online. He's up to something – I know he is, but he's not one for emails and I haven't picked up any useful chatter from the others.' Heidi groaned. 'I don't want to be doing any of it. I want to rescue Greta and Erica from that bloody cult. We haven't really got any idea what's going on inside.'

'Uncovered anything more on New Eden?'

'Yeah some, but still not enough. I know the place is a front, but can't seem to get my brain to work long enough to produce anything useful.'

'That's because you're in love, my dear.'

Heidi humphed and changed the subject. 'What's the news from Milebrook?'

'Oh, usual stuff, although…'

'Although what?'

'Your mother seems intent on paying me a visit. She's worried about Greta.'

'No, she isn't,' Heidi snapped. 'She doesn't care about any of us, the only person she worries about is herself. Did she say when she's planning to travel down?'

'Vague as usual.'

'Tell her to stay away, Pa. Tell her we don't want her.'

'I'm not sure I can ban her from the manor, she is my wife.'

Heidi snorted. 'You know my views on that. Make sure you tell me when she's expected so I can keep out of the way.'

'Why don't you come and talk to her, try to sort things out?'

'Now is not the time, Freddie.' Heidi took a deep, calming breath. 'What do you suggest I do about Erica?'

'Watching brief. If your lady was in trouble I'm convinced we would have heard. Have some faith.'

Heidi hung up, logged on her system and saw Daffydd Owen was online. He was surfing the net, the usual stuff men without enough to do looked at. He browsed YouTube, watched a few cage fighting bouts, some porn, news channels and spent time in a couple of far-right chat rooms. She checked the computers of his stooges and found more of the same. Heidi had noticed early on in the investigation they didn't communicate via email and the only texts she'd been able to glean from their mobiles were short, usually just to confirm or arrange a meeting, nothing more.

The surveillance teams were still shadowing Daffydd, but couldn't get close enough to hear what he talked about with his crew. The leaders of Cenedl Cymru ate breakfast together each morning but always in different cafes, so there was no chance of planting any bugs. All three lived in digs but didn't meet at home, so that wasn't a possibility either. The only chance she had was to set up something in The Prince Llewelyn. Heidi smiled. She'd make a trip to the pub tomorrow and see what was possible. Being busy might stop her worrying about Erica so much.

Chapter twenty-six

Daffydd and his friends sat on a low wall at the edge of Brecon Industrial Estate, eating their breakfast. Overstuffed rolls from the burger van.

'This is good,' Rhys said, egg yolk running down his chin. 'You kept this place quiet, knocks spots off the cafe in town.'

'Glad it's not raining,' Geraint said. 'Wouldn't be much fun in the rain. Why are we out here?'

'Cos I don't want anyone to overhear us,' Daffydd said. 'I want to tell you my plan and don't want eavesdroppers.'

'OK, so spill,' Rhys said. 'What are you planning to use Granda Owen's goodies for?'

Daffydd grinned and wiped his lips with a tissue. 'I'm going to cut Wales off from England at the River Severn. We've got enough TNT to plant devices on both bridges and in the entrance of the Severn Tunnel. Set them all off together and it'll be weeks, maybe months before the English sort it all out, and anyone wanting to come to Wales will have to take the long way round.'

'The hauliers won't like it,' Geraint said. 'The extra fuel will cost a fortune and everything will be delayed. It's a great idea. Have we got enough explosive?'

'Never mind that,' Rhys said, 'does Daffydd know what he's doing with it? Blowing open seams in slate is one thing, but blowing up a bridge or a tunnel, that's something else entirely.'

'It'll be fine,' Daffydd said. 'Granda wrote instructions for setting the charges and let's be honest here, if a kid in London can build a bomb in his mother's pressure cooker which shuts down the transport system for days, I'm sure we can build suitable devices. There'll be something online. I'll do some research.'

'You can't do that,' Rhys said. 'You start looking up bomb making on the web and the police will be all over us.'

'That's what everyone thinks, but they're wrong. Looking can't get you into trouble. How on earth can the government or the security forces monitor every single search? It's not physically possible, even with their new GCHQ cyber department.'

'People do get caught though,' Geraint said. 'I read about them every day in the paper.'

'A few get caught,' Daffydd said. 'For example, you read about a drugs bust, tons of cocaine discovered on a fishing boat off the coast of Scotland, the biggest bust the country has ever known. Have you ever heard of a coke shortage?'

They shook their heads.

'Exactly, look how much gets in undetected. I'm not planning on spending weeks researching and I won't download anything – that's when people get nicked. I know what I'm doing and I'll be careful.'

'It's a cracking idea,' Rhys said. 'Cause bloody chaos for months, especially if we could strap bombs to the towers on the bridges. We probably wouldn't be able to topple them, but just a small crack would be a disaster.' He laughed. 'If we pull this off, we might bring down the government.'

Daffydd grinned. 'Probably not.' He drained his tea. 'So, are you with me on this?'

'Count me in,' Rhys said. 'If your plan works, they'll write poems and songs about us and school kids will perform them at the Eisteddfod.'

'Yeah, me too,' Geraint said. 'I'm up for it.'

'Good,' Daffydd said. 'I've found a barn on the edge of the army ranges near Aberbran and stashed the gear there. It's well hidden and will be safe until we're ready to build the bombs. Remember, not a word to anyone about this. The only way we'll get sussed is if someone shoots their mouth off. Did you organise a meeting for Cenedl Cymru?'

'Yeah, I passed the word. We'll meet tonight in The Prince. The boys want to celebrate after the rally and a few are calling for a march in Cardiff.'

'Now there's an idea,' Daffydd muttered. 'Keep the police busy elsewhere.' He threw his polystyrene cup in an overflowing metal bin. 'Right then, lads, on with it. I'll catch up with you soon, let you know what I've been able to find out online.'

* * *

Heidi pulled up in the car park of The Prince Llewelyn, checked her pockets to make sure the bundle of tiny microphones was where it should be, climbed out of the car and headed to the entrance. She pushed open the door and walked in.

A large man stood behind the bar, stacking glasses in a dishwasher. He looked up and did a double take when he saw Heidi.

'Can I help you?' the barman asked.

'Coffee please. Strong, black and sweet, just how I like my men.' She grinned.

The man frowned, turned away without passing comment and busied himself with a complicated-looking coffee machine on a counter behind the bar. Heidi glanced around. Unsurprisingly the place was empty, a touch dingy and chilly. A fire had been laid in the grate, but not lit. A coffee cup appeared in front of her, she paid and carried her drink to a table in one of the front windows. Removing a tablet from her bag she woke it up and asked it to display the plan of New Eden.

She examined the small screen carefully, disturbed that the red dot representing Erica still hadn't moved. According to the blueprints, the GPS device was situated high up beneath the eaves of the Victorian house. Erica might have taken the necklace off and left it on a bedside table, but Heidi doubted that. Erica didn't remove it at home, so why would she at the commune? She also didn't understand why Erica hadn't sent her any word, other than the single text when she first went inside. It was possible the phone had broken, or needed charging, but again unlikely. Erica would have planned better than that. Heidi was beginning to feel very concerned about her partner and if the dot didn't move in the next couple of hours, she would need a new plan.

Heidi stirred three sachets of sugar in her coffee and took a sip, not bad, she thought. She looked up at the landlord who was regarding her coldly.

'You're not from round here, are you?' he asked.

'What gives you that idea?'

'Haven't seen you before, that's all.'

'I don't get out much,' Heidi said. She sipped her coffee. 'Lively place you have.'

'It's early. Busier in the evening.'

Heidi picked up her cup and ambled around the room, peering through the windows, running her fingers along the mantel, lifting horse brasses down from the wall for a closer look. In a little over five minutes, she had planted ten mini-microphones and was sure the barman hadn't noticed a thing. Draining her cup she put it on the bar.

'I'll have another. Bring it over, will you?'

Heidi sat by the window and stared at the tablet. Erica's red dot hadn't moved. Her coffee arrived. The landlord returned to his post and Heidi tapped her screen, smiling as each of the bugs came online. She finished her coffee and took the empty cup to the bar.

'Good coffee,' she said. 'I may call in again, next time I'm passing.'

Heidi left the pub and returned to her car. She checked the tablet again and was happy to see the signal from the bugs was strong and constant. She turned the volume up and was sure she could hear the glass washer churning behind the bar. Should be no problem now to pick up conversations. Satisfied, she started the car and headed back to Brecon. She needed a chat with DI James.

Chapter twenty-seven

Erica pushed her empty plate back under the door and wished she had something other than water to wash the unpalatable food past her tonsils. She'd never liked lentils in stews and plain lentils were disgusting.

'Pixie,' she called. 'You OK?'

'Yeah, I suppose. You?'

'Pissed off,' Erica said. 'I need to get out of here. How long do you think Adam will keep us locked up?'

'No idea. He kept one guy in seclusion for a couple of weeks last year. He didn't stay though, as soon as Adam let him out, he legged it.'

'I don't understand why any of you stay. This place is mad. It's a racket, you know that, don't you? Adam's a fraud.'

'I'm not sure he is,' Pixie said. 'He took me and Felix in when we had nowhere else to go and it's been good… until recently.'

'You said you've been here three years, why did you join?'

'Dad threw me out. I got caught with weed and fined. He said I'd brought disgrace on the family and basically disowned me. Felix and I decided we'd find a new life for ourselves and moved to Cheltenham. It didn't work out. We lost our digs and couldn't get jobs.'

'How did you hear about New Eden?'

'Saw the bus. Adam used to come to the town centre to preach and everything he said made perfect sense. Felix spoke with him and was told we could move to the commune if we wanted to. We jumped at the chance, anything to get off the streets.'

'Why did you stay so long?' Erica asked.

'We loved it here, Felix especially. He didn't get on with his mother. That was the main reason he came away with me, to get away from his mum. It was good for the first couple of years, then it started going weird.'

'How?'

'Adam chose me to spend the night with him and Felix didn't like it.'

'I'm not surprised.'

'It was all so stupid. It wasn't like I was having an affair or anything. Adam sleeps with all the women at least once.'

'Why? And why the hell do they put up with it?'

'I don't know,' Pixie whined. 'It's what's done and everyone accepts it. Adam tells us he is spreading his seed, the seed of God. He's the father of Clover's baby and two more besides that I know of. I didn't fall pregnant.' She sounded wistful and her longing disturbed Erica more than anything she'd heard before.

'Where are the babies now?'

'Adam finds adoptive parents within the church. We don't have children here.'

'And that's OK with everyone?'

'Yeah, I guess. Certainly no one questioned it, until Greta. She didn't like it much and Adam sent her up here for three days.'

'Why didn't she leave when he let her out?'

'I don't know, being up here changes people. Felix rang his mum, don't ask me why but he confessed what he'd done to Adam and was sent here. He left New Eden as soon as the door was opened.' Pixie sobbed. 'Didn't even tell me he was going. I might have gone with him and not be stuck in this bloody room now.'

'Do you pay Adam anything to live at the commune?'

'No. I haven't got anything, but had to fill out housing benefit forms, I think he gets that. I haven't had money in my pocket since I moved here.'

'Have you ever left the place?'

'No, haven't felt the need. Everything I wanted was here, until Felix left. Now it feels as though everything is going wrong and I don't know what to do. It's not like I have anywhere to go.' Pixie sobbed harder and Erica wished she could comfort her.

'Hush, love,' she said. 'It'll all work out, I promise. If you still want to leave when Adam lets us out, I'll take you away. Find you somewhere to be.'

'Adam won't let us leave.'

'Do you honestly think he can keep me here if I don't want to be?'

'It's not as easy as you think. Mala and Eleanor watch us all the time and we're miles from anywhere. It'll be impossible.'

'I don't make promises I can't keep,' Erica said. 'As soon as they unlock the doors, we're off, both of us.'

* * *

Lizzie Wild was holding a team briefing in the squad room, but Heidi wasn't paying attention. She wanted to speak with DI James, but he wasn't due in until later.

'So, here's where we are,' Lizzie said, standing in front of the incident board. 'Daffydd and his cronies made a trip home two days ago, called in at his granddad's house and were seen leaving with three large, heavy crates. Unfortunately – due to a mix-up between the surveillance teams – we know he drove them back down south, but don't know where he stashed them or what was inside.' She glared at Tegan who blushed and looked away. 'Sloppy police work won't get us anywhere, so for God's sake, you lot, get with the programme.' She glared around the room. 'We now possess a full list of Cenedl Cymru members and I've asked Bristol CTU to run the names to find out if we already know any of them. Our records are more extensive than yours,' she boasted.

Heidi humphed but kept quiet.

'DC Holtz has been monitoring the group's internet use and so far has turned up nothing useful.'

'Nothing to find,' Heidi said. 'They don't use email or texts to communicate. They all surf the net for the same sort of stuff and trawl far-right websites, but nothing we can nick them for.'

'They must talk,' Lizzie said.

'Yes, over breakfast each morning,' Oliver said, 'and we can't get close enough to hear what they're saying. I'm sure they've sussed us and reckon we're wasting our time with any more stake-outs. We need to be able to hear what they're talking about, maybe one of our lads should infiltrate the group, get inside.'

'The brass won't sanction it,' Lizzie said. 'Told me it was too dangerous.'

'They'll talk in the pub, won't they?' Heidi asked. 'The Prince on the A40.'

'Probably, but we still can't get close enough to overhear what they talk about, especially if what Ollie says is true and they've sussed us.'

'Good job the place is bugged then.' Heidi stood and handed over the tablet.

Lizzie stared at the screen. 'What's this?'

'I planted ten bugs in the lounge bar this morning. Plug the tablet into a speaker-set and you can listen to each independently. All you need to do is have someone monitor them and record any useful conversations.'

'Who told you to do this?'

'No one. Used my own initiative… and my own equipment. I shall want it back eventually.'

Lizzie glared at her before exploding. 'You're out of order, constable, you do not go off reservation like this. How dare you take matters into your own hands without talking to me? You don't know who you're messing with. You're stuck out here in the boonies and think these people are just a bunch of louts. Believe me, they are so much more than that and any information we collect from your bugs could well be deemed inadmissible.'

'And there's me thinking you'd be pleased,' Heidi said. 'Should have known better. All you've done is flounce in here, take over, order us about and thoroughly piss everyone off.'

'How dare you speak to me like that! I'm going to report you to your commanding officer. You'll be lucky to have a job this time next month.'

The door swung open, DI Ben James walked in and immediately picked up on the tension in the room.

'What's going on?' he asked.

'Get her out of here!' Lizzie yelled, pointing a finger at Heidi. 'I cannot work with such an insubordinate officer.'

'Fine with me,' Heidi said, slapped off her system, unplugged her laptop and slipped it in her backpack. 'Funnily enough, sir,' she said, glaring at DI Wild, 'I can't work with such an inflexible, short-sighted, up-herself officer as her, so I'm off.'

Heidi stormed towards the door and Ben snagged her arm as she passed.

'Go to my office, DC Holtz. Do not leave the building before we talk.' He gave her a shove in the right direction, then turned to face the room.

Heidi trotted down the stairs, listening to his voice as he tried to restore order. She hesitated at the second floor wondering if she should just leave, but eventually turned left and headed towards her boss's office.

Chapter twenty-eight

The office door banged open, Ben entered and dropped on his chair looking stressed.

'Let's hear your side of things, Heidi,' he said, running a hand over his short hair.

'What's the point?' Heidi asked. 'I can't work with that woman, she doesn't think outside the box. How she ever got to be a DI I have no idea. I planted ten bugs in The Prince this morning, gave them to her on a plate and she roasts me in front of the entire squad for going off reservation.'

'Might have been a good idea if you'd spoken to someone before, but hindsight is a wonderful thing.'

'It just made sense to me to hear what these nasty bastards are talking about when they're together. Now we can. There's nothing going on online, they don't communicate in cyberspace and they are planning something. I know they are.'

'Any idea what?'

Heidi shook her head. 'No, but it's something big. Another march wouldn't have them driving all over the country. What was in the crates they picked up? If the tail had paid attention and not lost them on the way back from Porthmadog, we'd at least know where they've stashed the stuff and be able to take a peek. As it is we haven't a clue, could be anything.'

'OK. I'll have a word and clear things up with Lizzie Wild, tell her what an asset you are.'

'Not good enough, sir.'

'Pardon?'

'I'm not cut out for coppering, can't cope with all the rules and the forelock tugging, and let's be honest, it's not like being a copper is helping me at the moment.'

'What do you mean?'

'My sister has been kidnapped by a cult. Yes, I know she went of her own free will, but I can't get to her. Erica has gone inside to bring Greta out and I haven't heard anything from her for days. The GPS device she wears round her neck hasn't moved for over twenty-four hours now and no, she hasn't removed it and I'm sure she isn't spending her days in bed. Something has gone wrong. I want to go in, but you tell me I can't.'

'We've been through this, Heidi. We can't unless there is clear evidence of laws being broken.'

'That's why I'm leaving,' Heidi said.

'Leaving?'

'The force. I resign. Effectively immediately. I cannot see the point of an organisation I'm part of which won't – or can't – help me rescue my sister and my partner. I'm bound by the rules if I stay. If I leave I can do what I like.'

'That's not strictly true.'

'OK, so everyone has boundaries, has to act within the law, but as a copper I have to leave the cult alone, as an individual I don't.'

Heidi dug in her pocket, pulled out her warrant card and dropped it on the desk in front of her boss. He stared at the square of plastic.

'Don't do this, Heidi,' he said. 'We need you here, you're a good copper, if a little unconventional. Give me some time with this and I'll see if there's a way around it.'

'We don't know if we have any time, sir, and the CTU is working the Cenedl Cymru case. You don't need me.'

She stood, slung her backpack across her shoulders and headed for the door.

'Heidi, wait.'

She turned back and smiled at him. 'I'm sorry, sir, I've made up my mind.'

'You can't just walk away,' he protested, but Heidi had gone.

* * *

Daffydd switched on his computer in the bedsit and began surfing the net for bomb making instructions. Most of what he found was rubbish and he quickly moved on until he came across a site that seemed to know what it was talking about.

He scrolled down the page and made notes on a pad next to the keyboard. He didn't need to know how to make explosives, he had plenty of that, just how to construct a viable device. He was nervous, worried that someone somewhere might be looking, but pushed the thought to the back of his mind. As he'd told his friends, it was unlikely he was being monitored and wasn't planning on spending hours online, just long enough.

Daffydd was surprised how relatively straightforward building a bomb was. He'd thought it would be more complicated and was heartened. The three crates of TNT would be more than enough to do the job. He might not be able to topple the bridges, or destroy the Severn Tunnel, but he'd create a series of large explosions that would make the English sit up, make everyone sit up, and cause chaos.

He switched off the computer, lifted a loose floorboard beneath frayed carpet and tucked his notebook inside. He took a quick shower and dressed in clean clothes before heading downstairs and out to the car. Cenedl Cymru members were meeting at The Prince and he wanted to speak with Geraint and Rhys, ask if they had anything to add to the plan that was beginning to take shape. He grinned, the lads were right. If they pulled this off, songs would be written about them, about how they saved the Welsh nation from the swarming hoards threatening the country. Cenedl Cymru would be the next generation of folk heroes.

* * *

DI James stood at the head of the squad room and addressed the team.

'I'm sure some of you will have heard that DC Holtz will not be working with us for the foreseeable future. She has been granted compassionate leave for a personal matter, so you will have to take up the slack.'

'That's all well and good, sir,' Oliver Langdon said, 'but no one knows what she actually did. No one can work out how to use her computer and even if we could, it's all password protected.'

'Bloody typical of the girl!' Lizzie Wild snapped. 'Irresponsible and unprofessional. We're in the middle of a major investigation and she's an important part. Who will monitor Cenedl Cymru members' internet use?'

'Surely the CTU in Bristol could help with that?' Ben asked. 'You've more resources than we have and must have a cyber-terrorism section.'

'Of course we do, but it's not convenient. You don't seem to have any understanding of what we're trying to do, that there could be the possibility of a terror attack. The force is not a private club, Inspector, but you seem to run your department as though it is. Two officers now released on "compassionate leave". CID is understaffed, we don't even have enough beat officers to maintain a successful tail on Daffydd Owen and his bunch of cronies.'

'That's enough, DI Wild,' Ben said. 'If you wish to carry on this discussion, I suggest we go to my office. This is not the place.'

'Fine!' she said. 'Lead the way. The rest of you organise yourselves, share out the work and will someone please contact Holtz and ask her for the passwords. Without them, we are effectively blind and won't know what Cenedl Cymru is planning if we can't monitor their internet usage. Connor?'

'Yes, boss.'

'Call the CTU, arrange for the cyber department to pick up where Holtz left off. I don't want any holes these bastards can slip through.'

She stomped from the room, face like thunder and Oliver was happy he wasn't in the firing line. He'd already felt the rough end of Lizzie's temper and had no wish for a repeat performance.

Chapter twenty-nine

Freddie was reading in the library at Milebrook Manor and glanced up from his book as Heidi burst through the door.

'Did I know you were visiting?' he asked, peering at her over his glasses.

'No. Last minute decision.'

'I'm surprised you've been given leave with all that's going on in your part of the country.'

'I haven't,' Heidi muttered. 'I've resigned.'

'Resigned? What's happened?'

Heidi flopped on an old chesterfield sofa and curled her feet beneath her bottom.

'Erica's in trouble, I know she is. That bloody GPS signal hasn't moved since I last spoke to you. I've heard nothing from her at all and I'm going to the commune to get her out… Greta too of course. I spoke to my boss, DI James, his hands are tied and I understand why, but so are mine while I'm a copper. So I'm not one anymore.'

'Just like that?'

'Yes, Freddie, just like that. I'm going inside the commune this evening, and not through the front door.'

'Can you tell me your plans?'

'Haven't got any really, other than I'm going to rescue Erica and Sis, but until I get in I won't know what I'm dealing with or what sort of opposition I'll meet.'

'Do you want me to whistle up some help?'

'Probably better not to, unless I get into real trouble. I haven't uncovered anything to suggest this bunch of loons are armed. I should be able to get in and out without anyone noticing until the morning, and by then it'll be too late. Even if I'm spotted, I can't see Adam Inverdale – or whoever he is – putting up much of a fight.'

'You've always been blessed with an inflated self-confidence, it'll get you into trouble one day,' Freddie warned.

Heidi laughed. 'How do you know it hasn't already?'

Freddie ignored the comment. 'If you're successful, I imagine you'll be coming back here.'

'If you've no objection, that is the plan. Erica will have to go back to work, but I'll be a free agent so can stay on and help with Greta if you need me. If she's been brainwashed, we could be looking at months to deprogram her.'

'Any idea what you'll do, now you've left the force?'

'One thing at a time, Freddie. Let's bring Greta and Erica home. There will be plenty of time for me to work out my future.'

'I still think you should have backup. I don't like the idea of you going inside the place alone. Religious types are always the worst in my experience, hide behind their God and think they can get away with anything they like as long as it's in His name.'

'If you think like that, why on earth did you force me and Greta to sing in the church choir when we were kids? We hated it.'

'Keeping up appearances. The locals like it if I'm seen to be taking an interest in their belief system. Doesn't mean I have to believe it.'

'But you didn't show an interest, you sent us instead.'

Freddie hauled himself upright. 'Let's get you fed, you can't go running around the county on an empty stomach. When are you planning to head over?'

'Soon. I want a couple of hours to watch the place, get an idea how much resistance I'm likely to meet and try to discover a way in.' Heidi uncurled herself from the sofa and followed Freddie towards the kitchen, realising she was very hungry.

* * *

Pixie was crying again. Erica had been calling under the door but hadn't been able to get the girl to answer.

'Pixie, please, talk to me. Don't keep crying, it won't help.'

Pixie didn't answer, but her sobbing increased. Erica was worried, it seemed as though the young woman was shutting down, retreating into herself. Erica looked under the door but couldn't see anything new, just a couple of feet of dingy corridor on either side. Pixie's sobs bounced off the damp walls and tore at Erica's heart. She hauled herself upright, rattled the door, tugged at the old handle and kicked the base, but made no impression.

She walked to the window and peered through the murky glass at the front drive lined with lime trees and saw no one. She yanked at the sash window – even though she knew it was nailed shut, she just needed to do something. Angling her head she looked down at the ground and wondered for the umpteenth time whether she could climb down if she broke the glass. Pixie was right, they were a long way up, too far to attempt an escape through the window. She returned to the door and knelt on the bare wooden boards.

'Pixie!' she snapped. 'Come to the door and talk to me – now!'

Erica heard shuffling, sniffing and eventually Pixie spoke.

'I'm here, but we shouldn't talk. Someone might hear us.'

'I don't care,' Erica said. 'Please, love, don't cry, it stops you thinking clearly. We need to find a way out and will be more successful if we work together.'

'I get that, but it's hopeless,' Pixie whimpered. 'There is no way out. We have to wait until Adam or Mala lets us out and who knows how long that will be. I feel like I've been here forever and can't bear it. How could Felix leave without me?'

'Things like that happen,' Erica said. 'You know they do. What we have to do is be ready when we're released so we can leave. I want to take Greta with us, so we'll have to find her before we leg it. I can't leave without her.'

'Why not? Do you know her?'

Erica wondered how much to tell her new friend and thought it was best to keep disclosure to the bare minimum.

'I don't actually know her, she's a sister of a friend of mine. I came here to convince her to come home, but obviously that didn't go according to plan.'

'So you never wanted to join the church?'

Erica snorted, 'No chance! Places like this are always bad news and New Eden doesn't seem to be any different. Just another cult like all the rest with a leader who's raking in money on the backs of his members.'

'It wasn't like that at the beginning,' Pixie protested, still unwilling to believe she had been tricked and used. 'Adam had a vision, a new way of doing things and it worked wonderfully. Things changed slowly and that was OK too, but now things have got weird. I wish I knew how Clover is, I've been so worried about her.'

'And I'm worried about you. Hold it together, Pixie, you must if we have any chance of standing up to Adam. You told me he'd try to stop us leaving, how would he do that?'

'There are cellars,' Pixie said, sniffing. 'Worse than up here. People are locked down there when they are caught trying to leave. Adam doesn't like people walking away.'

'Maybe that's where Felix is?'

'No, he isn't. One of the kitchen girls said they saw him running towards the road.'

'They won't shut us in the cellars either if we stay strong and united, but we must be ready and need to convince Adam we've changed. When he unlocks the doors we will pretend to be converted to buy us time to round up Greta and sneak away. As soon as we get out of the building we can call for help, but not until then.'

'You promised you'd find me somewhere to go,' Pixie said.

'I know and I will. Don't worry, Pixie, but be strong. Don't sink into despair. Nothing is ever as bad as you think it is.'

* * *

Inside the derelict barn near Aberbran, Daffydd broke open the wooden tea chests with a crowbar and spread out the explosives on a workbench. He examined the sausage shaped rolls of TNT. There were far more in the crates than he realised and plenty for what he needed. He'd been able to glean enough information from the net and planned to construct three devices. The process seemed straightforward and he was eager to get started.

He had decided the best way to deliver the bombs would be in cars, certainly the bridge bombs. The third for the tunnel would take more thinking about. He planned a trip to Rogiet Moor to check the layout of the tracks and how close he could get to the entrance. The bridges wouldn't be a problem. Geraint and Rhys could each drive a car, stage a breakdown next to the towers, set the timers, get picked up by a following vehicle and make their escape. Daffydd smiled, wondered how large the explosions would be and how much damage they would cause.

He began work and bundled sticks of explosive together with duct tape before packing them inside a large gas canister, with the top cut off. He buried a couple of detonators in the middle of the mass and wired a cheap, battery alarm clock to them. His hands were sweating even though the barn was cold. He'd never worked with explosives before and hoped his Granda was right when he'd said the stuff was stable.

He worked long into the night and shortly after midnight he had managed to construct the first device. He had no way of knowing whether it would explode the way he planned, but he'd followed the instructions exactly and saw no reason why it wouldn't. It was a shame he couldn't actually test it, but an explosion out here – even this close to the army ranges on the Epynt – might attract unwelcome attention.

Soon after one he'd had enough, stashed the gear at the back of the barn in a storage space beneath the floor, extinguished the lanterns, chained and bolted the door, climbed in his car and headed back to the main road.

Oliver Langdon and Tegan Hedges shrank down in their car as Daffydd drove past without a second glance. As soon as his headlights vanished from view, Oliver struggled out and stretched his cramped body.

'Bloody hell, I thought he was there for the night,' he grumbled. 'What do you think he's been doing all this time?'

'Only one way to find out,' Tegan said. 'Let's take a look.'

They walked quietly along the lane and turned onto a dirt track which led to the old barn. They slowed as they drew closer, kept to the shadows in case someone else was still inside. They circled the building warily, established there was only a single door, and that was chained and locked. Tegan peered through a knothole in the wood while Oliver tried to shine his torch through a second.

'See anything?' he asked.

'Not much. Some mouldy straw bales, odd rusty lumps of ancient farm machinery, some old Calor gas bottles, but no crates and nothing that looks like it came in one.'

'There must be something,' Oliver grumbled. 'What was he doing in here all night?'

'Perhaps he's restoring the rusty junk?'

'Does any of it look restored?'

'Not really, but I can't see much. We need to get inside.'

'Not tonight,' Oliver said. 'We'll drive past Daffydd's place – make sure he went home – then hand over the surveillance and report to Loopy Lizzie. No way am I doing anything she hasn't sanctioned, not after the way she ripped into Heidi.'

Tegan straightened up. 'Fair enough.' She chuckled. 'Heidi didn't roll over though, fired right back at her. How long do you think she'll be off?'

'Forever, I reckon,' Oliver said and unlocked the car. 'I've heard she told the boss to shove it and walked.'

'Why would she do that?'

'Pissed off when he wouldn't help rescue her sister from the cult.'

'God, I hope not. Heidi's pretty strange, but I really like her and she's good at what she does. That bloody CTU woman. I won't forgive her if she's bullied Heidi out of the job.'

Chapter thirty

Heidi had been hidden near the front entrance of the building for over an hour, tucked between a low wall and a set of descending stone steps. The hall's lights had all been extinguished by midnight and Heidi hadn't seen or heard anything or anyone moving about since. Satisfied she wouldn't be detected, she stood, stretched her constricted limbs, rolled her shoulders and bounced on her toes to encourage blood flow.

She was dressed entirely in black, tight-fitting clothes, a woolly hat pulled over her white-blonde hair. A small body pack was strapped to her chest. She carried a torch and a small, but weighty, lead-filled cosh confiscated from one of the gang masters during the slavery case earlier in the year.

She checked the location of the GPS tracker on her tablet and calculated she was standing directly beneath its signal. She craned her neck and stared up at the roof. The moon flashed briefly between the clouds, shedding a second of white light and Heidi spotted the glimmer of glass. Windows. Servants' quarters? Why was Erica up there and why hadn't she moved? The only answer that made any sense was she was probably locked in and that possible truth warned Heidi to be extra careful.

She worked her way slowly around the building, checking each window and door searching for a way inside. Everything was secure until Heidi drew level with the door to the kitchen. A transom window to the right of the door was propped open half an inch. Heidi hauled herself up the wall, hung on to the windowsill for leverage, slipped three fingers into the gap and pulled herself higher. As soon as both hands were on the frame, she popped open the metal latch and posted her petite body through the opening.

She dropped into a long, narrow room, lined with shelves loaded with pickles, jams, sacks of flour and sugar, trays of tinned food and bottled fruit. The place smelt dry, dusty and spicy. Heidi stifled a sneeze and then moved between the shelves and tried the door. It was locked and she swore silently until she noticed the bottom section had a metal air vent fixed in the middle of the panel.

Heidi rummaged in her pack and removed a multi-tool which she used to unscrew the vent's fixings. She frowned at the small hole, dipped her head and tried to wriggle through. She was too wide. Backing out she removed her pack, fed it through the hole, tried again and by twisting and turning her head, shoulders and hips, finally managed to squirm free. Strapping her pack on, she headed for the kitchen door. Cracking it open, she listened hard and heard nothing, so slipped through and headed towards the large hall at the front of the house.

Voices! She froze, looked around frantically for somewhere to hide and flattened herself in a doorway, heart beating faster than she would like. A large group of people were trooping down the stairs, mumbling to each other. All looked tired, but strangely, most were smiling. Heidi held her breath as they passed, eyes opening wide when she recognised her sister in the middle of the group.

Once they had passed by, Heidi nipped out of her hiding place, set off after them and turned a corner just in time to see a large door at the end of the corridor close. She crept closer to the door and heard a deep voice saying something about being nearer to God. Peering through the keyhole she saw people sitting on the floor and Adam perched on a low stage, preaching. She quickly checked the screen on her phone. Erica's tracker wasn't in the room, it was still at the top of the house. Heidi changed direction, headed for the main staircase and began the climb towards the top of the building.

On the third floor, Heidi discovered a door which concealed a narrow staircase leading to the servants' quarters and crept higher. Her nose wrinkled at the damp smell of fungi, fingers cringing at the touch of wet plaster and peeling paint. The stairs led to a narrow corridor with four doors on one side, two open, two shut. She knelt and peered under the first closed door, but the room was dark. She tapped her nails on the boards and hissed quietly.

Almost immediately a face appeared in the gap.

'Heidi! What are you doing here?' Erica whispered fiercely.

'Rescuing you, of course. Are you OK?'

'Will be as soon as you open the door.'

Heidi rummaged in her pack, pulled out a picklock and began work.

'How long have you been here?' Heidi murmured quietly.

'Too bloody long. Did you meet anyone on the way in?'

'Just passed a large gang of loonies, they all went inside a room near the back of the building. What are they up to?'

'Early meditation, lasts about an hour, so we have some time before they'll come back upstairs.'

There was a muffled click as Heidi sprung the lock and the door swung open. Erica dashed out and wrapped her partner in a tight hug.

'Later,' Heidi said and shook her off. 'Let's go and find Greta and get out of this nuthouse.'

'Not yet. We have to take Pixie with us.'

'Who's Pixie?'

'In the room next door. I promised I'd take her with me. Anyway, we can't get to Greta until the session in the hall is over and everyone's back in bed. Adam has followers, we'll be overpowered.'

'Rubbish!' Heidi snorted. 'I'm just going to drag Greta away. I don't care who sees me and we can't take anyone else.'

'Hello?' Pixie's voice floated under the door and her pale, tearstained face appeared in the gap. 'What's going on? Erica?'

'Hush, love,' Erica whispered. 'My friend is here and she'll get you out, but you must be quiet, we don't want anyone to hear us.'

Erica glanced at Heidi who shrugged, cracked her knuckles and started work on the second lock. As the door opened Pixie fell into Erica's arms.

'Now what?' Erica asked.

'Easy,' Heidi said. 'Find my sister and get the hell out.'

'Be better if we could creep out rather than cause a ruckus. As I said, Adam has around thirty acolytes and they might try to stop us leaving. Also, there's a room at the rear of the house I'd like to take a peek inside. I'm fairly sure it's the office, that's where we might find out what's really going on here.'

'OK,' Heidi agreed reluctantly. She checked her watch. 'It's well after three, will they all be back in their beds now?'

'More than likely, but we'll have to keep our wits about us.'

'So lead the way,' Heidi said. 'Pixie, stay between us and keep really quiet.'

Pixie nodded and followed close to Erica as she negotiated the narrow stairs. They reached the bottom of the main staircase without meeting anyone and Erica guided them through the dark corridors to the locked door. Heidi worked her magic and all three slipped inside.

The room was indeed an office, filing cabinets lined the walls and a computer squatted on a desk near the window.

Heidi switched it on. 'Erica, do you know where Greta will be now?'

'Yes, upstairs in the dormitories.'

'Go and round her up so we can leave. I'll see what I can do with this while we wait. If I can get round the password, I'll download everything and we can read through it later.'

'What about me?' Pixie asked, voice quavering.

'Stay with Heidi,' Erica said. 'I won't be long and she'll keep you safe while I'm gone.'

'I want to come with you.'

'No, love, stay here. I'll be back before you know it.'

Erica left the room while Heidi worked at the computer and linked it to her tablet, ready for the download. Pixie watched over her shoulder.

'How did you get in?' she asked.

'Through a window.' Heidi's fingers flew across the keyboard as she worked at cracking the password.

'Are you Greta's sister?'

'Yes, I am.' Heidi wished the girl would shut up so she could concentrate.

'And Erica's your friend?'

Heidi sighed. 'Erica's my partner. Could you just give me a second?'

Pixie wandered away, opened drawers and filing cabinets, riffled through paperwork. She jumped when the office door opened and Erica returned with Greta in tow.

Greta squealed with delight when she spotted her sister. 'Heidi!' She flung her arms around her neck and Heidi shook them off.

'Not now, Sis, I'm busy, and keep your voice down.'

'How much longer do you need?' Erica asked. 'I want to leave this place.'

'Not long.' Heidi watched the screen as the download began and a couple of minutes later, she unplugged the device, turned off the computer and stood to face the others. 'Done. Now, let's go. Keep together and move quietly. We don't want to wake up any of the loons.'

Heidi slipped the tablet inside her pack, led the way from the room and headed towards the front of the building. She hesitated at the bottom of the staircase before striding towards the front door.

'Who the hell are you?' said an angry voice from the shadows. 'What are you doing in our house?'

The women spun around and Erica recognised Mala as she moved towards them, two young men at her side.

'We don't want any trouble,' Erica said. 'We're leaving.'

'No,' Mala said, 'I don't think you are. Adam won't like it. Joe, Mack – grab them.'

One of the men moved towards Erica and stretched out his hand to take hold of her arm. Heidi withdrew the cosh from her pocket and whacked his wrist, sure she heard the bones crunch. He howled and Mala pushed past him to take a swing at Heidi, who dodged the blow easily, gave her attacker a vicious shove and grinned as Mala tumbled to the floor.

'Stay down,' Heidi growled, 'or I'll really have to hurt you.' She glared at Mack who backed off.

'You can't get out,' Mala sneered. 'The door's locked and Adam has the only key.'

Heidi glanced around the hall, spotted a heavy chair next to the stairs, picked it up and hurled it with all her strength through the nearest window. She grabbed hold of Pixie's arm and pushed her towards the shattered glass.

'Go on, kid,' she said. 'Climb through. Make sure you don't cut yourself and take Greta with you. We'll meet you at the end of the drive. Go!'

Pixie scrambled towards the smashed window and pulled Greta with her.

Heidi turned her attention back to the room. 'E, go with them. I'm right behind you.'

Erica backed closer to the window while keeping an eye on the cult members. She was just about to climb onto the windowsill, when a door banged open and Adam appeared, face like thunder.

'In God's name, what is happening? Mala, what's going on in my house?'

‘Greta and Pixie have gone,’ Mala said. ‘Erica’s still here – obviously – but I don’t know her.’ Mala pointed a finger at Heidi. ‘She attacked Joe. I’m sure she’s broken his wrist.’ Joe sat on the stairs and cradled his injured arm, groaning.

Adam moved closer and glared at Heidi. ‘Tell me who you are and why you’re here,’ he ordered.

‘I’ve come for Greta. That’s all you need to know.’

‘Maybe you’ll be more forthcoming with the police.’

‘I doubt it,’ Heidi snapped.

A movement to her left caused her to spin around in time to see Mala wrap an arm around Erica’s neck. She spotted a bright flash and saw Mala held a long shard of glass to Erica’s throat. Heidi took two steps forward.

‘Don’t!’ Mala spat. ‘I’ll do it.’

‘Then what? What will you do then?’ Heidi sank to the floor and began fiddling with her shoe. ‘Do you even have a plan?’ she asked. She suddenly powered her small body upwards and sprang catlike to cover the distance between her and Mala, smashed the hand that held the glass with her cosh and shoved Erica away. Heidi whirled to face Adam.

‘Did you say you’d called the police?’ she asked angrily. ‘Oh, no, you didn’t, you just threatened me with them. Don’t worry though, Adrian, they’ll be here soon enough. Erica, let’s go.’

Adam could do little but watch as the women hoisted themselves through the shattered window and chased after Greta and Pixie.

Chapter thirty-one

Lizzie Wild listened intently as Oliver and Tegan delivered their reports, one hand covering her eyes.

'So, the only way we'll know what he's up to,' Tegan concluded, 'is to get inside the barn. We wondered about taking a look last night, but thought it best to update you first.'

'Quite right,' Lizzie said. 'Daffydd went home after he left the barn?'

'Yes, we followed him to his digs, then the second team took over,' Oliver said.

'No chatter online to give us a clue what he's up to?'

Oliver shook his head. 'I managed to open Heidi's system and continued the monitoring, but they're not saying anything and still surfing the same websites. Nothing new. The bugs in The Prince have given us a lead though. Seems as though Cenedl Cymru are planning a march in Cardiff.'

Lizzie leaned back in her chair and smiled. 'Good work, Ollie, didn't know you had it in you. Find out exactly where and when this march is happening and we'll make sure we have a welcoming party in place. We'll film the crowd so we can identify them. Some are bound to have outstanding warrants so those who do, we can nick and take off the street.'

'What about the barn?' Tegan asked. 'Daffydd was in there for hours last night, we need to know what he's up to.'

'We'll learn more by watching. If we bust the place we'll nick Daffydd but the others will walk away and they're all involved. I know they are.'

'I still think we should infiltrate a copper into the group,' Oliver said. 'A man on the inside and we'd know everything that's going on. Heidi thinks they're planning something big.'

'Don't talk to me about her,' Lizzie growled. 'Heidi and Erica have dropped us all in it; unprofessional, both of them. A major operation like this and they go AWOL. And I've already told you, the brass won't sanction an undercover operation. We've covered all the bases, Daffydd and his cronies can't fart without us knowing.'

'Except we don't know what they've got in the barn,' Tegan grumbled.

'Probably nothing. Swastikas and banners, neither of which are illegal. We watch until Bristol CTU tells us otherwise and if anything is agreed, it'll be the CTU that carries out any operation, not you.' Lizzie stood, smoothed wrinkles out of her trousers and left the room.

Tegan lobbed a ball of paper at the door. 'Bloody woman,' she said. 'If DI James was running things, we'd already have these scumbags under arrest. We're messing about on the edges of the investigation achieving nothing, while Cenedl Cymru are running around as though they're untouchable. If anything bad happens, you know who'll get the blame, don't you?'

'Yeah,' Oliver said, 'us, the coppers from the boonies. Still, it'll give the *Daily Mail* something to write about and if I get the chance, I'll make bloody sure they know who was responsible. Come on, Tegan, let's get some shut-eye, we'll be back on shift again before you know it.'

* * *

Freddie stood at the old range in the large kitchen and fried sausages and bacon. He listened to the chatter around the table while he put together a full English and wished he hadn't given Cook a day off. The young girl, Pixie, wasn't saying much and Freddie was worried about her. After they'd eaten, he intended calling the local doctor to visit, check her and Greta over. Greta was quieter than usual, but he wasn't so concerned about his daughter. She was a tough woman and had bounced back from far worse. He broke eggs in the pan and listened to the conversation behind him.

'Did you find anything useful on New Eden's hard drive?' Erica asked.

Heidi slurped coffee to clear her mouth of toast. 'Yeah. Once I've been through it all properly, I reckon we can put Adam and his sidekicks away for a long time. Forever if I have my way.'

'Did you find out where the money has been coming from?'

Heidi nodded. 'He's selling babies.'

Freddie turned away from the range. 'Did you say, "selling babies"? You're kidding.'

'Unfortunately, I'm not,' Heidi said. 'Remember the £125,000 I found in his account, Erica?'

She nodded.

'It would seem that's the going rate. Pixie has been at the commune more or less since it formed and she's aware of three babies being born there, says they were adopted by other church members living outside the hall. I've matched the dates, as best I can, with large payments into Adam's personal stash. All three were made electronically and all three have been bounced around the financial system to cover their origin. Can't work out exactly where they came from yet, but I will.'

Freddie carried the enormous frying pan over to the table and unceremoniously dumped the food on a large central platter. 'Dig in, ladies,' he said. 'There's plenty more, so don't be shy.'

'I've been dreaming about your breakfasts, Pa,' Greta said. 'I'm never going to eat muesli again… ever.'

'I've never eaten it once,' Freddie said. 'Rabbit food with added sugar as far as I can tell.' He pulled up a chair and sat at the head of the table. 'So then, what do we do next?'

'Bring New Eden down,' Heidi muttered. 'Now the police can get involved. A good starting point would be unlawful imprisonment of a police officer and we'll take it from there.'

'Where do I go?' Pixie asked, her voice quavering.

'You'll stay here for as long as you wish,' Freddie said. 'Have you got family?'

She nodded. 'I have but they won't want to see me. Dad chucked me out, that's how Felix and I ended up at New Eden. Adam was so kind.'

Erica slapped the table angrily. 'Stop thinking that way, Pixie. Adam is a user, a conman, a criminal. He wasn't kind to you unless it suited his purpose. All of you were slaves, working for him, running the shops. None of you were paid.'

'We didn't need money,' Pixie protested. 'Everything we wanted was at the commune.'

'You can't defend him,' Erica said. 'You were effectively held prisoner. You may have signed up willingly, but you were coerced – all of you – to feather Adam's nest. He isn't even called Adam, his name is Adrian Ingham. Everything he told you was a lie.'

Pixie stared at her in horror, before jamming sausages between two slices of bread and escaping from the room. Erica made to follow, but Heidi held up her hand.

'Don't,' she warned, 'give her some space. You should ring DI James, update him with our news, find out what's going on in Wales and return to work. I'll stay here, search through what we've found and look after Pixie. There's an organisation in London, the Cult Information Centre, I'll speak with them, find out the best way to handle her. She's been living at New Eden a long time.'

'What do I tell Ben?'

'The truth. Let him know what we've already discovered and tell him if he needs to speak with me he knows the number.'

'You should come back to Wales with me.'

'No chance. I'm done with Dyfed Powys Police – for good.'

'Ben will smooth things over. He'll want you back.'

'Tough! I told you, E, I'm not interested.'

'What will you do?'

'Why does everyone keep asking me that? I'll think of something, but at the moment I have my hands full. I'll care for Pixie and help her through this. Then I'll find out as much as I can about New Eden from here, work on where those baby payments came from. As soon as we discover that, we can destroy this dreadful man and his cohorts and reunite the little ones with their mothers.'

'I can help with Pixie,' Greta said, 'if Pa lets me stay.'

'Why the hell wouldn't I let you stay?' Freddie asked, eyebrows bouncing. 'This is your home. I find it difficult to understand why you became involved with the cult in the first place, but I'm not sure you really know either.' He sipped his tea. 'Your mother's been in touch. She's concerned.'

'She's not planning on coming down is she?' Greta asked.

'She has mentioned a visit, yes.'

'Well, I don't want to see her. She'll cause ructions if she turns up. Tell her to stay away, Pa.'

Erica stood. 'Can I use your phone, Freddie? Heidi's right, I ought to check in.'

'Yes, of course. Use my study, you won't be disturbed.'

Erica left the kitchen, anxious not to become embroiled in a family dispute.

'This situation with your mother can't continue,' Freddie said. 'Everything happened so long ago we ought to sort things out and behave like a family.'

'There's no statute of limitations in a situation like this,' Heidi said. 'That woman abandoned me. I'm only here now because of you, so don't tell me I have to kiss and make up. It'll never happen and you surely understand why. I'm going to find Pixie and get some work done. I'll see you two later.'

Heidi stomped out of the room.

'Give it up, Pa,' Greta said. 'You'll never get those two together and I'm firmly on Heidi's side. Mother's had years to put this right, but hasn't made the slightest effort. How can you expect either of us to welcome her with open arms? What she did was appalling and you know it. I cannot understand why you think there'll be a happy ever after to this story.'

'As I said, it happened so long ago. We're all adults now and ought to be able to deal with this.'

'Not going to happen. Now, if you don't mind, I need a lie-down.'

'Are you OK? Heidi said you might suffer ill-effects from the brainwashing.'

'I wasn't there long enough and I'm over it. Don't worry about me. Help Pixie, that's something you can do.'

Greta left the room and Freddie stared at the uneaten mound of food. He rested his head on his arms and for the first time in years, actually felt like crying. He might be a powerful man in Whitehall, but seemed to be powerless in his own home. He realised he had little choice but to phone his wife and do as his daughters asked… tell her to stay away.

Chapter thirty-two

Daffydd pulled up in the centre of Brecon and waited for Rhys and Geraint to arrive. The planned march in Cardiff was due to kick off at one and they had plenty of time to get there. Five minutes later the doors opened and his cohorts climbed in.

'Morning, boys,' Daffydd said as he pulled away. 'Ready to cause a row?'

'Yeah,' Rhys said, 'been looking forward to it. Should be a good turnout. Cardiff won't have seen anything like this before.'

'How are you getting on with your research?' Geraint asked. 'Built any bombs?'

'I have, actually,' Daffydd said. 'Wasn't hard. Can't test it – obviously – but it should work fine.'

'What's the plan then?'

'This is how I see it,' Daffydd said, as he pulled across a roundabout and headed towards Merthyr Tydfil. 'We'll deliver the bridge bombs in cars. The explosives will be packed inside gas canisters, thirty sticks in each. It only takes six sticks of TNT to flatten your average semi-detached, so thirty should be a bloody enormous bang. The canisters will be in the boots, so we pull off the road just before the bridges, set the timers, drive to the towers, leave the cars and walk away.'

'That won't work,' Rhys said. 'The bridges are watched twenty-four seven. If a car breaks down the tow trucks are there within minutes, we'll get caught.'

'I thought about that,' Daffydd said. 'We'll need second cars following, then when we leave the cars, the driver can hop in the follower and head to England. You'll drive up through Gloucester, swap the cars and hightail it back to Brecon. If we set the timers with a ten-minute delay we can make our escape and get off the bridges before the bombs explode. Even if the tow truck gets there fast, not being able to find a driver with the car will slow things down. Ten minutes will be enough.'

'What about the tunnel?'

'Even easier. The tunnel appears above ground about two miles from the coast at Rogiet Moor and a minor road runs alongside the track. I'll park in the road, carry the canister to the mouth of the tunnel, set the clock and leg it. An explosion as large as the one I've planned, will shatter the arched roof and bring the whole lot down.'

'Will the bridges collapse?' Rhys asked.

'Unlikely,' Daffydd said. 'The new bridge is a cable stay bridge, that means the road hangs from the towers, so we attack the towers, maybe blow a hole in one, then the authorities will have to shut the bridge. The first Severn crossing is a suspension bridge. The road bed hangs from chains, so we need to place the bomb on the concrete structure at the end of the bridge where the chains are anchored. If we blow one chain, the road bed will tip.'

Geraint laughed. 'Shame we can't watch,' he said. 'I'd love to see that. The government will piss its pants. Bet they blame ISIS.'

'Yeah, probably, but we'll claim responsibility so they'll know it's the Welsh who have struck back.'

'Are we going to phone through a warning, like the IRA used to?'

'No warning,' Daffydd muttered. 'Maximum impact.'

'Got a date in mind?' Rhys asked.

'Soon. I'll build the other bombs while you two sort out four cars and two drivers, but tell them as little as possible. Secrecy is what will make this work and keep us safe.'

'I know a lad with a scrapyard in Ammanford,' Geraint said. 'I can round up the cars we need from there and he won't ask questions.'

'Perfect. Now all we have to do is stop any violence in Cardiff this afternoon. We want to be heard, not shut down because one of the lads loses the plot. And no Gurkhas.'

Geraint chuckled. 'Yeah, the lads have got that now.'

* * *

Lizzie had been able to round up an impressive force of uniformed officers and a few members of the Bristol CTU had travelled over from England. They were all in place around Cardiff city centre before Cenedl Cymru members began to gather and this time Daffydd ensured there was no trouble.

A large crowd of shoppers congregated to listen to what Daffydd had to say and it was disturbing how many of the audience cheered and clapped. Lizzie had spotted the reporter woman from Brecon and made sure she kept her distance. She didn't like journalists, especially the print variety and hadn't been happy to see her name in the paper after the Brecon rally. Connor Haskins stood by her side, bright eyes watching the crowd.

'Bloody hell, boss,' he said. 'This lot are better organised than last time. Daffydd has them eating out of his hand.'

'It's all talk,' Lizzie said. 'A load of bullshit and bluster and until Cenedl Cymru get themselves banned, we can't do much about it.'

'They killed that Romanian girl,' Connor pointed out.

'Two of their members did, but we can't prove Daffydd guilty of incitement, or even joint enterprise. The only link is that the nasty little scrotes were members of his gang. Not enough, unfortunately.'

Another ripple of applause ran through the crowd and Connor tensed.

'This could kick off so easily,' he muttered. 'Good job we're here.' He hesitated. 'Have you heard from Holtz or Bevan?'

Lizzie nodded. 'Bevan's on her way in, nothing from Holtz.'

'Do you think Holtz is right when she says the XRW are planning something in Wales?'

'No, I don't. All this lot are trying to do is reinvent themselves as a serious political party. They'll carry on making a noise, but I doubt they'll resort to violence and if they do, we'll nick them.'

A woman pushed her way through the crowd and Lizzie recognised Stacey Logan from *The Mid Wales Times*.

'Oh shit,' Lizzie grumbled. 'Not you again. I've told you, I've nothing to say.'

'Aw, come on, DI Wild, I'm only doing my job. Can you tell me why Bristol Counter Terrorism Unit is involved in this investigation? Do you have reason to believe this is about more than rallies? Are you worried about a terrorist attack?'

'How did you find out I was from the CTU?'

'I'm a great investigative journalist. Well?'

Lizzie sighed and launched into the standard reply about how – in these times of heightened threat – all extremist groups would be investigated, and asked for the public to remain vigilant.

Stacey chuckled. 'I bet you spout that rubbish in your sleep. What can you tell me about Cenedl Cymru? Two of their members beat Daniela Stoica to death… allegedly. Any comment?'

'None,' Lizzie snapped. 'Now I'll have to ask you politely to get out of my face so I can do my job. If you don't leave, I'll have DS Haskins shift you, or arrest you for obstruction. I'm not fussy which.'

Stacey laughed. 'Yeah, of course you will. Is it twelve forms for an arrest these days?'

DS Haskins took a step towards her and Stacey held up her hands.

'It's OK, I'm going, got a front page to write. Last chance to have your say…'

Lizzie glared at her, Stacey grinned, tucked her camera away and disappeared into the crowd.

Chapter thirty-three

Erica rapped on DI James' office door before pushing her way in. Ben was surrounded by mounds of paper; he glanced up and smiled.

'Erica! Good to see you. Take a seat and tell me what's been going on. I could do with a break from this lot. I'm convinced paperwork breeds.'

Erica sat and said, 'I'm still waiting for the paperless-society we were promised decades ago.'

Ben chuckled. 'Never happen. Now tell me, how's Heidi?'

'She's fine. I was so bloody glad to see her when she turned up at the commune. Inverdale had me locked up and if it wasn't for Heidi I might still be there. We rescued Greta and another young girl, Pixie, they're both at Milebrook Manor – Heidi too.'

'Is she planning to return to work?'

'Not at the moment, maybe never – sorry.'

Ben frowned. 'Be dreadful to lose her. Can you do anything?'

'I'll give it a go, sir.'

'So what's New Eden up to? Any proof of wrongdoing? Apart from kidnapping a police officer.' He raised his eyebrows. 'Are you sure you're OK?'

Erica nodded. 'I'm fine, sir, but the New Eden thing is a racket,' she said. 'The members living in the commune are little better than slaves, controlled utterly by Inverdale and a woman called Mala.' She hesitated. 'It looks as though they are selling babies.'

Ben looked shocked. 'Did you say, "selling babies"?'

'Yes, sir. Three have been born at the commune since its inception and are not there now. Heidi has uncovered three payments of £125k into Inverdale's personal account. She's trying to trace the origins, but the money has been shipped all over the place before landing with him.'

'Have you spoken to Gloucester force about any of this?'

'Not yet. Heidi's working through a copy of a hard drive she downloaded from a computer at the commune. I'll speak to her later and let you know if she's had any luck.'

'How did you leave things with Inverdale? Any problems I ought to be aware of?'

'He caught us leaving.' She hesitated. 'There was a bit of a scene but he doesn't know I'm a copper.'

Ben looked a question across the desk.

'The front door was locked,' Erica explained. 'Inverdale refused us the key so Heidi lobbed a chair through one of the windows.'

Ben threw back his head and laughed. 'That sounds like DC Holtz. No one tried to stop her?'

'As if they could!' Erica grinned. 'Proper firebrand my partner. We weren't followed.'

Ben leaned back in his chair, stared at the ceiling and rocked back and forth, deep in thought.

'OK, leave it with me,' he said. 'I'll have a chat with Gloucester. Keep me up to date with anything Heidi uncovers and talk to her, please. She's a useful member of our team and I want her back. If she returns soon, I should be able to smooth things over.'

'I'm pretty sure she won't consider it while Lizzie Wild is on the scene, but I will talk to her. What's happening with Cenedl Cymru?'

'Still monitoring them, but we've found nothing to link them with the murder – or anything we can nick the ringleaders for. They're holding a rally in Cardiff city centre as we speak… DI Wild is in attendance.'

'Any clues whether they are planning anything? Heidi thinks they are.'

'Zilch. Oliver Langdon took over the online surveillance after Heidi left and says there's nothing. She planted bugs in The Prince before she walked out and Ollie's been listening.' Ben paused. 'Where does she get her kit? It knocks spots off anything the force can get its hands on. The tracking device she used to find you is dead impressive.'

'Tracking device?'

'A GPS something or other; in the necklace you're wearing.'

Erica removed the chain and peered at the locket suspiciously. 'Heidi put a tracker on me?'

Ben nodded. 'Didn't you know?'

'No, I didn't!' Erica frowned at the prospect of another difficult conversation with her partner.

'Still,' Ben said, 'good job she did, great to have you back. Might be an idea to keep you away from DI Wild for a few days though, so I'll speak with Gloucester about New Eden and name you as contact.'

'Thank you, sir.'

'If I can't get them interested in investigating the cult, we might have to handle it, and if this Inverdale character is selling babies, we need to stop him. Set yourself up in the office next to mine and keep your head down for a few days. You're definitely number two on Lizzie's shit list.'

* * *

Heidi had set up camp in her father's study and was running search programs, trying to discover where the payments made to Inverdale had originated. Pixie was curled up in an old leather chair in front of the wide fireplace, staring into the flames. Heidi glanced up from her work and noticed the girl was crying. Not very good at handling her own emotions, never mind anyone else's, she left her alone.

The study door opened and Greta walked in, carrying a tray bearing coffee mugs and biscuits. She placed it on a table, perched next to Pixie and draped an arm around the girl's shoulders.

'Hey, sweetie, hush now. All this crying won't help at all. Are you sure it wouldn't be a good idea to see Pa's doctor? Get him to check you over?'

Pixie shook her head. 'I don't want to, there's nothing wrong with me.'

'Something obviously is. You're not eating properly, or sleeping. I heard you wandering about at two this morning.'

'I'm fine, just used to waking up for early meditation, that's all.'

Greta handed her some coffee. 'Drink this, it's hot and sweet and will do you good. Biscuit?'

Pixie shook her head and tears began to fall again. 'I don't know what to do,' she sobbed. 'I miss New Eden. I loved living there and now I'm lost. I don't belong anywhere now, no base, no home, no nothing…'

Greta pulled her closer and squeezed as though she was trying to wring out the misery. 'Pa says you can stay here for as long as you like, he'll look after you.'

'I can't just move in,' Pixie said. 'I should go home.'

'So we'll ring your dad. Talk to him about what you've been through and I'm sure he'll take you back.'

'No!' Pixie yelled. 'Not there. Home. Back to New Eden.'

Heidi looked up from her screen, caught her sister's eye and sent a visual warning not to push.

'OK,' Greta said, 'I get it, but give yourself some time to adjust. Don't make any hasty decisions. Stay here with us for a while at least. Maybe we can track down Felix.'

Pixie looked up. 'How? I haven't a clue where he went and he won't have gone home.'

'Heidi will find him, she's a wizard at anything like that. He could stay here too, I'm sure.'

'That would be great,' Pixie said. 'I miss him so much. Can you really find him, Heidi?'

'I'll give it a go,' Heidi said. 'Tell me as much about him as you can and I'll start looking.'

'Where's Erica?' Pixie asked.

'Gone back to work in Brecon.'

'I still can't believe she's a copper. She didn't seem like one when we were in the commune. She was brilliant when we were locked up, I couldn't have got through that without her.' She hesitated. 'What will happen now?'

'About what?' Heidi asked.

'New Eden.'

'No idea,' Heidi said. 'Not my problem. I'm not a copper anymore and it will be up to the local force to work out how they want to play it.'

'Will Adam get in trouble?'

Heidi didn't want to tell Pixie what she was really planning – complete destruction of the cult and its twisted leader. The girl was only liberated a couple of days ago and three years of brainwashing wouldn't vanish overnight. Heidi was also concerned Pixie might tip off Inverdale and didn't want that to happen. She wanted to see him held accountable for the damage he'd inflicted over the years to vulnerable, unsuspecting individuals – and she wanted to find the babies. If Inverdale got wind of her plans he would skip, she was sure of it.

'Come and sit with me,' Heidi said. 'Tell me what you know about Felix and we'll see if we can find him. Greta, will you take this file to Pa? Ask him to read through it and tell him I'd welcome his opinion.'

Greta laughed. 'He won't believe me. He doesn't think you like his opinions.'

'I don't – usually – but this is one time I could do with it. Now, Pixie, come and help me find Felix.'

Chapter thirty-four

Daffydd and the brothers were eating a late breakfast at the Castle Kitchen in Brecon and drawing up final plans.

'I've got the cars,' Rhys mumbled through a mouthful of sausage. 'Stashed all four behind the industrial estate in town and two of the lads are happy to act as second drivers.'

'You haven't told them what we're up to?' Daffydd asked.

'No. They didn't ask much, to be honest, just pleased to be involved, fight for the cause and all that. I said we needed drivers and they jumped at the chance.'

'When are we going to do this?' Geraint asked.

'Couple of days. A few last glitches to sort out, then we're ready. You two will drive the bridge bombs. I'll deliver the one to the tunnel.'

'There are cameras on the bridges,' Rhys said. 'They'll be on to us in no time. We'll never get away with it. They'll trace the cars back to Ammanford and your mate'll grass us up.'

'Not Nigel,' Geraint said. 'Hard as nails and knows how to keep his mouth shut. As for the cameras, we'll wear disguises.'

'What, false beards?'

'No, you bloody numpty, baseball caps, sunglasses and keep our heads down. We won't be on film for long before we're picked up by our escorts and trust me… the cars won't be traceable. Nigel's switched number plates around with stuff in his scrapyard. There won't be much left of the cars carrying the bombs and we'll dump the others as soon as we reach England. Nigel's set up a meet with a bloke on the edge of Bristol, place called Westerleigh, another scrapyard owner. He'll have more cars waiting and will crush the ones we arrive in.'

Daffydd grinned. 'You've done well, boy, sounds foolproof to me.' He pushed his plate away and groaned. 'I've eaten too much. Right then, lads, go about your normal business for a couple of days and I'll give you a shout when we're ready for the off.'

'Can't wait,' Geraint said. 'Still a bloody shame we can't watch the explosions.'

'We'll watch them on telly when we get back,' Daffydd said. 'It'll be all over the news for weeks. Look at the fuss when the Twin Towers were attacked. This is our day of protest. Cenedl Cymru will go down in history.'

* * *

Erica shoved open the door to her new office, dumped her bag on the desk, hung her coat on a wobbly hat stand in the corner and flopped on the chair. She had managed to reach the office without bumping into Lizzie Wild and had caught up with Oliver and Tegan yesterday afternoon. It sounded as though the CTU inspector was making their lives a misery. The pair had given her an update on the current case and Erica wasn't impressed. Like Heidi she thought Cenedl Cymru were up to something, but DI Wild seemed convinced they were just making a noise. Loopy Lizzie didn't have a very high opinion of the locals and seemed to believe that no one in Wales was intelligent enough to even plan a terrorist attack, never mind execute one.

The phone rang and she snatched it up.

'DS Bevan.'

'Hi, E. How you doing without me?'

'Heidi! How are you getting on? How are the girls?'

'Greta is fine, feeling stupid now she was caught by the cult in the first place, but Pixie's not doing so well. She's been there a long time and has been well and truly brainwashed. It's so sad, she says she doesn't feel as though she belongs anywhere and is utterly lost, like a teenager with a broken satnav.'

'Have you found anything we can beat Inverdale over the head with?'

Heidi chuckled. 'Where shall I start; money laundering, benefit fraud, coercive behaviour, property fraud and theft, and that's without the baby supermarket he's been running. Round up the troops, E, and we'll pay him a visit.'

'Not so fast, Heidi. DI James is on our side, but he needs proof. He must convince Gloucester force to become involved and they don't know you're always right like we do. The boss has set me up in the office next door to his and is allowing me to spend some time on this cult stuff, not least because Inverdale locked me up.' She hesitated. 'He told me there's a GPS bug in the locket you gave me, is that true?'

Heidi didn't answer and the silence between them stretched.

'Why didn't you tell me you'd planted a bug around my neck?' Erica asked.

'Cos you wouldn't have worn it if I had and, as things turned out, it was a bloody good job I did.'

'You should have told me.'

Heidi remained silent and Erica was sure she heard her partner cracking her knuckles. She decided not to push the issue now, they had more important things to deal with.

Heidi eventually spoke. 'Not working the XRW case anymore then?'

'No. Nothing seems to be happening with that. Lizzie has Daffydd followed everywhere and once Oliver managed to open your computer, he's monitored the cyberspace stuff and found nothing.'

'What did Lizzie have to say when she found out Daffydd was researching bomb building online?'

'Bomb building? What are you talking about?'

'He's visited a few sites detailing how to put together viable explosive devices using TNT. He only looked once, soon after I walked out, but once is enough. If he's got his hands on any go-bang gear, we could have a big problem on our hands.'

'Bloody hell. I haven't heard anything about this. Ollie hasn't said a word and Lizzie still reckons it is all bluster. She says Daffydd's talking the talk but has no intention of walking the walk.'

'She's wrong!' Heidi said. 'Make sure she knows what he's been researching as soon as you can and ensure you convince Gloucester force to take the cult case. If they don't, I'll deal with it myself. We'll talk again.'

Heidi hung up abruptly and Erica was left listening to dead air. She was about to head upstairs to the CID room to talk to DI Wild when her phone rang again. Thinking it was Heidi, she grabbed it.

'Knew you'd ring back.'

'Uh, DS Bevan? Front desk. There's a Jon Williams here with his nephew. Says he'd like a word.'

'Is it urgent?'

'He said it's important. Refuses to discuss the matter with anyone but yourself. Will you come down?'

'OK. Stick them in an interview room and I'll be there in a minute.'

Erica slammed down the phone and wondered what Williams wanted. She decided to pop downstairs and get the chat out of the way, then have a word with Lizzie Wild.

That way she'd have more time to work out what to say without antagonising the woman.

Erica left the office and ran down the stairs. Jon Williams and a young man were waiting for her in room two. Jon stood as she entered and dragged his nephew upright.

'DS Bevan,' he said. 'Thank you for making the time to see us.'

'No problem. What can I do for you and…' Erica looked at the lad.

'Matthew Williams,' Jon said. 'He's my nephew and he's got something to tell you.'

'OK, Matthew,' Erica said, settling on a chair. 'What's up? How can I help?' She studied him. He was flushed, sweating, as twitchy as a dreaming dog and obviously had no desire to be in the police station. A small lad, the sort you wouldn't notice, with a baby face and dark floppy hair.

'Speak up, boy,' Jon snapped and dealt his nephew a clip round the ear, the sound ricocheted off the tiled wall.

Erica held up her hands. 'Whoa, Jon. I've no idea what this is all about, but I can't allow you to whack him, so calm down, and will one of you please tell me what's going on?'

'Go on, Matt, tell DS Bevan why we're here.'

The boy covered his face and mumbled into his hands. Jon shot out an arm and angrily knocked them away.

'I was at the rally in Cardiff,' Matthew finally blurted out.

'Cenedl Cymru's march?' Erica asked.

'Yeah, got taken along by one of my mates, group of us went.'

'Well, so far you've not told me about anything illegal,' Erica said.

'After the march… we… we robbed a newsagents, the one near the station,' he said. 'The others, they beat the owner and trashed the place. I didn't know they were going to do any of it.'

'Tell me the names of the others.'

Matthew shook his head. 'I can't. They'll come after me.'

'If you don't, you'll take all the blame. True you'll get a lighter sentence for handing yourself in, but not much. Give me some names though and your prospects could change.'

Matthew allowed a sob to escape his lips and Jon growled, 'Man up for God's sake. You've been a bloody idiot getting involved with that lot and now you have to face up to what you've done.'

'How did you get involved?' Erica asked.

Jon cut in, 'Got himself radicalised, looking up crap on the internet. Bloody fool!'

'Please, Jon,' Erica said. 'Let him speak for himself. Matthew?'

'I joined their chat room and agreed with some of what they said about the Welsh being endangered. I mean, if you've got a pedigree dog, you don't let it shag anything do you?'

Erica cringed internally but said nothing and let Matthew talk.

'Anyway, I was invited to their club house, The Prince on the A40, and I went.'

'How long ago?'

'A few months. Been on a couple of rallies and took some local kids to Penarth beach once. The group runs days out.'

'It's sick,' Jon muttered. 'Indoctrinating little kids? Sicker than sick.'

'What was different about this rally?' Erica asked.

'We were louder,' the lad grinned suddenly at the memory, 'and there were more of us. Loads of people stopped to listen to Daffydd, he gives a good speech. The boys were enjoying themselves, then when the rally was over they went to the shop, pulled out knives, stole the money in the till and whacked the Paki bloke. Then they wrecked the place. It wasn't right.'

'So you told your Uncle Jon?'

'No, not really. He heard me talking on the phone about it and dragged me down here.'

'Have you got your phone on you?'

Matthew nodded, removed it from his pocket and dropped it on the table.

Erica left it where it was and said, 'Before I arrest you, tell me how you fell in with this lot. Are you a racist?'

'No, I'm not, that's why this is all so mad. I only went along for something to do and some of what they said did make sense. They tell you things about the Muslims, about their religion and why they shouldn't be over here. You get sucked in and then – boom – you're part of it.'

Erica stood, palmed Matthew's phone and left the room. She beckoned Jon to follow and pulled the door shut behind them. She leaned on the wall and sighed heavily.

'You're going to nick him then?' Jon asked.

'Yeah, but have a word before I do. The more he tells us, the easier things will be for him. I'll send DC Langdon down, you've met him already.'

'Can't you deal with this?'

Erica shook her head. 'No, sorry. I'm working a different case. I'll go and find Constable Langdon, let him know where we are with this while you talk to your nephew. Make sure he understands how important it is that he helps us.'

'I'll do my best.'

'Good. Sit tight.'

Erica called Oliver from the phone on the front desk. He met her downstairs and Erica brought him up to speed.

'If this kid is a member of Cenedl Cymru,' Oliver said, 'and wants to get himself out the shit, why don't I suggest he snitches for us? Be our man on the inside. We can cut him loose today, but only if he tells us everything he can find out about The Three Stooges.'

'That's not a bad idea, Ollie, but run it past DI Wild, see if she'll go for it. Catch you later, I've got stuff to do.'

Erica ran upstairs to the squad room. Lizzie Wild was absent from her desk, so Erica made a mental note to speak to her and returned to her own office.

Chapter thirty-five

Heidi swirled brandy in her glass as she sat with her father in front of the library's impressive fireplace. She noticed he looked tired, older than his years somehow, guessed his wife was probably hassling him, but didn't want to become embroiled in another heated discussion so kept quiet.

'Did you read through the file I gave you?' she asked.

He nodded. 'Disturbing stuff. There's no doubt I suppose?'

'None. Inverdale has received £375k in exchange for three babies. Pixie was helpful, she knew when the children were born and the payments were made a week or so before the births.' Heidi sighed heavily. 'She also told me Inverdale is the father. He enjoyed sleeping with the female disciples and convinced any who fell pregnant they were host mothers for God's children.'

Freddie snorted, 'And when they were born, he sold them. How did he persuade the mothers to hand them over? Were they paid?'

'Pixie says not. Refused to believe me when I told her the babies had been sold.'

'Have you shown her this?' Freddie asked and tapped the file. 'All the proof is here.'

Heidi shook her head. 'No, she's not in the right frame of mind to assimilate the information, and all the proof isn't there.' She sipped her brandy. 'I still can't trace who made the payments and until I can do that, I've no chance of locating the babies. They could be anywhere, may not even be in the UK.'

'There's plenty of evidence of Inverdale's other misdeeds though,' Freddie said. 'The fraud and money laundering alone gives you more than enough to arrest him.'

'Not me, Freddie. I left the force, remember, and I'll be honest, I don't really care about his financial shenanigans, that's only money. All I want is to find the children, return them to their mothers and then make Inverdale vanish. Given the chance, I'll bury him so deep he'll never crawl back to the surface.'

'This business has really upset you, hasn't it?' Freddie asked.

Heidi shrugged, cracked her knuckles and helped herself to another couple of fingers of brandy.

Minutes passed, Freddie sighed, wiped his eyes and said quietly, 'As soon as I knew about you, I came looking.'

Heidi stared at the fireside rug, but didn't storm out as she had in the past. Freddie took that as a positive sign and continued.

'Took me far too long though,' he muttered. 'Even my contacts couldn't help. You'd been well hidden and six years had passed since you were born. Memories fade, grow fuzzy with time, but I did find you and brought you home.'

'Home?' Heidi snapped. 'I'd never lived here. Wasn't anything to do with you. Why did you even bother?'

'Do I have to have a reason?'

'Makes more sense if you did.'

Freddie gulped a large mouthful of spirit and winced as it burned his gullet.

'When I found out what your mother had done, I was appalled, you have no idea. I was angry, furious and utterly ashamed by what she had done. I had to do something to try to put things right.'

'How did you find out I existed?' Heidi asked.

'Quite by chance. Bumped into one of your mother's friends from Italy outside Harrods. She asked me how you were, how you were doing at school and I didn't even know you'd been born.' He groaned. 'I came home, confronted Miriam and eventually she confessed. She told me she'd had an affair soon after we had married, fallen pregnant and, anxious to conceal the fact from me, travelled to the villa in Italy, where she gave birth then returned home as if nothing had happened.'

'And left me behind.'

'Yes, and left you behind. She found you new parents, swore them to secrecy and walked away.' He slumped in his chair, chin resting on his chest and his breath was laboured as though he'd been running.

'I still don't really understand why you came for me, why you brought me here,' Heidi said. 'I had a life, a family, and wasn't unhappy. What did you say to them? How did you convince them to give me up?'

Freddie raised his eyes and stared into Heidi's. 'I paid and they handed you over. That was what convinced me I'd done the right thing.'

'Who would sell their child?'

'Someone who was paid a lot of money to take the child in the first place.'

The pair fell silent, gazed into the flames, listened to the crack and spit of the logs.

'I love you, Heidi,' Freddie said. 'You are as much my child as Greta, always have been and always will be. I've never regretted my decision, not for an instant.'

Heidi stretched out a hand, grasped her father's and squeezed. 'Neither have I, Pa, but you must see why I can never forgive Mother. She betrayed you and sold me. She doesn't deserve to be forgiven and why you stay married to her, I just don't understand.'

Freddie smiled. 'Nor me. Maybe it's just easier than the alternative. Most of the time she stays away and it's not like I want to remarry. No sense in changing things for the sake of change.'

'When is she coming here?'

'Tomorrow, after lunch. Around two she said.'

'I'll keep out the way. You'd better let Greta know, she won't be overjoyed either.'

Freddie flapped the folder. 'So what do we do with this? Pass it to the police?'

'I'll speak to Erica. She says Ben has her working the New Eden case to keep her away from Lizzie Wild who's investigating the XRW business… not very well in my opinion.'

'You did rather drop the woman in it, walking off the job like you did.'

'Better that than thump her! I don't get on with her type, never have.'

'What type is that?'

'Bossy, know it all, by the book, unintelligent, woman of a certain age…'

Freddie held up his hands. 'OK, I get it.'

'What really annoys me is she thinks everyone in Wales is a numpty. The police don't know what they're doing and the criminals aren't capable of putting together a decent job. She's wrong, I know she is. Daffydd Owen has been researching bomb making online. I've been monitoring his internet use since he came to our attention,' Heidi explained, 'and all he looks at is porn and far-right sites, until now. The bomb making stuff is new and I think it's serious research, not idle curiosity.'

'Does Lizzie Wild know?'

Heidi nodded. 'I told Erica this morning when we spoke and she was going to have a word, we don't need to worry.' She uncurled from the chair and stretched her tiny body, arms reaching towards the lofty ceiling. 'I think that's enough for me, Pa. Too much brandy and too much family history.' She bent to hug his neck and plant a kiss on his cheek. 'Thanks,' she muttered, 'for everything,' and padded out of the library.

In her room, she pulled out her mobile and rang Erica.

'Hi, E. How did you get on with Gloucester force? Are they going to take the case on?'

'I'm fine thanks, Heidi, and you? Are you enjoying your stay with Freddie?'

Heidi sighed. 'You can't do sarcasm, so give it up. I'm fine and enjoying my time at the family seat. Now, tell me, how did you get on with Gloucester?'

'So so. I'm coming over your way first thing tomorrow. A couple of local officers have planned to pay Inverdale a visit.'

'A visit? What does that mean?'

'What it says, knock on the door, ask some questions and see how Inverdale reacts.'

'You've told them what he's been up to, haven't you?'

'Yeah, they know everything I do, but their bosses would like to, "information gather" before they break down doors. Can't say I blame them.'

'But we're wasting time,' Heidi whined. 'Inverdale might be planning to leave right now and who knows where he'll pop up again.'

'I don't think he'd run. He'll be licking his wounds having lost a few of his converts. I reckon he'll stay put, after all he doesn't know how much we know, or that we are – uh, were – police officers.'

'Not convinced. Are you coming over here after the visit or are you expected back in Brecon?'

'Coming to you. Got a day off so thought we could catch up.'

'Mother's due here tomorrow afternoon,' Heidi mumbled.

'Your mum?' Erica was surprised.

'Yeah, wants to check on Greta. She's arriving at two, just so you know. Sleep well.' Heidi disconnected the call.

Erica glared at the phone and wished her partner would learn some telephonic etiquette.

Chapter thirty-six

Erica waited in the car as DS Colin Amos and DC Andy Boswell, members of Gloucester CID, walked up the gravel drive towards the crumbling Victorian hall. She had a good view of proceedings and was happy to wait. The Gloucester officers were anxious not to tip off Inverdale that their visit was anything other than routine. If anyone from the commune spotted Erica they'd know the visit was more than that. Amos yanked on the bell pull, then stood back from the door and gazed up at the front of the building.

'Didn't realise this place was so big,' Amos said. 'Never been called out here. When did DS Bevan say this lot moved in?'

Boswell checked his notebook. 'About three years ago.'

There was a rattling sound on the other side of the door and it swung open to reveal Adam and Mala standing side by side. Adam was dressed in his usual black suit, Mala wore baggy trousers and a colourful jumper, long hair twisted into a bun.

'Good morning, gentlemen,' Adam said. 'Can I help you?'

Amos flashed his warrant card. 'Morning, sir. Gloucester Police, DS Amos and this is my colleague, DC Boswell. I wonder if we could come in for a moment.'

Adam smiled. 'Can I ask why?'

'Why what, sir?' Amos asked.

'Why you want to come inside my house.'

Boswell checked his notebook again. 'Are you Adam Inverdale?'

'Am I under arrest, officers?'

'Uh, no, sir, nothing like that.'

'Then I don't need to tell you my name. I ask again, why do you want to come into my house?'

'I thought it was a commune,' Boswell said.

'New Eden is so much more,' Mala said. 'New Eden is a church. You are both standing on sacred ground.'

'I'm still waiting to learn why you're here,' Adam said. 'Have you received a complaint?'

'Ah, no…' Amos struggled to construct a suitable answer. 'There have been some break-ins locally.' He nodded at the boarded-up window. 'Looks like the bad guys got here before us.' He laughed but no one joined in. 'We're calling at isolated properties to offer owners a free security check.'

Mala grinned. 'You're not a good liar, sergeant, you're blushing.' She linked her arm in Adam's.

'I respectfully refuse your offer, DS Amos,' Adam said. 'I am a religious man and I am protected. I know God and God knows me. He sees how we all live our lives, there are no secrets from Him and I am not afraid of His judgement. Are you?'

The officers shuffled their feet and knew they weren't going to get past the front door.

Amos pulled out a business card and offered it to Adam. 'Well, sir, if you change your mind, give me a call and we'll set something up. Sorry to have bothered you.'

Erica watched from the back seat of the car and saw Adam shut the door. The officers trudged down the drive, opened the doors and dropped in the front seats.

'That was a bloody waste of time,' Amos grumbled. 'No way we're getting in there.'

'What did Inverdale have to say?' Erica asked.

'Bloody load of mumbo-jumbo, God-crap,' Boswell said. 'I can't stand these holier-than-thou types. Wear a religious badge and do what you like. Religion should be banned in my book.'

'Did he say anything useful?' Erica persisted. 'Get a look inside the place?'

'No. There was a woman with him, fiftyish, thin, hair in a bun.'

'Probably his right-hand woman, Mala, mother of Clover, the young girl who recently gave birth. Did you see anyone else?'

'Nope,' Amos said. He started the engine and pulled away. 'Trouble is, without good reason, we can't insist on gaining entry – you know that.'

'You've got plenty of evidence of financial improprieties,' Erica said. 'Benefit fraud, tax evasion, money laundering. You'd get an arrest warrant with no trouble, then you could look into the baby selling business.'

'I agree with you, but I'm not the boss, and he wants more time to review the stuff you gave him. Cautious man, my governor.'

'Inverdale will run,' Erica said. 'Trust me, if we don't make a move on him soon, he'll leg it and we'll never find the kids.'

'If they were even there,' Boswell muttered.

'Did you say something, constable?' Erica asked.

'I said, "if they were even there". It's very difficult to prove something has happened when the evidence of the something isn't here anymore. We have nothing to prove babies have been born at all, no medical records, no photographs, nothing at the registry office, only your word, and even you didn't see them.'

'Are you suggesting I'm making this up?'

Boswell shrugged. 'No, sergeant, but maybe you were mistaken.'

Erica flung herself back in the seat angrily, she knew Gloucester Police weren't in a hurry to pursue Adam Inverdale, that nothing would be done for weeks, and weeks would be too late. She groaned. Heidi was going to be seriously pissed off when she heard the news.

* * *

Lizzie glanced up from the paperwork as Connor plonked a mug of coffee on the desk in front of her.

'Ta, I could do with that.' She sipped and winced at the bitterness. 'Christ, they drink crap stuff here. So, any news?'

Connor sat opposite and shook his head. 'Same old, same old. The bugs in the pub haven't told us anything we don't already know, that we're dealing with a bunch of racist idiots who have nothing better to do with their lives. Honestly, if you listen to some of the tapes, they all seem to think they're related to Owain Glyndŵr. It's pathetic, like me saying I'm the many times great grandson of St George.'

Lizzie snorted, 'Hardly, St George wasn't even English. Any sign of this plot Holtz seemed convinced they are planning?'

'Nope.' Connor sipped his coffee. 'Langdon has continued to monitor their internet use – nothing, and the tail on Daffydd hasn't been useful either. If you ask me, the murder of the barmaid wasn't planned, certainly not by Cenedl Cymru. More like a couple of their lads got a bit enthusiastic, like Daffydd says.'

'Can we nick any of them for anything?'

'Can't see it. Cenedl Cymru isn't a proscribed organisation and free speech is still very much alive in the UK.'

'Bloody wouldn't be if I had my way,' Lizzie grouched.

'What does head office say?' Connor asked.

'Give it another couple of weeks, then we can leave this godforsaken country and go home, back to proper coppering and let the locals handle their own muck. I really don't know why we were sent here in the first place, complete waste of time. We've enough real terrorists in Bristol to keep us busy.'

'Any chance we can leave early?'

'None. The CTU want to make sure we've covered everything. I've told them there's nothing here for us, but they want to be sure. Guess I can't blame them, it's their asses on the line.'

'So we keep on with the tails and the online snooping?'

'Yeah, leave it all in place. You and me will visit Cardiff nick and re-interview the louts who killed the barmaid, maybe they'll have more to say. Do me a favour and check in with Ollie Langdon. Ask if Matthew Williams has been able to tell us anything useful.'

'The kid who owned up to trashing the newsagents in Cardiff?'

'Yeah, him. Ollie cut him loose on the understanding he'd report anything interesting.' Lizzie chuckled. 'I'd put money on him not having anything to tell us either. This investigation is in injury time and I for one will not be unhappy to go home. I'm cheesed off with Wales.'

* * *

Erica pulled up on the gravel drive at the front of the imposing, yellow-stone building, tyres popping pebbles. Heidi appeared on the front steps and crunched across the loose stones to the car.

'How did the visit to New Eden go?' she asked, pulling open the driver's door.

'Bloody hell,' Erica grumbled. 'Can't I even have a cuppa before you interrogate me?'

'What? Oh, yeah, come in.' Heidi plonked a kiss on Erica's cheek. 'We're in the kitchen.' Heidi reached into the back seat, dragged out Erica's overnight bag and slung it on her shoulder. 'What the hell have you got in here?' she asked.

'Just the usual. How are Pixie and Greta?' Erica followed her partner towards the grand entrance.

'Greta's OK... well, seems to be. Pixie is all over the place, doesn't know what she wants or where she wants to be. Very much a work in progress, but the Cult Information Centre in London is proving useful.'

'Has your mother arrived?'

'No. Not yet.'

Heidi led the way downstairs to the large kitchen. Pixie leapt to her feet as soon as they entered.

'Erica!' The girl wrapped herself around her friend. 'I didn't know you were coming, no one told me. How are you?'

'I'm good, how about you?'

'Alright, I guess. Heidi thinks she's found Felix for me, we're going to try and get in touch with him and Freddie says if we find him, he can come and stay here.'

'That's great,' Erica said and gently extricated herself from Pixie's fierce hug. 'Where is Freddie?'

'Upstairs,' Heidi said, 'waiting for the royal visit. Mother's expected any time now.' She placed a full coffee pot on the table and flopped on a chair. 'So, tell me, E, how did the visit go?'

Erica glanced at Pixie.

Heidi noticed her gaze and said, 'Pix, will you go and find Greta for me please? Tell her coffee's ready.'

Pixie left the room and Erica sighed heavily. 'I don't think Gloucester's up for it.'

'What happened?'

'Two CID officers went out this morning. I went with them but stayed in the car so wasn't spotted. They knocked on the door, Adam refused them entry, and they came away. Said their boss wants more time to review the evidence before they do anything more. They told me Mala was at the door with Adam, said both spouted a lot of religious rubbish then shut them out.' Erica topped up her mug.

'This is no bloody good,' Heidi snapped. 'We must do something, smash this poisonous cult to bits, lock up Inverdale and find the children. Whatever's wrong with Gloucester force?'

'DI James told me he'll be willing to pursue the case from Brecon if we have to, but he'll need to talk to his opposite number first. I'll give him a call, start things moving.'

'We'll lose Inverdale. He will run, I'm sure he will.'

'Have you discovered where those payments came from yet?'

'Getting closer, but it's a slow process. The cash bounced all across the planet before it landed with him. If I could talk to the mothers of the babies born at the commune that would help, but can't do that if I can't get to them.'

The kitchen door opened and Greta peered in.

'Heidi. Mother's here, in the study with Pa. Are you planning to put in an appearance?'

'No, I'm not,' Heidi huffed. 'I've nothing to say to her and she's only here to see you. She has never wanted to see me.'

'Pa would like it if you talked to her.'

'Well, I wouldn't and that's an end to it. Where's Pixie?'

'Upstairs, says she's tired. I'm worried about her, we really ought to call the doctor and have her checked over.'

'I'm sure she's OK, just needs deprogramming and that takes time. If I can find Felix I'm sure that will help and I'm in touch with the CIC. They've sent some very useful info. It's all on the desk in the study, if you want to take a look.'

Greta hovered in the doorway and asked, 'So you're not coming upstairs?'

'Not planning to.'

Greta backed out and banged the door behind her.

'What is it with you and your mum?' Erica asked.

Heidi sighed. 'I'll tell you, but I don't want to discuss it, so no third degree.'

'OK.'

'I was the result of an affair early in her marriage to Pa. She gave birth to me in Italy and left me there. Freddie learnt about my existence some years later, found me when I was six years old and brought me here. Now you know and I really don't want to talk about it. What we need to do is work out what to do about Inverdale and find the babies.'

Chapter thirty-seven

Daffydd and the Jones brothers sat in their usual corner at The Prince Llewelyn drinking whisky. The remainder of Cenedl Cymru filled the bar, some drunk, others so pissed they couldn't stand and slumped on chairs, or propped themselves against the walls. An elderly couple pushed through the main door, took one look at the clientele packing the room and decided to find somewhere else for supper. Rhys went to the bar and collected more drinks. Daffydd nodded his thanks.

'We're all set then?' Geraint asked.

'Yeah,' Daffydd said, 'everything is more or less in place for the end of the week, just need to move the cars about. We could get that done tomorrow.'

'Where shall we meet?' Rhys asked.

'Usual place, usual time, bring the drivers with you.'

'Will do.' Rhys nodded across the room. 'They're over at the bar. I'll have a word, tell them to lay off the sauce.'

'We all should,' Daffydd said. 'We'll need clear heads.'

'Any idea what time we'll be back on Friday?' Geraint asked.

'Why?' Rhys asked. 'Somewhere to be?'

'Got a date with the girl who works at the Castle Kitchen in town.'

'If all goes according to plan, it'll be over by early evening.' Daffydd chuckled. 'You'll have plenty of time for a wash and brush up before you meet her.'

* * *

Oliver Langdon hunched over Heidi's old desk, listening to noisy chatter in The Prince. The place sounded packed and he struggled to concentrate on the many conversations. He had put in ten hours already and was beginning to fantasise about bed linen. He switched from one bug to another and picked up The Three Stooges. They were talking about drivers, it didn't seem very important.

The conversation moved to an upcoming date with the lass from the cafe in town and Oliver grinned. He wouldn't mind a date with Megan either, she was well fit. He listened harder and heard Daffydd say something would be, "over by evening". He wondered what exactly, but nothing further was said. He clicked on the audio file and replayed the conversation. The Stooges were definitely discussing an event planned for the end of the week – sounded like Friday. Another march perhaps? Bit soon after Cardiff. Something else? He composed an email to Lizzie Wild and sent her a copy of the recording, she could decide what to do with it. Her pay grade allowed her to make decisions, his didn't. The email sent, he switched on another bug and closed his eyes as he listened to members of Cenedl Cymru spout their racist vileness and wished he was home.

The squad room door suddenly opened and DI James stomped in.

'Ollie. Where is everyone?'

'Knocked off, sir. I drew monitoring duties this evening, but I'll be off myself soon. Connor Haskins is taking over in an hour.'

'Anything interesting?'

'No, not really. Usual sort of boozed up bollocks, I'll be glad when I don't have to do this anymore. I go home feeling grubby. The Stooges are in The Prince chatting about something happening on Friday, but no clues what. Here, have a listen.'

Oliver played the snippet. DI James shut his eyes and concentrated on the recording. He asked for it to be played a second time.

'What do you think they're talking about, sir?'

'No idea. Has DI Wild heard this?'

'Just sent her a copy in an email.'

'Good, it's her case after all.'

'And don't we bloody know it,' Oliver muttered.

DI James laughed. 'Won't be forever, constable, nothing ever is. Personally, I think the CTU overreacted and now don't want to look foolish. They should have let us deal with Cenedl Cymru, but as they're here they need to justify their presence. They'll be gone before you know it.'

'Will Heidi come back when they've left? We've really missed her input, sir, it's one of the reasons we're all working overtime.'

'I don't know,' Ben admitted. 'I hope so, but the longer she's away, the more unlikely it is she'll be able to return.

I've done what I can, but she hasn't contacted me and things are getting awkward.'

'Where is she?'

'At her dad's place. I've spoken to Erica who is less than impressed with Gloucester force's reaction to the New Eden situation, so I think we're going to have to deal with that too.'

'How, sir? We're pushed already what with having to follow Daffydd Owen around the countryside, and the Cotswolds isn't exactly on our patch.'

'I know, but I'll have a word with head office, maybe they can let me have some bodies and we'll pay the commune a visit. Inverdale did unlawfully imprison one of our officers so I'll probably get permission. Would you like to be on the team?'

'Definitely, if Loopy Lizzie will let me. Tegan would be up for it as well.'

'Leave it with me, we'll talk again when you clock on tomorrow… and I'll pretend I didn't hear your remark about DI Wild.'

Chapter thirty-eight

Ollie, Tegan, and a uniformed officer from Builth Wells, Sergeant Dan Briggs, crammed into Ben's office. Erica was on the phone from Milebrook Manor and updating the team.

'Adam refused Gloucester CID entry to the hall,' she said, 'and their boss isn't at all keen on getting involved with the cult. I'm assuming DI James has shown you the evidence?'

The group mumbled their agreement.

'Good, then you have an idea of what we're dealing with. We have been able to obtain a warrant to seize any paperwork and all computer records. Another for the arrest of Adam Inverdale – otherwise known as Adrian Ingham – on charges of the unlawful detention of a police officer for starters, and yet another for his right-hand woman – known as Mala – for aiding and abetting.'

'Do you think we'll get any trouble from the commune's members?' Briggs said. 'You told us there's around thirty people in there.'

'Yeah, but a right mix, from young to old. It's not like Inverdale has a private army.'

'If he has,' Briggs muttered, 'this could go badly wrong. We might end up with another Waco on our hands.'

'I think that's unlikely,' Ben said. 'The whole thing appears to have been set up as a cover. The converts are human shields to keep eyes away from what's really going on. Inverdale's motivation is money, not God, I'm sure of it. He's squirrelled away a fortune over the last few years.'

'By selling babies,' Tegan snapped. 'What sort of twisted individual would come up with a scheme like that? It's medieval. Are we looking for the little ones?'

Erica cut in, 'Heidi is. She's trying to trace the payments, but once we're inside the hall and have access to the mothers, we should have more clues to work with. Trust me, if anyone can find the kids, Heidi can.'

'OK, let's finalise the plan,' Ben said. 'We'll call in at Milebrook Manor after lunch to collect you and Heidi and aim to be at the commune by five. With a bit of luck, Inverdale will let us in to do our job. If he doesn't, our only alternative will be to force entry. With so many people inside, I'm reluctant to do that, but if it's necessary I have a transit van full of uniforms borrowed from local nicks. Gaining entry shouldn't be a problem, but it will be Gloucester's call – not mine.'

'I'm not sure Heidi will be here,' Erica said. 'She went out early this morning and I have no idea where she's gone.'

'Don't you two talk to each other?' Ben asked.

'Not as much as I'd like, sir. You know how she can be.'

'Yes, I do. OK, with or without Heidi we'll stick to the timings. You'd better warn Mr Holtz we'll be descending on him.'

'I will, but he's got his hands full at the moment, what with caring for Pixie and trying to keep the peace between his wife and daughters. I don't think he'll even notice you're here.'

* * *

Daffydd pulled up at the back of Brecon Industrial Estate and tucked his car behind an old rusted container. Two young men climbed out, walked over to a pair of old bangers, started the engines and followed Daffydd as he drove out of the lot.

Daffydd glanced in his mirror to make sure the boys were keeping up and noticed a dark blue Montego travelling behind the convoy, matching their speed. He wondered if he had a tail and thought he might have seen the car before, but couldn't be sure. He kept one eye on the mirror. It was difficult to be certain on these roads, wasn't as though he could make a few odd turns to expose the tail as he could if he was in town. He decided to keep on to Aberbran. If the car followed them along the lane towards the barn, he'd know for sure and would abort the mission.

Ten minutes later he passed through Trecastle and was sure the car wasn't anywhere in sight. The two lads were still close behind, but the road behind them was empty. He chuckled to himself. Nerves did funny things to a man. Why on earth would the police be following him? As if they even had the manpower. He grinned, turned left and headed towards the Epynt mountain firing ranges and the old barn tucked in a valley.

He pulled into the muddy yard, jumped out of the car and quickly unlocked the chain securing the huge wooden doors. By the time the lads arrived, the doors were propped open and they drove inside. Daffydd pulled the doors closed behind them.

'Well done, lads, nice driving,' Daffydd said.

'What are we doing here?' the older one asked.

'Just dropping the cars off. We won't need them for a couple of days, but they're better under cover than on the estate.'

'What will we need them for?' Matthew Williams asked.

Daffydd thumped him lightly on the arm. 'Need to know basis, boy. Just make sure you're both available on Friday morning. I'll pick you up at the war memorial in town at 9.30. Be there! If anything changes, one of the others will be in touch.'

Daffydd stepped out of the barn, wrapped the chain through the metal handles and snapped the padlock shut. The group climbed in his car and headed back down the hill chatting, laughing and failing to notice the dark blue Montego tucked behind a wall in the village.

As soon as Daffydd was out of sight, Connor started the engine and headed up the lane. His companion, a constable from Builth Wells called Will Deacon, glanced up from his phone in surprise.

'Shouldn't we be following Daffydd?' he asked.

'He's only going back to town. I want to see what's in the barn.'

Connor turned off the lane and splashed into the yard.

Will opened his door and stepped out. 'Bloody hell, sir, the place is ankle deep in mud.'

'Then watch where you put your feet.' Connor skirted the puddles, caught hold of the chain and gave it a rough shake. 'Not getting in there,' he grouched. 'There are lots of tyre tracks. Go round the back, see if there's a window or anything.'

Connor tried peering through the gaps in the door. In the semi-darkness, he saw two tatty cars parked side by side, some old straw bales, a few rusty Calor gas canisters and little else.

Will returned, grumbling, and said, 'My feet are bloody soaked. We should have brought wellies.'

'Any luck?' Connor asked.

'No, solid walls all round, no windows. Can you see anything inside?'

'Not much. The cars are there, but that's about it.'

'Nothing odd about keeping cars in barns round here,' Will said. 'My brother's renting one off an old boy on the other side of the hill. He's renovating a Riley Pathfinder – ex cop-car, late 1950s,' he explained when he spotted Connor's blank face.

'Yeah, I guess. Let's get back and check that Daffydd's safely back at his digs.'

* * *

The manor's kitchen was busy. With Pixie's help, Cook was rustling up lunch. Erica and Greta were deep in conversation at one end of the long table, while Freddie sat at the other, a stony-faced Miriam by his side.

'Why do I feel like a stranger in my own house?' Miriam complained under her breath.

Freddie couldn't think of anything appropriate to say, so patted her hand and made what he hoped were soothing noises.

'And where is Heidi?' Miriam continued. 'I haven't seen her since I arrived.'

'Did you really expect to?' Freddie asked as gently as he could. 'She's stayed away from you for nearly twenty years.'

'Well… I thought…' She sighed. 'After all this time, you'd think she'd have forgiven me. I was young and I'm sure I suffered some sort of post-natal depression. I was ill, not responsible.'

'If you do get a chance to speak to Heidi, I wouldn't say that to her. She hates excuses.'

'What's she like?' Miriam whispered.

Freddie grinned. 'She's the most amazing young woman I have ever known… in every respect.' He paused. 'I am immensely proud of our daughter and everything she has achieved during her short life. She is driven, talented, incredibly intelligent and strikingly beautiful – she's unique.' He sighed. 'I love her dearly, Miriam, and I absolutely forbid you to upset her. If she decides to speak to you, it will be her decision. I wouldn't force her – even if I could.'

Cook and Pixie carried dishes of vegetables to the table and Pixie sat next to Erica to eat. The meal had just begun when the door opened and Heidi marched in, followed by a thin, nervous-looking, young man.

'Felix!' Pixie squealed and leapt from her seat to fling herself at him.

'Hey, Pixie,' he mumbled and tried to hug her into submission. 'Good to see you. You OK?'

'Brilliant now!' she squeaked. 'This is fantastic! Come and eat, Freddie won't mind.' Pixie released him reluctantly before throwing herself at Heidi. 'You found him. Thank you sooo much. Where was he?'

'Cheltenham,' Heidi said and wriggled out of Pixie's exuberant hug. 'In a homeless shelter.'

Pixie grabbed her hand, dragged her to the table and pushed her in a chair. 'Sit here, I'll fetch you some food.' She looked at the others around the table. 'Everyone – here… is… Felix.'

Heidi perched on the chair, swept her eyes around the room and fixed them on Miriam, who stared back, a look of utter astonishment on her face. In her eyes, Heidi was certainly unique. Her tiny form was a surprise, but the almost white hair and pale grey eyes were shocking.

Heidi looked away. 'Erica, what did DI James have to say this morning?'

'We've got warrants and are planning a visit later today. The Inspector has rounded up a team and will swing by here on the way to pick me up. You too, if you want to tag along.'

Heidi snorted. 'I'm at the front of the queue. Glad the boss is prepared to stick his neck out on this. Can't wait to see Adam's face when he sees us outside his pad.'

'I'm hoping he'll open up and let us in. If he barricades himself inside, we'll have a stand-off. Ben isn't keen on smashing his way in, bearing in mind New Eden is registered as a religious movement and of course, Gloucester have the final say.'

'People are so touchy,' Heidi grumbled. 'Say "religion" to your average copper and they run a mile, terrified they'll be accused of racism or godism or something, it's baloney. Crime is crime whether you do it for God or not.'

Heidi heard Miriam call her name and without looking up from her food growled, 'What?'

'I wondered, ah… whether we could talk? Later maybe?' Miriam stammered.

'No. We couldn't.'

'But, I want to say…'

'Tough. I'm busy later,' Heidi snapped. 'I don't have the time for you.'

Miriam opened her mouth to speak, but Freddie warned her with a look to stay quiet. The remainder of the meal was eaten in silence and as soon as it ended, Erica and Heidi went to prepare for the raid, Pixie and Felix vanished upstairs for some catch-up time. Greta also slunk away, leaving Freddie alone with Miriam.

'Come on,' he said and pulled his wife upright. 'Let's take a wander around the grounds, see if we can devise a plan to save our family.'

Chapter thirty-nine

DI James led the way along the drive towards the New Eden commune; a transit van full of uniformed officers and a couple of cars followed closely behind. Oliver sat next to his boss in the front seat, Heidi, Erica and Tegan squashed in the back. The light was fading and the vehicles' headlights swept the hall's facade as they parked close to the front door. DI James climbed the steps and yanked the bell pull, while Heidi hammered on the door with her fists.

'Open up, Inverdale,' she shouted. 'We know you're in there and we want a word.'

Some time passed before a small flap in the door dropped open and Adam's face appeared in the gap. His eyebrows raised when he recognised Heidi and Erica.

'You two!' he spat. 'What are you doing here? Why have you brought the police to our church?'

'Church?' Heidi sneered. 'Money making racket would be more accurate. Open the bloody door.'

Adam grinned and snapped the flap shut.

'That went well,' Erica said. 'What now?'

Ben swung on the bell pull again and shouted through the door.

'Adam Inverdale, or Adrian Ingham, whichever you prefer, we have an arrest warrant for you. Open the door so we can talk. We're not going away. You have questions to answer, so let us in and we can try to sort things out.'

The flap dropped down again and Mala peered out. Heidi had a sudden urge to reach through the gap and drive her thumbs into the woman's eyes, but wisely kept her hands in her pockets.

'Adam has told you to leave,' Mala said, 'so I suggest you do just that. We're not letting you in. This is a church, a place of worship, sanctuary. Go home… all of you.'

The flap slammed shut.

Ben rubbed a hand across his face and turned to his team. 'OK, split into two groups. One lot stay here while I take the rest to the back of the hall. Maybe we can discover another entry point.'

'I don't know why we don't just smash our way in,' Heidi grumbled. 'We've got warrants and the muscle. We should go through the front door and drag them out, right now, before they can organise themselves.'

'We can't do that, Heidi, not yet,' Ben said. 'We must explore all options before taking rash actions and don't want to endanger anyone inside. Come with me and check out the rest of the building. Erica, stay here and keep an eye on things with Tegan. Ollie, with us.'

Ben led the way to the rear of the hall and Heidi stomped along bad temperedly by his side.

'We should be inside, sir,' she grouched. 'All this crap about sanctuary, it's rubbish and you know it. We have warrants and we know offences have been committed, so we have every right to go in. New Eden isn't even a real church… whatever the hell that is.'

'The hall has been registered as a place of worship,' Ollie said. 'That effectively makes it a church.'

'Bollocks!' Heidi snapped and increased her pace, the rest of the group struggling to keep up. They circled the entire building, but all the doors were locked and wooden shutters covered the windows.

'Any luck?' Erica asked when they met up at the front.

'No.' Ben hammered on the door again and again the flap dropped open. Adam's grinning face appeared.

'Still here?' he asked.

'I told you. We're not leaving until you open the door so we can talk.'

'And I told you, we're not going to do that.' Adam snapped the flap shut.

Ben marched back to the vehicles and the gang of officers.

'Break the place open, sir,' Heidi said. 'We've no idea what's happening inside. If we leave it too long, when we do get in we might only find bodies. These situations never end well.'

'Not yet,' Ben said. 'I'll report to the boss, find out what he advises. Inverdale can't leave without being seen, so there's no danger of him legging it, and how long can he hold out – realistically?'

'Not long if we cut off the services,' Heidi said.

'I'm not sure that's an option.'

Heidi snorted and strode away.

'Erica,' Ben said, 'go and have a word. Calm her down or I'll have to send her away.'

'I'll do what I can.'

Erica dashed after her partner and caught up with her in the kitchen garden.

'Heidi,' she called. 'Wait, will you?'

Heidi turned and glared at Erica, face flushed with anger.

'This is bloody ridiculous,' she yelled. 'We could be stuck out here for weeks while that bastard Inverdale laughs at us, or worse, convinces his followers to top themselves for Jesus… or whatever. I thought DI James had bigger balls than this.'

Erica slipped her arm in Heidi's. 'You must see why he's being cautious,' she said. 'This isn't his patch and he's only just been cleared by the inquiry generated by the slavery case. He could have lost his job.'

'He was safe. Made too many arrests to get the old heave-ho. He could collar at least two more today if he'd only break down the door. Sanctuary! Yeah right, this is the twenty-first century.'

'There's a family up north who have lived in a chapel for years to avoid deportation,' Erica said.

'Exactly! How long is James going to wait? We need to know what's happening inside that dreadful place. He wants to keep his head down and I get that, but if we find thirty dead acolytes in the hall, no one will ever forget that. Now, please, E, leave me alone for a bit. I need some space or I'm going to break something.'

* * *

Lizzie Wild put the phone down, stood and stretched. She glanced across the squad room at Connor Haskins who was bent over the bank of computers. He looked as bored as she felt and she moved to his side.

'Anything?'

'Nothing,' he said. 'The pub is empty and it looks as though Daffydd is in for the night. What a waste of time this whole thing has been,' he grumbled, shoving the keyboard away from him. 'Even head office are agreeing with us now. How much longer do we have to give it?'

'Our last day is Friday. That was Bristol on the phone telling us to draw stumps. They haven't been able to uncover any serious threat from Cenedl Cymru and agree with me they're no more than a bunch of loud-mouthed racists with nothing better to do.' She sighed heavily. 'We've been tailing Daffydd for weeks and haven't learnt anything significant. The bugs in the pub haven't picked up anything and he's not using the net for anything he shouldn't.'

Connor said, 'I can't wait to get home. This place drives me nuts, nothing to do and nowhere much to go, only pubs full of Welshmen. Why can't we leave now?'

'Oliver Langdon overheard a conversation about something possibly happening on Friday. Bristol want us to hang around until then – just in case – but realistically, what are we talking about? Another march? Another trip to the seaside with the kids? A bit more shouting in Brecon? Who knows, we might get lucky and they'll take on some more squaddies. I could do with a laugh.'

'What about getting inside the barn at Aberbran?' Connor asked. 'Daffydd's been in and out of the place for a couple of weeks. He took two cars up there yesterday.'

'Not worth the paperwork to obtain a warrant and not enough to go on. As your partner said, old cars in a barn is nothing unusual here, not suspicious enough to take things further without other evidence of wrongdoing.'

Connor shrugged and glanced at the screens. 'Well, I've been at this for hours and nothing rings any alarm bells, even the porn they look at is legal. No basis at all to back up Holtz's mad theory. Like you said, boss, all mouth and no trousers.'

Lizzie grinned. 'Did I say that?'

'Something pretty much like it.'

'Is the tail arranged for tomorrow?'

'Yeah, for all the good it'll do us. I've pulled surveillance duties on Friday, then it's back to sunny Bristol for us. Thank God.'

Chapter forty

The sound of a vehicle crunching gravel on the drive to the commune shook Heidi awake. She saw it was early, struggled out of the untidy heap she had fallen asleep in on the back seat of Ben's car and peered through the misty windscreen. A second transit van was pulling alongside the car, the next shift clocking on.

Heidi climbed out and went in search of Erica. She found her leaning against the wall at the front of the house chatting to DI James. She looked over as Heidi approached.

'Hi, sleepyhead,' she said.

Heidi said, 'Stake-outs have never been my thing, if I stop moving, I go to sleep. Any signs of life?' she asked, nodding towards the hall.

'No. Haven't seen anything all night.'

Heidi yawned. 'Now would be a good time to bust in then, sir.' She looked pointedly at DI James. 'So how about it – while they're all asleep.'

Ben shook his head. 'We can't. The governor of Gloucester force is coming out this morning to make his own assessment and he'll be in charge of any operation.'

'Finally woken up to the fact he's got a problem on his patch, has he?' Heidi sneered. 'Three years this lot have been here and he hasn't been interested until now.'

'That's because there hasn't been a problem until now,' Ben said. 'You've been a copper long enough to know how this works.'

'Yeah, I have, and it's the main reason I'm not one now.'

'Not coming back then?'

'Not a chance. In fact, I'm going to leave you with this mess and go home. I can't see the point of being here if we're not going to do anything. I can be better employed searching for the missing children.'

Ben opened his mouth to speak, but Erica cut in, 'I'll borrow one of the cars and give you a lift.'

'Don't bother. You stay here. I'll make my own way back.'

'How? The Manor is miles away.'

'I'll ring Greta, she'll fetch me. You know where I am if you need me.' Heidi reached into the car, dragged out her hoodie, pulled it over her head and marched away down the drive. She moved to the verge as a dark car passed her, a high-ranking copper sitting in the back. She dialled Greta's number to arrange a lift and even though her sister was not best pleased at having been woken so early, she agreed to make the trip. Forty minutes later a Land Rover pulled up by Heidi's side; she opened the door and climbed in.

'What's happened?' Greta asked as she turned the vehicle to face the other way and headed back towards Milebrook.

'Nothing!' Heidi snapped. 'Absolutely, bloody nothing. Gloucester has finally become involved but they're all pussy-footing around, scared to death of causing offence because the commune is, "a place of worship". Bloody ridiculous. Inverdale and his cronies have barricaded themselves inside and who knows how long they can hold out. I said we should cut off the water and electricity, but DI James won't even do that.'

'They'll have to come out eventually,' Greta said, turning off the main road.

'Will they? What if Inverdale convinces his disciples God is waiting for them and they all commit suicide?'

Greta stared at her in horror and the Land Rover surfed the grass verge.

Heidi grabbed the wheel. 'Keep your eyes on the road, Sis, I'm way too young to die.'

'You don't really think that will happen, do you?'

Heidi shrugged and cracked her knuckles. 'Many similar situations in the past have ended just like that. The death toll has been horrendous; eighty-three dead at Waco, thirty-nine at Heaven's Gate in California and a massive 909 in Jonestown, Guyana.'

'But this is England,' Greta protested. 'Things like that don't happen here.'

'Not yet,' Heidi muttered, 'but if James and the others mess about, there's nothing to say it won't.'

'What do you think they should do?'

'Smash down the doors, get everyone out and throw the book at Inverdale and Mala.' Heidi sighed. 'How's it going at home with Mother?'

'Sticky, I think is the best way to describe it. Pa's doing his best and I'm keeping away as much as possible, but it's not great. Are you ever going to talk to her?'

'Not if I have a choice,' Heidi mumbled. 'Luckily I can hide away while I'm searching for the kids. I've plenty to do to occupy myself.'

'Did the police talk to you about returning to work?'

'Yeah and I told them where to shove it. I'm never going back.'

* * *

Ben watched as the Chief Inspector of Gloucester Police climbed back into his chauffeur driven car and was taken away. The man had promised more officers to bolster the force at the hall, but refused to sanction a raid until he had spoken with his bosses. Ben couldn't believe the man wouldn't act. Heidi's warnings rattled around in his brain, he was frustrated and, had to admit, alarmed about the possible outcome. He marched up to the front door and hammered on the wood.

'Adam Inverdale,' he yelled. 'Come and talk to me. You can't stay inside forever, we must resolve this and soon.'

The flap dropped down and Adam's smiling face appeared in the gap.

'Do you have anything different to say, Inspector?' he asked.

'Things are going to get very difficult for you if you don't open the door,' Ben said. 'The services will be cut off, you won't have water or electricity and you've thirty people to feed. How are you going to do that without access to food?'

'None of us are going hungry,' Adam said. 'But thanks for your concern… and the warning.' He turned away and shouted into the building. 'They're going to cut off the water, so start filling containers!' He turned back to face the front. 'Is there anything else? I have a meditation to conduct. God waits for no man – not even me.'

'This is ridiculous. Just open the bloody door, let us in and we'll sort this out. We must be allowed to check on the well-being of your residents and can't do that if you don't let us in.'

'Everyone is fine, Inspector, you really don't need to worry. We have our own medical staff, plenty of provisions and, if necessary, can stay here until Christmas. God knows us and cares for us. He will not forget us.'

He snapped the flap shut and Ben leaned on the door and groaned.

Erica approached him and asked, 'What did he say?'

'That he's not coming out. Do you think he'll do something stupid?'

Erica shrugged. 'I have no idea,' she said, 'but Heidi thinks he will. While Greta was inside we carried out extensive research into cults, and situations like this don't tend to end well. I don't know how to advise you, but how often have you known Heidi to get things wrong?'

'Have you heard from her since she left?'

'Yeah, a quick call. She's at Milebrook searching for the kids. Surely, sir, if she manages to find them we could bust in?'

'I'd be in there now if it was left to me, but it isn't and Gloucester are still not convinced.' He groaned and rubbed his face. 'The force doesn't want us on their patch, so aren't leaning towards helpful.'

'Can't the brass in Brecon have a word? Make Gloucester realise how potentially serious the whole situation is?'

'Trust me I have tried, but we're out of our jurisdiction and DCI Ambrose is on leave. The rest are only interested in Daffydd Owen and his crew, anxious to put on a good show for Bristol CTU. Let's take another walk around the place, maybe there's a way in we haven't spotted yet.'

Chapter forty-one

Heidi was in the study following threads in cyberspace, desperate to track the large payments to Inverdale so she could locate the missing babies, but it wasn't happening fast enough. Nothing ever did for Heidi. She snatched up her phone, tapped in a number and fidgeted as she listened to the ringing tone.

It was answered quickly. 'Hi, this is Angus.'

'Hey, matey, it's Heidi.'

'Ms Holtz! What a surprise. Haven't heard from you in yonks. How's it hanging?'

'OK thanks, but I need help with something.'

'You? Need help? Don't make me laugh.'

'Yeah, funny. I want to get inside somewhere tonight and think I'm going to have to climb to do it.'

'So you call me cos you know I'm a stone monkey?'

'That's about the size of it. Are you interested?'

'You'll have to tell me a bit more than that,' Angus said. 'Is it a matter of life and death?'

'Actually it could well be. Where are you?'

'At work – GCHQ.'

'Good, you're not far away. You know Milebrook Manor, don't you?' Heidi heard him giggle.

'Of course, I know your place,' he said. 'Not likely to forget it after that mental New Year's bash you threw a few years ago. Did your dad ever get over it?'

'Once he'd recovered the suits of armour from the roof and calmed down Cook. She wasn't at all impressed when she found you in her larder wearing nothing more than a pair of budgie smugglers. So, are you in or not?'

'Of course I'm in. When do you want me?'

'I'd like to go in tonight, so ASAP really.'

'Do we need anyone else? There's one or two chaps here who'd be well up for a touch of breaking and entering.'

'This is serious, Angus, not a boys' night out. Things could get nasty.'

'OK, just us. I'll finish up here and leave soon, be with you in time for tea. Does your cook still make those delicious cheese scones?'

'Yes, she does, but I'm not sure she'll give you any after the larder episode.'

'She'll forgive me – everyone does – I'm so lovable.'

'Just get here as quick as you can.' Heidi disconnected the call as the study door opened and Freddie wandered in.

'Hello, you,' he said. 'How are you getting on?'

'Not as well as I'd like. My programs are trying one last time to trace those bloody payments to Adam Inverdale. I'm still hopeful we'll eventually learn where they came from. In the meantime I've been in touch with a mate of mine from Cambridge, you'll probably remember him, Angus Hickman.'

Freddie smiled. 'Yes, the lanky lad who hid all the armour and caused a ruckus with Cook. How could I forget?'

'He's coming over later. I'm planning to break into New Eden tonight and he's agreed to help me. If I can get the doors open, DI James and his crew can just walk in. They'll have no excuse then for their inactivity. In fact they'd have a duty to make sure the property is secure. I'm very concerned for the people inside. Inverdale is unstable. I don't trust him not to do anything ghastly and his followers' brains have been so warped, they'll more than likely go along with whatever he says.'

Freddie perched on the desk and stared at his daughter. 'You mean it, don't you?'

'When do I ever say anything I don't mean? The police are twisted up in red tape, terrified about being accused of heavy handedness and we're wasting time. I have a dreadful feeling about this. If Inverdale can sell his own children, he's capable of anything.'

'Do you need any help from me?'

'Don't think so. Like I said, if Angus and I can get inside, we'll open the door, hightail it back here and pretend we were never there.'

Freddie nodded and muttered, 'Miriam's been asking for you. I don't know how much longer I can keep her away.'

Heidi sighed heavily. 'I know it's difficult for you, but I've got too much on my mind to worry about her now. Any chance you can keep distracting her until tomorrow? I'll have time then.'

'Does that mean you will speak with her?'

'Guess I'll have to, but not yet, and don't ask me what I'm going to say, I have no idea. Now, if you don't mind, I need to organise for tonight, more calls to make.'

'Yes, of course.' Freddie stood. 'Don't forget, if you need extra help, holler.'

'I will, thanks.'

Freddie left the room and Heidi picked up the phone and dialled.

'Hello, Stacey Logan.'

'Good morning, Ms Logan. Heidi Holtz here, we met earlier in the year during the slavery case.'

'I remember and it's Stacey. What can I do for you?'

'I thought you'd be interested to know about a developing situation. There's a siege in progress at the premises of a cult – new religious movement – in the Cotswolds. I know it's a touch out of your area, but Dyfed Powys Police – including your partner – are involved and having a member of the press in attendance seems like a good idea.'

'Give me the details and the address and I'll pop over. How serious is this siege?'

'Could be very if things go wrong and I feel the public should be informed, hence my call to you. Cults like this are dangerous but receive little adverse publicity. I want you to write a piece to warn people off these crackpot organisations.'

'Yeah, I can do that. I'll be there in a couple of hours. Thanks for the tip-off.'

'No problem. I'll text you the details but make sure you protect your source. I can't be seen to be involved.'

'I'll never name a source.'

'Good.'

Heidi hung up, glared at her screens, watched rubbish scroll past and felt like throwing them through the window. Why couldn't she trace those bloody payments?

* * *

A red Mazda MX-5 skidded to a halt outside the manor house. The driver's door was flung open and a tall, good-looking lad unfolded himself gracefully and stepped out. He stretched his lanky body, walked to the back of the car, opened the boot and lifted out a jangling rack of climbing devices, karabiners, spikes and cams. He slung it on his shoulder, grabbed a rucksack and headed for the main entrance. Heidi was waiting for him on the top step.

'Angus, you made good time.'

'Knocked off early. Told the boss I had somewhere to be.'

'And he just let you go?'

'I'm the best he's got and he knows it, so he's happy to cut me some slack.'

'Come to the kitchen. Looks like Cook's forgiven you, she's been baking.'

Heidi grabbed the rucksack, carried it inside and dumped it in the hall on a mound of wellies and waterproofs. They trudged downstairs and entering the room Heidi was relieved to see Miriam wasn't in attendance. Pixie and Felix were sitting so closely together a cigarette paper couldn't separate them; Greta was helping Cook and smiled when she recognised Angus.

'Hey,' she said. 'How are you? Haven't seen you in ages.'

'Good thanks,' Angus said. 'You?'

'Not bad, still getting over my spot of bother earlier in the year.'

Angus chuckled. 'I heard. Sent down for contempt. Read about the whole sorry episode in the local rag. What was it you called the judge?'

Greta grinned. 'Can't remember, surprised that wasn't reported.'

Angus dumped his burden in a corner and sat at the long table. He peered at Pixie and Felix who sat at the far end and asked, 'Who are you two?'

They introduced themselves as Cook transferred food from the Aga to the table. The smell of baking filled the air and Angus breathed in deeply, a wide smile on his face.

'Mmm, cheese scones. Cook, you're an angel.'

Cook humphed and bustled out, leaving the group to it.

'Where's your pa?' Angus asked, through a mouthful of crumbs.

'Keeping Mother occupied, I guess,' Heidi said.

'Your mother's here?'

'Couple of days now. Things aren't easy.'

'I can imagine.' Angus slurped tea to clear his mouth. 'Right then, what is it we're up to this evening?'

Heidi leaned close to her friend and lowered her voice. 'I need you to help me get inside an old place not far from here. A cult set up home there three years ago and things are going badly wrong. The police are camping on the doorstep, unwilling to break down the doors, and I'm worried the situation will escalate. There are around thirty people inside, controlled by a charismatic sociopath – Adam Inverdale – supported by an evil and twisted cow called Mala. He's deeply unstable and utterly despicable.'

'So you want us to get inside and do what, exactly?' Angus asked. 'There's only two of us. We can't take on thirty, plus a nutter and his assistant.'

'All we have to do is open the door and let the police in. They can't continue to sit on their hands when they don't have to do any smashing in stuff. Easy as that.'

'Why do we need the climbing gear?'

'No entry on the ground floor, but I reckon we should be able to get in through the servants' quarters in the eaves. How good are you at climbing buildings?'

'I can climb anything,' Angus bragged and helped himself to another scone. 'An old house will be no problem.'

Pixie and Felix finished their food, nodded at Heidi and left the room while Greta cleared the plates.

Heidi got to her feet. 'Come to the study and I'll show you what I've got. You might also be able to tell me what's going wrong with a program I'm trying to run, it's not doing what it's supposed to.'

Angus raised his eyebrows. 'You? Struggling? I don't believe it.'

Heidi humphed and stomped out of the kitchen, Angus on her heels.

* * *

Connor was clearing his desk ready for the off tomorrow evening. He hated everything about Wales and couldn't wait to return to Bristol. All he had to do tomorrow was follow Daffydd about for a few hours, then he was free. This investigation had been a waste of time, and without a decent result hadn't furthered his career in the slightest. The desk sergeant had taken his place at the bank of computer screens, but Connor could tell he wasn't interested. Lizzie walked in carrying coffee.

'Thanks, boss,' Connor said. 'I could do with that, keep me awake.'

'How's it going?'

'Just the same. I'm rounding up my stuff so as soon as I'm off duty tomorrow we can leave. I'm not expecting any trouble. We'll follow Daffydd about, he won't break any laws and that'll be it. Leave the locals to handle their own bad boys.'

'Who's working with you in the morning?'

'Will Deacon, like yesterday.'

'I'm so fed up with all this scrabbling around for staff,' Lizzie grumbled. 'DI James should never have taken personnel to the Cotswolds, not even his patch. Why the bosses allowed it I have no idea.'

Connor shrugged. 'They certainly do things differently over here, it would never have happened in Bristol. It's as though Wales and the Welsh are at least twenty years behind England.'

The desk sergeant cleared his throat noisily to remind the CTU officers he was still in the room.

'When does your shift start?' Lizzie asked.

'Eight till three.'

'You'd better get off then. I'll be in the office all day tomorrow, so anything I need to know, get in touch.'

'Sure thing, boss.'

Connor closed the lid of the cardboard box and stuck down the flaps with parcel tape. He drained his mug, slipped on his jacket and lifted the box.

'Right, I'm off. See you in the morning.' He chuckled. 'Our liberation day.'

He pushed through the door and Lizzie heard him run down the stairs. She gazed around the room and her eyes settled on the incident board. At the top of the middle section was a photograph of Daniela Stoica's destroyed face and Lizzie winced. At least Daniela's killers were locked up and wouldn't be released for years, but she wished she had been able to find a link to Daffydd Owen. She'd never uncovered any evidence he'd been involved with the murder or anything else she could nick him for. What a bloody waste of time this investigation had been. Like her sergeant, she couldn't wait to get out of Wales.

Chapter forty-two

Angus carried his gear out the front entrance and loaded it in the back of the Land Rover. Heidi climbed in the driver's seat, turned the key and the diesel engine shook itself awake, rumbling loudly in the darkness.

'How far away is this place?' Angus asked, settling himself in the passenger seat.

'Not far, should be there just after midnight, give us a couple of hours to get organised before the converts get up at two.'

'Why do they do that?'

'Early meditation, part of the brainwashing process. Comes under the heading of sleep deprivation and fatigue. Adam probably slips in a touch of hypnosis during the session. Greta was lucky, she was so nearly sucked in, even though she wasn't there very long. I'm worried about Pixie, she's been with New Eden since the place opened and is very confused, lost.'

'She'll recover though, won't she?'

'Given time and the right care. Having somewhere safe to stay is a huge bonus. Good old Freddie, he's always been a soft touch for waifs and strays.'

After thirty minutes' driving, Heidi turned off the main road and onto a narrow lane.

'We can't go in the front way,' she explained. 'Like I said, there are coppers camped on the doorstep.'

'Do they know what we're up to?'

Heidi shook her head. 'No, this is a freelance operation. Only Freddie knows what we're doing.'

'Won't you get into bother? Your boss won't like it if we make him look daft.'

'Not my boss anymore,' Heidi said, pulled the vehicle off the lane and parked at the edge of a muddy field. 'I've left the force.'

Angus chuckled. 'Knew you wouldn't stick it. You're way too clever to be a copper. I can put in a word at the office if you like.'

'Thanks, but I don't like. To be candid, I haven't a clue what I want to do, but know it isn't that. Now, to the job in hand.' She pointed across the dark expanse of grassland. 'New Eden's place is that way. If we cut across these fields, we should end up next to the kitchen garden at the rear of the building. We'll try to get in that way. You fit?'

'Yep.' Angus dragged out the rack of climbing gear and slung it around his body while Heidi slipped her arms in the straps of the rucksack. In silence they began the trudge across the fields.

Fifteen minutes later they reached the wall that surrounded the vegetable garden and Angus peered through a small pair of light-gathering binoculars, reconnoitring the climb.

'If we get on the wall,' he muttered, 'we can use the roof of the extension as first base. I'll lead, attach a rope to that ugly gargoyle above the guttering and then you can shimmy up.' He raised the glasses and studied the higher floors. 'The only real problem will be the overhang on the roof, but it's possible.'

Heidi checked her watch. 'Twenty past midnight. We should get a move on.'

After checking the windows of the hall to make sure he wasn't observed, Angus sprang up, grabbed the top of the wall and pulled himself higher. He balanced on the crumbling bricks, reached a long arm down to Heidi and dragged her up beside him. He made sure she was steady before creeping onto the roof of the single-storey extension and beginning the climb, rock boots searching out tiny crevices in the old stonework. In minutes he was hanging by one hand from the gargoyle. He unwound a rope from his shoulders, fastened it around the lump of ornate stone and dropped one end down to Heidi. She clipped it to a karabiner on her belt, placed her feet on the wall and hauled her compact body towards the roof. As soon as she reached Angus, he made sure she was securely attached to the rope, then swung himself on the gargoyle and flicked his feet up and over the guttering. His toes snagged the edge and with some frantic wriggling he was soon perched on the roof. He peered over the edge and signalled to Heidi.

'Just do what I did,' he whispered loudly. 'Don't worry if you slip, I've got you.'

Heidi mimicked his movements and with the help of a swift tug on the rope, she reached the roof without incident and sat next to her friend. They grinned stupidly at each other, pleased with themselves.

'The windows for the servants' quarters are at the front of the house,' Heidi said. 'We'll have to work our way round.'

'Slowly,' Angus advised. 'Some of these slates are well dodgy. If we kick any off we're sure to be spotted.'

They moved cautiously and were soon on a narrow ledge running along the front of the house. Heidi peeped through the first tiny window they came to and saw the room was empty.

'The windows are nailed shut,' she hissed. 'We'll have to get one open without breaking the glass, someone might hear us.'

Angus leaned precariously over the edge of the roof. 'Can't see anyone. The fuzz must be in their vehicles keeping warm.' He rummaged in his bag, removed a multi-tool, unfolded a screwdriver and began working at ancient putty. It came out in chunks and revealed eight small panel pins holding the glass in place. Another attachment on the tool became a pair of pliers. Angus winkled out the pins, rested a hand on the small pane and levered it away from the frame using a narrow blade. He passed the glass to Heidi who leant it against the tiled roof, edge tucked securely in the guttering. They unclipped from the rope and slithered inside, relieved when their feet touched the boards.

Heidi grinned. 'That was fun. Follow me.'

She crept out of the room and shone a small beam along the narrow hall. All the doors were open, no one in seclusion. She pulled open the door at the far end, checked the coast was clear and beckoned Angus to follow her downstairs to the third floor.

The building was in darkness. The pair stood still listening hard but heard nothing, so scooted along the landing towards the main staircase and slowly began to descend, testing the treads for squeaks. They arrived at the bottom without incident and Heidi crossed the hall towards the front door.

Suddenly she was bathed in a bright spot of light and turned to see Adam and Mala standing side by side. She took a single step towards them before realising Adam held a large torch in one hand and a short stubby revolver in the other.

'Welcome to New Eden,' Adam sneered. 'We've been expecting you. Heidi, isn't it? And Angus?'

'How…?' Heidi spluttered.

Adam waved a mobile phone. 'Pixie sent me a text, told me you were coming… and who you were.'

Mala chuckled and Heidi felt a shiver tickle her spine. She wasn't a match for firearms and wasn't reckless enough to think she was.

'What happens now?' she asked, wondering how she could wake the officers on the doorstep. If Adam could be encouraged to use the gun, they'd be sure to hear the shot. She took another step closer and Adam frowned.

'I will shoot you,' he said and waved the gun. 'I'm a homeowner defending my property and won't make the mistake of shooting you in the back. No jail time for me. Now, take off your bags and climbing gear, remove your mobile phones and put your hands behind your backs, both of you.'

Angus hesitated, he wasn't sure Adam would use the gun, but equally wasn't sure he wouldn't. He considered throwing the rack of climbing gear in the man's face, but was too far away, wasn't worth the risk. He hadn't got involved in this to end up dead, that was a price too high to pay for a moment's lack of judgement. He complied and Mala secured his and Heidi's hands with cable ties.

'Good,' Adam said. 'Now, let me show you to your room. Move!' he shoved Heidi roughly in the back and she turned quickly to glare at him, eyes flashing.

'Go on,' Adam implored, 'try it. Give me the excuse.'

She turned away reluctantly and followed Mala who opened a door beneath the staircase and descended a flight of stone steps. Heidi could hear Angus breathing heavily behind her, felt his fury and impotence while struggling with her own. There were thirty steps, Heidi counted them. The cellar was damp, dark and silent. Mala led the way to the far wall and dragged open a door. Adam shoved his prisoners inside and locked it. There was a metal grille in the wood and he rested his face against it, smiling, eyes sparkling.

'Well, that's something I don't have to worry about,' he said. 'Good old Pixie, I knew she wouldn't let me down.'

'Why?' Heidi asked. 'Why did she contact you?'

'Because I own her. Pixie is mine, always has been and always will be. She found the path to God with my help years ago. She loves God and loves me just the same. I am her God.'

'You're mad!' Angus growled. 'Utterly stark raving bonkers. It's you who should be locked away.'

Adam laughed. 'But it's not, is it? It's you.'

'So now what?' Heidi asked. 'What happens next?'

'Nothing much. You and Angus will die of dehydration in a few days unless the police do decide to storm the place. In that case you might be useful as hostages, but I don't think that's going to happen any time soon. None of them want to make the decision to raid a church. We could be here for months and that will be too long for you.'

'You're just going to leave us here?' Angus asked.

'You've got it, that's exactly what I'm going to do.'

'We'll be missed,' Heidi said. 'My father will come for me.'

'Yes, he might, but he won't get in any quicker than the police. They'll ask about you, I'll tell them I haven't seen you and that will be the end of the conversation. I'll leave the light on.'

Adam retreated from the door followed by Mala who cackled nastily as she passed the cell, peeking in and waving a middle finger in Heidi's direction. They climbed the steps, Heidi heard the door slam then silence. She studied Angus who looked paler than ever.

'You OK?' she asked.

'If I was in superhero mode I'd say "spiffing", but if I'm being truthful... not really. This is bloody awful, Heidi. What do we do now?'

Chapter forty-three

Daffydd drove slowly past Brecon's war memorial and was pleased to see Matthew and Kev, the extra drivers, sitting on benches. He pulled up and they hopped in.

'Morning, boys. Everything OK?'

'Yeah, mate. Looking forward to a day out,' Kev said. 'Where are we going?'

'The barn to pick up the cars and meet the others. We'll tell you more then.'

'Why all the secrecy?' Matthew asked. 'Why can't you tell us where we're going?'

'You'll find out soon enough,' Daffydd growled, unwilling to encourage further discussion while they were on the move.

He drove out of Brecon, made good time before turning off towards Aberbran. He didn't notice the blue Montego following at a distance or see it park behind a high wall. Pulling up in the yard outside the barn, he saw Geraint and Rhys leaning against two tatty cars. They raised their hands in greeting and Daffydd turned his car around, tucked it close to the building and got out. He unlocked the padlock, dragged open the heavy doors and they went inside.

'OK then, lads,' he said. 'Today's the day Wales finds its voice again. Friday the thirteenth, couldn't be better.'

'How's it all going to work then?' Rhys asked. 'What's the plan?'

'I'll leave first,' Daffydd said. 'I'll drive to Rogiet Moor where the Severn Tunnel pops up and set my bomb to explode at noon. I can park in the lane, carry it to the tunnel and get well away before it blows.' He laughed. 'When it explodes, every copper in the country will head there, leaving you and Geraint a clear run to your own targets.'

Matthew wasn't sure he'd heard correctly. 'Did you say "bomb"?'

'Yes, boy, I did. We're going to remind the English government we still exist and maybe put people off coming here. Wales for the Welsh!'

'Where did you get bombs?' Matthew stammered.

'Made them. Come and take a look.'

At the back of the barn three large gas canisters stood in a row. The tops had been cut off and a cheap alarm clock dangled from the neck of each one, attached to wires which snaked inside the metal bottle.

'They're packed with TNT,' Daffydd explained, 'and a detonator is wired to the clock. All you have to do is set it with the hands fifteen minutes apart, put the battery in the back and drop the lot inside. There are wires soldered onto the hands and when they cross… BOOM!'

'Are they safe?' Geraint asked. 'I'm not sure I fancy driving one of those about.'

'Safe as houses. Nothing can happen until you set the clock and put in the battery. Stop just before you reach your targets, set fifteen minutes' fuse, drive the cars onto the bridges and fake a breakdown. Then, with Matt and Kev's help, hightail it to England, swap cars and come back home. Now, give me a hand to load them up, they must be strapped down so they can't roll about, then I'll get off.'

'I'm still not sure,' Geraint muttered.

'It's fine I tell you. Wait till you watch the news tonight and you'll know it was worth the risk.'

As soon as the devices were loaded, Daffydd patted each of his boys on the back and shook their hands.

'Rhys, you set off at noon, time your explosion for three and Geraint, you've the shorter distance to travel, so you leave at one. With a bit of luck your bomb will explode at the same time as Rhys'. Good luck,' he said. 'Don't get nicked for speeding or anything stupid and remember, after midday, all the coppers will be at the tunnel so you'll have a clear run.' He checked his watch. 'Ten thirty. That's me off. Keep your radios tuned to the news so you know what's going on and pay attention to the traffic channels.'

He climbed in his vehicle, drove towards the A40, and passed Connor and Will hunched down in their car behind the wall.

'What do we do?' Will asked. 'Follow him or wait for the others?'

'Oh God,' Connor groaned. 'Follow him I guess. It's crap trying to do a job like this without enough manpower.' He started the engine and set off in pursuit. 'Give DI Wild a call, let her know what's going on, just in case she wants us to do something different.'

* * *

Erica was walking around New Eden's kitchen garden with DI James and Stacey Logan, who had appeared out of the blue yesterday evening. Her phone buzzed, she checked the screen and was surprised to recognise Freddie's number.

'Good morning,' she said. 'What can I do for you?'

'Have you seen Heidi?' Freddie asked.

'No, not since yesterday.'

'Are you still at the New Eden place?'

'Yeah, still here, kicking our heels while Gloucester make up their minds what they'd like us to do. Why did you ask about Heidi?'

'She went to the commune last night with a mate from uni, had the idea of breaking in and opening the doors for your lot.'

'That sounds like Heidi. No, I haven't seen her. What time did she leave you?'

'Just after eleven. She was planning to arrive around midnight.'

'I've been here all night,' Erica said. 'There's a good dozen with me and no one has said they've seen anything. Maybe she changed her mind?'

'She was very determined,' Freddie said. 'You must have noticed how distracted she's been by the situation, worried the whole thing will end disastrously?'

'Yeah, I have, that and her mission to find the kids.' Erica sighed. 'I'll talk to DI James and call you back as soon as I know anything.' She disconnected the call.

'What's up?' Stacey asked, her sharp ears had picked up the anxiety in the air.

'Sorry,' Erica said. 'I need to talk to Ben – operational matter. Will you give us a moment?'

'Sure,' Stacey said and set off for the front of the house.

'That was Freddie Holtz, sir,' Erica said. 'He's lost Heidi. Seems she roped one of her friends into a scheme.'

'What scheme?' Ben asked.

'To break in here and open the doors so we can gain entry to do our job.'

'Bloody hell. Why would she do that and if she did arrive, where is she?'

'That's what Freddie wanted to know.'

'Check with the others, ask if anyone saw anything and I'll take a look around, see if there's any sign they've been here.' He yawned. 'Although, I didn't get a wink of sleep last night and heard nothing, so they must have abandoned their crazy plan. I do hope so.'

Erica dashed to the front of the house and found Stacey chatting to a group of coppers lounging against the side of the van. They straightened up when Erica approached and Stacey slunk off to sit in her car.

'Any of you see or hear anything last night around midnight?' Erica asked.

They all shook their heads and mumbled a negative.

'Nothing at all?'

'No, boss,' Oliver said. 'Why, what's happened?'

Erica lowered her voice. 'Seems Heidi and a friend were planning to break into the hall last night. I've had her father on the phone asking if we've seen her.'

'Why would she break in?' Tegan asked.

'Cos we haven't. She's afraid if we mess about much longer we'll find corpses inside and for all we know, Heidi might be one of them.'

'You don't really think she's in there, do you?' Tegan asked. 'If she was, she'd have opened the doors.'

'Unless she was caught, or never got here, or changed her mind or…' Erica ran out of options. 'Ollie, take Tegan and have a scout about. If Heidi is here, she'll have a vehicle parked close by. She drives a black Land Rover, go and see if you can find one anywhere and call me if you do.'

'Will do and if anything happens here, call us.'

* * *

Angus paced in the cellar and rubbed his wrists incessantly, even though Heidi had cut the cable ties hours ago, using a tiny blade incorporated in the catch of her belt buckle. He was starting to irritate her but she said nothing. Arguments would be futile and probably counterproductive. In a situation like this, they needed to be on the same side.

'Why don't you have another go at trying to make the pager work?' she asked. Adam had only asked for their phones, so that was all Heidi had given him. They hadn't been searched so the tiny device hadn't been found. She briefly wondered why they hadn't been given a pat down, but guessed it was because Adam knew there wasn't a way out of this room – other than the door.

'It won't work,' Angus mumbled. 'I can't get anything like a signal down here.'

'Is there no way to boost it?'

'Nothing springs readily to mind. Do you really think the nutter plans for us to die down here?'

'Yeah, I do,' Heidi said. 'That's why we have to help ourselves. At least we've got our hands free. How are your wrists?'

'Bloody sore,' Angus grumbled and began rubbing them again. 'That bitch pulled the cable tie so tight I lost feeling in my fingers in minutes. God, what's wrong with these people?' he yelled, voice bouncing off the walls.

'Keep calm, matey,' Heidi said. 'Use that considerable brain of yours to come up with a plan to get us out of this pickle.'

'I have done and there is no way out. The door is too thick and the wood sound, so we can't kick our way out. We're underground and don't have any picks or shovels so can't dig a tunnel and no one will hear us if we scream until Monday. About the only thing we've got going for us is your pa knows we were coming here. We just have to hope he convinces the force to break in before it's too late, and that they find us.'

'At least you're not totally negative.'

'Your pa's definitely our best bet at the moment,' Angus said. 'That and finding our own underground spring and would you believe it? I left my divining rods at home.'

Heidi giggled and eventually Angus joined in.

'I should know better than to get involved with you,' he said. 'I might have taken the blame for the armour episode, but it was your idea.' He walked to the door and examined the metal grille. 'I wonder if we can do anything with this. Pass me that nifty little blade of yours.'

Chapter forty-four

Daffydd parked in a gateway on the B4245, at the edge of Rogiet Moor. From where he sat he could see the second Severn crossing spanning the river, a graceful structure which, if all went well would soon be marred. He smiled and congratulated himself on the plan. Granda would be so proud, this will make his year, he thought.

He left the car, leaned on a rickety fence and stared across an area of grassland towards the entrance of the tunnel. He checked his watch, time to set the timer and carry the canister to the railway track. He opened the boot, unstrapped the metal container, lifted it out carefully and stood it on the mud. He fiddled with the clock and made sure the wires were still attached. He slipped a hand inside the neck of the bottle and discovered the bundles of TNT felt wet, but decided it was condensation, built up during the time it was stored in the barn.

Some distance away a second car sheltered Connor Haskins and Will Deacon. They watched their quarry through binoculars.

'What's he up to, boss?' Will asked, craning his neck, trying to see what was going on. 'What's he taken from the boot?'

'Don't know. He's blocking my view. Move over, Daffydd, can't you?' Connor muttered.

'What's he doing here? Do you think he's meeting someone?'

'I don't bloody know!' Connor snapped. 'I'm not a mind reader.' He refocused the glasses but still couldn't see what Daffydd had removed from the boot. 'He's fiddling with something… ah, he's shifted at last… looks like a Calor gas bottle, the sort you put in the back of those dreadful fires.' Connor frowned beneath the glasses and a disturbing niggle rumbled in the back of his brain. Where had he seen gas bottles recently? He watched as Daffydd carried the canister across the road and put it down by the fence. The man looked around, failed to spot his watchers, lifted the bottle high over the fence and dumped it in the field.

A monstrous explosion rocked the air. Great gouts of roaring flame shot towards the sky, earth and fence posts were flung in all directions, tangles of barbed wire scythed through the air like enormous cheese cutters. The sound of the blast was immense, shock waves rocked the Montego and assaulted the occupants' eardrums. The horrified officers crouched low, cringing as clods of earth and stones smacked against the windscreen, cracking the glass. Ears ringing, Connor straightened and with shaking hands, trained his binoculars on the edge of the field. Daffydd's car was nowhere in sight, neither was Daffydd. Connor saw nothing apart from a deep crater, some twisted metal and a few wisps of smoke rising from the devastation.

'Christ!' Will said. 'What the hell was that?'

'A bomb that exploded prematurely,' Connor gasped. 'Get Lizzie Wild on the line, we have a serious problem.'

'A serious problem which is over surely?' Will said. 'Daffydd's blown himself up, couldn't have happened to a nicer bloke,' he sneered. 'And no one else is injured. That's a result in my book. Case closed.'

'What about the other cars, you prat?' Connor snapped.

Will's face paled. 'You don't think…'

'That's exactly what I think. There were three canisters in the barn when we checked it out a couple of days ago and we saw four other cars there this morning. There could be more bombs. For crying out loud, get Wild on the blower – now!'

Will fiddled with his phone, tapped in the number and handed the device to Connor who snatched it, eyes still fixed on the smoking crater.

'Boss? Connor. We have a problem.'

'What's happened?'

'Daffydd's blown himself up. We followed him to Rogiet Moor and he parked close to the entrance of the Severn Tunnel. He took a gas canister out of his car, dropped it over the fence on the edge of the road and the bloody thing exploded.'

'You're kidding!' Her voice trembled, reluctant to believe her sergeant.

'No, I'm not and there could be more. I saw several canisters in the barn earlier in the week and there were those other blokes in cars there this morning. What if they're delivering bombs as we speak?'

'They can't be!' Lizzie said. 'We've been all over them the last few weeks and haven't seen anything to indicate this.'

'We've been following Daffydd – not the others. I'm sure they've planned further explosions.'

'Where? What would they attack?'

'Looks as though Daffydd was planning to collapse the entrance to the Severn Tunnel, maybe the others are going to attack the bridges.'

Lizzie didn't speak and the silence stretched.

'What do you want us to do, boss?'

'Where are the other cars?'

'How would I know?' Connor snapped. 'You told us to follow Daffydd. I haven't a clue where the others went.'

'OK. Stay where you are. I'll alert CTU and the bomb squad. We'll have to close the bridges.'

'I'm only guessing that's where the others are heading,' Connor warned, 'they might still be at the barn. I don't even know for sure there are any more bombs. Fucking hell, this is a mess.'

'Sit tight. I'll be in touch.'

Connor hung up and Will raised his eyebrows.

'Told us to stay here. Bomb squad on its way.'

'Horse and bolt spring to mind,' Will mumbled.

* * *

Erica had explained the situation to Freddie. Told him Oliver and Tegan had discovered Heidi's Land Rover parked in a field a mile or so from the hall, but found no sign of the occupants. The officers camped outside the building had widened their search, but so far uncovered nothing to indicate Heidi and Angus were inside. Freddie wasn't happy and for a moment, Erica thought he was planning to storm the place himself. She hoped she had managed to convince him to pay the commune a social visit first so he could assess the situation before he did anything rash.

Her phone rang again. 'Freddie. I told you…'

'It's DI Wild. We have a problem.'

'What?' Erica asked.

'Daffydd Owen has blown himself up trying to plant a bomb in the mouth of the Severn Tunnel. We think there could be at least two more devices and they might be planning to attack the bridges. Tell DI James to leave what he's doing and get back here. This is a major incident and we need every officer.'

'You tell him,' Erica said. She passed her phone to Ben and watched his face cloud as he heard the news.

'No,' he said, 'we can't leave here. We have reason to believe that DC Holtz is inside and may be in trouble. Give Builth Wells station a ring.'

Erica heard Lizzie's angry voice squawk out of the phone and Ben shook his head.

'No, I'm sorry. The incident at New Eden is still very much ongoing and we can't leave. You've got the bomb squad and the CTU. You'll have to manage.'

More angry noises filled the air, like the buzzing of a wasp trapped in a matchbox.

'Yeah, you can try to close the bridges, but you'll need to be sure there is a threat.' Another pause. 'I realise that and I agree with you, there is a chance, but it's not me you need to convince. We'll speak later.'

He hung up on Lizzie mid-flow and frowned.

'How could she have let the situation get so out of control?' Ben grumbled. 'She's been watching this group for weeks now.'

'It might be my fault,' Erica said, knees suddenly weak.

'How can this be your fault?'

'Heidi told me days ago Daffydd was looking at bomb making sites online and told me to inform DI Wild. I didn't. Got sidetracked. Oh shit.'

'This isn't down to you,' Ben said. 'If Heidi had spotted what Daffydd was up to, why didn't DI Wild? Took her eye off the ball. No excuse.'

'But…'

'No, I don't want to hear another word. What did Freddie Holtz have to say?'

'He wants to launch his own raiding party. He's convinced Heidi and her mate, Angus, are being held inside and wants to rescue them. He's on his way over. I told him he should take a look at the situation before he sets anything in motion.'

'I don't suppose Heidi wears a GPS locket does she?'

'Not that I'm aware of, so we can't even prove she's in there.'

Ben sighed and rubbed his eyes. 'OK, let's have another chat with Inverdale, maybe he's changed his mind about staying inside, we can but hope.'

* * *

Matthew Williams had followed Rhys through Abergavenny and wished he was anywhere else.

His mind twisted and turned thinking about the bombs and couldn't work out how he'd got involved in this mental plan. It wasn't what he'd signed up for and wondered if Daffydd had gone mad. Shouting at rallies and waving swastikas was a completely different ball game to this. He watched the car in front turn onto the bypass and head towards the motorway and made a sudden decision. He drove around the roundabout, turned back onto the A40 and pulled up in the first lay-by he came across. He removed his phone from his pocket with trembling hands, tapped in Uncle Jon's number.

Rhys glanced in his rear-view mirror and noticed Matthew wasn't behind. He slowed and checked again… no sign of the lad. He pulled off the road and stared in the mirror. Five minutes passed and still no Matthew. Rhys tried calling Daffydd but the call went to voicemail so tried calling Matthew, the phone was busy.

Rhys didn't know what to do. Without Matthew to pick him up on the bridge after he'd set the timer, he couldn't see how the plan would work. He'd have no way of escape. He called Daffydd again and still couldn't get through. He thumped the steering wheel in frustration and checked his mirror again… nothing. Maybe Matt had car trouble and was ringing the AA or something. Rhys decided to drive on to Magor services. By the time he arrived Daffydd should have blown the bomb in the tunnel and would be close by. He could act as follower and pick him up if Matthew hadn't reappeared.

He pulled into the traffic and turned on the local radio. He wondered if Daffydd had blown the tunnel, surely there would be something on the news if he had, unless the authorities were keeping it quiet, which was a possibility.

He reached the end of the A4042, joined the M4 at junction 25a and headed east. Matthew was still missing so perhaps he had broken down, but why didn't he answer his phone? He concentrated on the motorway traffic, spotted the sign for Magor services, indicated, pulled in and parked close to the building. He tried calling Daffydd, no answer. He called Geraint, but couldn't get through. A message informed him the mobile he'd called was unavailable. He decided to have a coffee and think things through. He wasn't keen on being anywhere near the bridge when the bomb went off, but without a lift couldn't see how he could get away and realised he might have to forget the whole thing.

He quickly checked the contents of the boot, locked the car and walked into the onsite McDonald's. He bought a large coffee, a burger and a bag of fries and carried the food back to the car to eat. He gazed through the windscreen. The service station wasn't very busy for a weekday, lots of space, the car park was usually packed. A helicopter flew overhead, rotor blades thumping through damp air. Rhys peered up but it had already passed on. He finished his meal, dropped the waste in a nearby bin, started the engine and headed for the slip road.

A plain-clothed CTU officer, positioned next to the entrance of the car park, saw Rhys start his car and called in the sighting.

'Subject on the move. Silver Fiesta, W plate, one male occupant.'

'OK, on it.'

Rhys turned onto the slip road, drove downhill towards the main carriageway and slowed as he spotted some sort of a blockage in the road, stop signs placed along the verge. Too late he realised he was heading towards a police roadblock. He slammed on the brakes and checked his mirror, wondered if a U-turn was possible. He saw a rolling bank of vehicles barricading the road behind him and knew he was sunk. It was over. He pulled on the handbrake, turned off the engine, got out of the car and raised his hands above his head.

'Down on the ground,' a voice screamed. 'Face on the road – now!'

Rhys knelt on the tarmac then lay prone. His cheek brushed the oily smelling surface and gravel pricked his skin. He felt a weight on his back, his arms were yanked roughly together and wrists cuffed. A boot rolled him over and he stared up at a circle of angry faces and gun muzzles. He was dragged to his feet and turned to face a large angry woman with windswept grey hair. For a moment he thought she was going to punch him. Looking past her, Rhys saw a man dressed in body armour approach the car and open the boot before moving quickly away.

'Viable device,' he yelled. 'The explosive is old and unstable, so everyone who doesn't need to be here should leave and close the motorway. Right now!'

The large woman pulled Rhys towards a police car, shoved him in the back seat and glared at him.

'My name is DI Wild,' she growled. 'Bristol Counter Terrorism Unit. Where's the other bomb? Tell me where it is.'

Rhys shook his head. She raised a hand and backhanded him so hard across the face, one of her rings drew blood. He was so shocked tears formed in his eyes.

She leaned in close. 'Where is it?' she hissed, face so close he could feel her breath on his skin and tried to sink into the seat. 'You will tell me,' she said, 'and the sooner you do that, the better for you. Now, where – is – the – other – car?'

'I don't know,' Rhys whined. 'Could be anywhere.'

'Where is it heading?' Lizzie raised her hand again.

'Severn Bridge – the old one,' Rhys mumbled.

Lizzie stood, slammed the car door shut and yelled, 'First crossing, everyone. Get as many cars over there as possible and close the bridge. Move! We don't know how much time we have.'

Chapter forty-five

Heidi sat on the cellar's dirty floor, back against the wall and fiddled with the useless pager. If only she could pick up a signal they'd be out of here in minutes. She wondered what was happening upstairs, whether Ben had finally taken the decision to break down the doors, and where was Freddie? She looked at her watch. She'd left Milebrook well over twelve hours ago, surely he'd worked out something had gone wrong.

Angus was by the door, working at the metal grille with Heidi's small knife. He grabbed the wire and gave it a tug. There was a splintering sound. Encouraged he tugged harder and stumbled backwards as the panel came free.

'Hey,' he crowed. 'Look what I've done.' He waved the grille in the air, grinning.

'Very good,' Heidi said. 'Now what?'

'Do you reckon you could wriggle through?'

Heidi laughed. 'I may be small, but I'm not a Lilliputian.'

Angus pushed his face close to the gap and stared through. 'It is tight,' he agreed. He turned his attention to the woven wire. 'Maybe we can do something with this,' he said.

'Like what?'

'I don't know, pick the lock, use it to work on the hinges, dig a tunnel, gouge out Inverdale's eyes… something.'

Heidi pulled herself upright and took the metal. 'Pass me the knife.' She wriggled the blade between the strips of wire and worked at the soldered joints.

'Where's your pa?' Angus asked and rubbed his wrists again, his default position.

'Don't know,' Heidi said, 'but he won't be sitting on his arse in the library drinking brandy. He's probably on his way or already on the doorstep with his own personal SWAT squad champing at their bits.'

'Why did Pixie grass us up?'

'Because her mind is not her own.' Heidi scraped with the knife. 'She has been utterly brainwashed, it's going to be difficult to bring her back to the real world. I shouldn't have spoken about our plans in front of her, it's my fault we're here.'

'No,' Angus said. 'It's that bloody Inverdale's fault. When I get out I'm going to give him such a smack. How are you getting on?'

'Slowly, but if I can free a couple of these strands, I might be able to fashion a picklock.'

'Any luck with the pager?'

'No, it's useless.'

Angus began to pace again and Heidi wished he'd stay still.

'I'm bloody thirsty,' he said. 'I could murder something long and cool. I'm fantasising about a Pimms and don't even drink the stuff.'

'Think about something else,' Heidi advised and ground away more solder. 'Take a good look at the hinges, maybe you can lever out one of the pins so we can open the door. Use this.' She lobbed a strand of wire at him and began working to free a second.

Two minutes later the light went out.

* * *

Ben turned to face the drive when he heard a car approach and watched a dove-grey Bentley pull up next to the assortment of police vans and cars. Freddie Holtz stepped out and marched across the gravel. Ben moved to intercept him.

'Good afternoon, sir,' he said, hand outstretched. 'DI Ben James.'

Freddie grasped the offered hand briefly. 'I need an update, Inspector. Any sign of my daughter?'

'No, sir. As Erica Bevan told you we have found her vehicle, but no one has seen her and we can't be sure she's even inside the hall.'

'Where else would she be?' Freddie snapped. 'She told me her plan was to break in and open the doors so the force can do its job, so why would she not be inside? And – if she is – why hasn't she stuck to her plan? I can only assume that's because she's met trouble and has been prevented from doing so.'

'I'm beginning to come to the same conclusion,' Ben said.

'Does the cult leader have anything to say? Any clue what he's up to?'

'No. He's stopped talking to us. His second in command, a woman called Mala, comes to the door occasionally, but only flings insults and quotes from the Bible.'

'Then for God's sake, man, break down the bloody door and get us inside. You have no idea what's happening in there.'

'I can't, sir. DCI Andrews from Gloucester force is in charge here and I can't move until I'm told to do so.'

Freddie snorted, took out his mobile, selected a number and tapped an impatient finger on the device while he waited for his call to be answered.

'Ah, yes. DCI Andrews please. No – I don't want to hear he's busy or in a meeting, I want to talk to him. Tell him Frederick Holtz wants a word and he's in a hurry.' He waited some more, then said, 'Good afternoon to you. I understand you're in charge of the debacle at the hall in

South Hatherop. Why the hell haven't you got inside? This unacceptable situation has developed due to your reticence and I have to tell you, sir, it's not good enough! If you don't take some decisive action soon, I will bring in my own team and get the job done.'

He listened, frowning.

'I'll agree to that, but if you're not here in an hour, I will take matters into my own hands. If you doubt my word, run some checks. It won't take you long to find out who you're dealing with.' He hung up and looked around. 'Where's Erica?'

'Checking the back of the place – again,' Ben said. 'Follow me, sir, I'll walk you round.'

* * *

Lizzie Wild felt she was losing her grip on what was real. She couldn't understand how her investigation hadn't uncovered the bomb plot, or how things had spiralled so dramatically out of control. Rhys Jones had been carted off to the police station under heavy guard and the bomb disposal unit had destroyed his device. Lizzie was shocked to see the TNT in the canister, more so when the man in command of the bomb squad informed her it was more than large enough to have caused serious damage to the bridge. Connor and Will who had arrived from the site at Rogiet Moor, stood by her side and waited for instructions.

'We must find the other car,' Lizzie said. 'It cannot be allowed to reach the first crossing. Have the motorways been closed?'

'Yes, boss,' Connor said. 'Traffic is gridlocked which will make it impossible for Geraint Jones to reach the bridge, but also makes it difficult for us to get around.'

'Has the helicopter reported any sightings?'

Connor shook his head. 'No, boss.' He pulled out a map and spread it on the bonnet of a nearby car. 'I don't think he'll use the motorway, he'll probably be heading along the B4598 towards Usk, then pick up the B4235 to Chepstow, quickest route to the first bridge.'

'Have we got cars on the roads?'

'As many as we can muster, but we don't really know what we're looking for – other than an old car.'

'Why the bloody hell didn't you take the registration numbers when you had the chance?' Lizzie muttered. 'If you had, we'd at least know the vehicle we need to stop.'

Connor stared at her. 'If you'd run the operation properly we wouldn't be in this mess.'

'I beg your pardon?'

'You heard. I don't think you've taken this investigation seriously since we got here, convinced the locals weren't clever enough to devise a decent plot. Well, look how wrong you were.'

Will stepped in. 'You know what? We really don't have time for this. We have to find that car and stop it.'

'We don't have enough manpower because of DI James' refusal to leave the siege at the cult,' Lizzie grumbled. 'He shouldn't be there, not his jurisdiction. This would never have happened in Bristol.'

'How many officers would be enough?' Will asked. 'We have to work with what we've got. Set up roadblocks on the approach roads and check every vehicle trying to drive through. Jones obviously hasn't reached his target yet cos we'd have heard.'

Lizzie tried to pull herself together. Will Deacon was right, she must use the resources she had and it was imperative to find the third car. If she didn't she'd never wear a uniform again, never mind work for the CTU.

Chapter forty-six

As soon as the chauffeur driven car pulled to a stop outside the commune, Freddie yanked open the back door, much to the surprise of DCI Andrews.

'At last,' Freddie grumbled. 'I'm assuming you did as I asked and checked to see who you're dealing with.'

The Chief Inspector nodded sheepishly. 'Yes, sir, I did.'

'Excellent, so now we all know who we are. I'm instructing you and your officers to break down the door so we can finally liberate not only the cult members, but my eldest daughter. I must admit, I'm struggling to understand why you've let this situation develop. If you'd dealt with it earlier, we wouldn't be in this position now. So let's get on with it.'

Andrews climbed out of the car and glanced around nervously. He didn't want to be here. He only had a few months to go until he could draw his pension and had no wish to be on the front page of any newspaper. He'd already spotted Stacey Logan in her car, parked to the side of the gravelled area and just knew she was press. He could smell journalists. This operation had to be carried out with as little fuss as possible and no dramatic scenes to make horrifying images in the papers. He didn't want an English version of Waco.

He cleared his throat. 'Is your daughter a cult member, sir?'

'No, she was trying to do your job because of your shameless inactivity.'

'A freelance operation by a civilian then?'

'Call it what you like, but for God's sake get on with it. We've wasted far too much time already.' Freddie stalked away to stand with Erica while Andrews reluctantly organised his troops.

Two officers dragged a metal battering ram from the back of the transit and carried it to the door. A group of others formed a solid block behind them, while a team made their way to the rear of the building to prevent anyone escaping. Andrews strode up to the front door and hammered on the peeling paint.

'Adam Inverdale, this is the police. Open up. If you refuse, we will have no option but to force entry.' He hammered some more and received no response.

Andrews gave the order.

The officers with the battering ram swung the heavy implement at the door and after two blows the lock splintered and the door burst open. Officers rushed into the gloomy hall, Erica in their midst.

DI James followed. 'Get the lights on,' he ordered.

'We cut the power,' Oliver Langdon reminded him.

'Then get it back on and open the window shutters. Where is everyone?' Ben asked. 'You said there are over thirty people living here, Erica, so where are they all?'

'Could be anywhere, sir, it's a big place.'

'So spread out, search it… and for crying out loud, get the bloody lights on so we can see what we're doing.'

'Can I look for Heidi?' Erica asked.

'Yes, but take someone with you. I don't want anyone wandering around on their own until we understand the situation. Take Tegan.'

Erica nodded, grabbed Tegan by the arm and set off towards the back of the house.

Officers split into groups. The first team began to search the ground floor, the rest took the stairs to the upper levels. Ben stood in the hall with Freddie Holtz and DCI Andrews who was trying his best to ignore everything going on around him, in case things didn't end well. Stacey snuck in through the shattered front door, passed through the hall without drawing attention to herself and into the maze of corridors and rooms, a camera hung from a strap around her neck.

There was a sudden shout from upstairs. 'Sir, we've found them. They're all in bed and we can't wake them.'

Ben felt the room spin, rushed to the staircase with Freddie at his side and climbed to the upper floors.

'Where, constable?' he asked.

The man pointed to his right and Ben dashed inside a large room filled with beds, a prone body in each.

'We've been trying to wake them, sir, but it's like they're in a coma or something, totally unresponsive.'

Ben squatted by the nearest bed and gently shook the occupant. He felt for a pulse and was heartened when he felt the thump of a heart, weak but steady.

'Whistle up ambulances,' he ordered, 'as many as local hospitals can provide and get them here. Inverdale has probably given them something, let's hope it isn't poison. If it is, we could be too late.'

'Is Heidi here?' Freddie asked.

'No, she isn't. Erica has taken Tegan to search for her.' Ben looked up from the bed. 'How many others like this?' he asked the officer standing by the door.

'All thirty-two of them. There are a couple of rooms full of women and they're in exactly the same state.'

'Any sign of Inverdale or Mala?'

'No, sir, not yet.'

'Well, find them!' Ben ordered. 'Fast! We need to know what's happened here and they will be able to tell us.'

* * *

'Please, Angus, sit down, will you?' Heidi said. 'Pacing in the dark is not a great idea, you've kicked me at least three times, so stop. Come and sit on the floor with me so I know where you are.'

‘Sorry,’ Angus muttered, felt his way along the wall to Heidi and sat next to her. He fumbled for her hand and grasped it tightly. ‘I don’t think we’re ever going to get out of here,’ he said. ‘Never thought it would end this way.’

‘Oh what utter rot,’ Heidi snapped. ‘Of course it won’t end like this. Freddie will find us, I know he will.’

‘He might,’ Angus agreed, ‘but will he be in time? It’s not like we can help ourselves… especially now we can’t see what we’re doing.’

Heidi rested her head on her knees, glad it was dark and Angus couldn’t see her. She felt as desperate as he sounded but knew sharing her feelings wouldn’t help. Maybe they would die in this place and hoped she wouldn’t go out screaming like a nutter. She lifted her head, was that a noise from upstairs?

She strained her ears. ‘Did you hear that?’ she asked.

‘What?’

‘A sort of thump from upstairs.’

‘You’re imagining things. I didn’t hear anything.’

‘Stay here so I know where you are,’ she said, stood and walked slowly along the wall until she reached the door. The basement was so dark she couldn’t tell whether her eyes were open or closed. She felt for the gap, pressed the side of her head close and was sure she heard a sound, a shuffling tapping sound. She held her breath, heard it again and spotted a brief flash of light. Was that someone walking down the steps to the cellar?

‘Hello?’ she called. ‘Is anyone there?’

‘Heidi?’

‘E! Thank God! We’re locked in a room at the back of the cellar. You’ll need the battering ram to get us out, we’ve been trying for hours but the door is solid.’

‘Tegan, go and bring the boys down here, quick as you like and pass the word to Freddie we’ve found his daughter. Heidi, I’m coming.’

Heidi peered through the gap and saw weak torchlight approaching. She dangled an arm through the gap and nearly fainted when Erica took hold of it and squeezed tightly. Heidi felt her partner brush a gentle kiss on the palm of her hand and shockingly, her eyes filled with tears which she angrily swiped away. Heidi didn't cry.

'How long have you been here?' Erica asked.

'Too bloody long, that's for sure. Angus is with me. We tried to get out, but nothing worked.' She hesitated. 'Inverdale planned for us to die down here from dehydration. If the siege had gone on much longer…' She gave herself a mental shake. 'What's going on upstairs? I take it Gloucester finally agreed to storm the citadel.'

Erica chuckled. 'Only because of Freddie. He turned up in his Bentley, gave DCI Andrews a right verbal going over, said if he didn't act he'd do the job himself. Wish I had such an effective father.' Erica glanced behind her. 'The team is here. Stand away from the door and we'll get you out.'

Two large uniformed men took up positions in front of the cell, swung the metal ram and smashed open the door.

Heidi flew out and like a cat wrapped herself around Erica.

'Thank you,' she whispered before turning and pulling Angus from the room. He blinked in the torchlight, his skin as pasty as a piece of overcooked pasta and he trembled with relief.

'Let's go and find that slime-ball, Inverdale,' Heidi said. 'Come on, Angus, shake yourself. You owe the bastard a smack, remember?'

Chapter forty-seven

Geraint had pulled into a picnic area off the B4235 and couldn't understand why no one was answering their phones. He'd heard about the explosion at the Severn Tunnel on local radio so had no reason to think everything wasn't going according to plan, but still hadn't been able to speak to Daffydd. Each time he tried to call a message told him the phone was unavailable, same with Rhys' phone.

'It's cos the signal's crap here,' Kev said. 'I couldn't even pick up any radio all along the last bit of road, so mobiles won't work.' He glanced up as a helicopter passed above the trees. 'That first bomb certainly shook them up,' he said. 'That thing's been over three times since we parked here.'

'Do you think they've sussed us?' Geraint asked.

Kev shrugged. 'Dunno. Unless they nicked Daffydd how would they know there were any more bombs?'

'I guess, but maybe that's why I can't speak to him, cos he's in custody.'

'He blew the bomb though,' Kev pointed out. 'If he was able to do that, he probably got away and if he didn't, he'll keep his mouth shut.'

'Yeah… maybe.'

Kev lit a cigarette and leaned against his car to smoke. 'We can't just stay here, so what we are going to do?'

'You could move away from the bloody cars,' Geraint snapped. 'I don't want this thing exploding when I'm anywhere near it.'

Kev moved. 'So?' he asked. 'What do we do?'

Geraint tried the radio again, fiddled with the tuning and through the static he heard:

> *…M4 closed at junction 23, both Severn crossings are also closed in both directions. Police are asking motorists to avoid the area completely. Anyone wishing to travel between Wales and England should use the M5 through Gloucester. The closures follow serious incidents at Magor services and Rogiet Moor. At this time we don't have any further details and don't know whether this was a terrorist attack or something else. Police haven't issued any statements. Stay tuned for further travel information.*

'That didn't sound right,' Geraint said. 'Rhys would have been close to Magor services.' He tried calling Rhys again but the message told him the phone was still unavailable.

'Perhaps his bomb went off,' Kev mumbled and moved further away from the cars. 'Did Daffydd really know what he was doing when he built the bombs?'

'Said he did.'

'So… what do we do?'

'Can't you just shut the fuck up a minute and give me some space to think!'

Kev wandered down the slope dotted with picnic tables and threw stones in the river, while Geraint stared at the cars. What should he do? He didn't want to let Daffydd and Cenedl Cymru down, but equally didn't want to get arrested… or die. Had a bomb exploded at Magor, miles away from the intended target? Was the TNT unstable or had Daffydd cocked it up when he built the devices?

He walked to the boot and opened it carefully. The canister hadn't moved and looked exactly the same as it had when it had been loaded. Geraint leaned his forehead on the open boot, felt cool metal on his skin and took a series of deep breaths. The plan had been such a good one, it was a shame to give up on it now. Maybe Daffydd was OK and just keeping his head down, lying low until the fracas calmed down, but maybe he wasn't.

He made a decision, unstrapped the canister, lifted it out and carried it carefully to the back of the parking area away from the road. Kev spotted him and wandered over.

'What are you doing?' he asked.

'I'm leaving this bloody thing here and going home.'

'You're giving up?'

'Yeah, I'm giving up and if you've got any sense you'll do the same. I'm sure we've been sussed. Both bridges are closed and it sounds as though one of the bombs might have gone off at Magor. That's wrong. It could either be because Rhys was caught or the TNT isn't stable, but either way, I'm getting out.'

'You're going to leave the bomb here?' Kev was surprised.

'I'm not driving around with it any longer. You take it if you want.'

'No, I don't. I want to go home too.'

'Then let's do that.' Geraint ripped the wires off the alarm clock, flung it into the river, climbed in his car and started the engine. He called to Kev. 'Stay away from me and Cenedl Cymru for a while. We don't want to be seen together, and don't phone. I'll be in touch when it's safe.'

Geraint put the car in gear and shot out of the picnic area, tyres scattering small stones and mud. Kev followed, anxious to be a long way away from the bomb. The cars sped along the winding road towards Usk, travelling as fast as they dared. A few miles from the car park, Kev misjudged a sharp bend and tried and failed to correct his error. The car left the road, burst through the undergrowth, took off and landed in the river below. Geraint saw the airborne vehicle in his mirror, but didn't stop. Kev was on his own.

As he approached the village of Llangwm, Geraint spotted a police car parked in a lay-by a few hundred yards ahead and slowed. He didn't want to get nicked for speeding after all he'd been through today. Too late he realised the car was one of a pair. The second had pulled across the road ahead and blocked it completely. Geraint slammed on the brakes, spun the car in a tight U-turn and headed back the other way. He glanced in his mirror, saw the cars weren't following and wondered why until he rounded a bend and discovered another pair of cars parked across the carriageway. He put his foot down. No way were they going to catch him, he'd ram his way through like in the films. He was still some distance away when he heard a bang and panicked before remembering he no longer had the bomb. The car slowed rapidly and he struggled to keep it on the road, belatedly realising he'd been caught by a stinger thrown across the tarmac.

As soon as the car skidded to a stop, police swarmed around it like bluebottles on a dead rat. Geraint was dragged roughly from the driver's seat and flung on the road, a boot on his back holding him down. He felt his hands cuffed and heard someone open the boot.

'Nothing here,' a bomb squad officer yelled.

Lizzie turned Geraint over, placed her foot on his groin and pushed hard. Geraint screamed and tried to wriggle away.

'Where is it?' Lizzie spat. 'What have you done with it?' She ground her heel into his balls. 'Tell me!'

'Where's what?'

'The bloody bomb. If you don't talk I'll castrate you.' She leaned heavily again.

Geraint spluttered. 'Picnic area. I left it at the picnic area.'

Lizzie removed her foot. Two officers grabbed Geraint, searched him roughly and stuffed him in the back of one of the cars. The bomb squad led the way back along the Usk road, while Lizzie got on the radio and organised a cordon at the Chepstow end. The idea of such an enormous bomb left unattended in a public area filled her with dread.

Chapter forty-eight

Erica led Heidi and Angus up the cellar steps to the hall. Freddie spotted them immediately and grabbed hold of his daughter in a suffocating hug.

'My darling girl,' he said. 'I am overjoyed to see you. Are you OK?'

'I am now,' Heidi said and returned his embrace. 'Knew you'd come for me, Pa.'

Freddie released her, offered a hand to Angus who grabbed it and shook it vigorously.

Freddie chuckled. 'I'm even pleased to see you, Mr Hickman. How are you?'

'Thirsty,' Angus said. 'I could drink an Olympic swimming pool, chemicals and all. Feels like my tongue has turned to polystyrene.'

Freddie beckoned to a uniformed officer. 'Can you fetch some water, Constable?' he asked.

The man nodded and went in search of a tap.

'What's been going on while we've been locked up?' Heidi asked.

Erica stepped closer. 'There have been developments with Cenedl Cymru. Daffydd Owen was killed on Rogiet Moor trying to plant a bomb in the Severn Tunnel.'

'I knew it!' Heidi said. 'Why on earth didn't Loopy Lizzie Wild nick him before things got silly?'

'I'll fill you in later,' Erica said. 'We need to sort things out here first. We haven't been able to locate Inverdale or Mala.'

'What about the others?'

'All unconscious upstairs,' Freddie said. 'Looks as though they've been drugged, haven't been able to wake any of them. We're hoping they've been given nothing more than a sleeping draft, but won't know until the paramedics get here and check them over. Ambulances on the way.'

Heidi turned, ran up the stairs, burst into the female dormitory and cast her eyes over the sleeping women. Clover was in the bed nearest the door and Heidi tried to shake her awake with no success. She brushed a lock of hair from the girl's cheek.

'Is someone searching the cottages and outbuildings?' she asked.

'Yeah,' Erica said. 'Since Gloucester force finally stepped up we almost have too many personnel. Boy, did Freddie give DCI Andrews a roasting. He was very impressive.'

'Yes, he can be.' Heidi checked the second room and saw more sleeping disciples. 'Where is Inverdale?' she growled.

'Haven't found him yet. We've been over the place once and no sign of him or Mala.'

'Pass the word he's armed.'

'What with?'

'Revolver. That's how he captured me and Angus. Have you checked his quarters?'

'Yeah, empty.'

Heidi dashed back downstairs to the hall and began her own search, Erica struggling to keep up.

'Are you sure he hasn't got away?' Heidi asked.

'Not possible. We've been camped outside for days, no one's gone in, apart from you, and no one's come out. He's in here somewhere.'

Heidi ran along the maze of hallways to the rear of the property and checked every room and every room was empty. Reaching the office door, she turned the handle and discovered it was locked.

'Go fetch Ben and a couple of likely lads. Have we any armed officers on site?'

'No, DCI Andrews wouldn't sanction it.'

'Well get some! Cornered animals are always dangerous and this cornered animal has a gun and thinks he's God.'

A few minutes later, Ben, Oliver and a couple of uniforms crowded the narrow corridor. Ben pounded on the door.

'Inverdale! Open up,' he shouted. 'We know you're in there. Do yourself a favour and put an end to this.'

They were greeted by silence.

'Maybe he's out cold like the others?' Erica suggested.

'He won't be,' Heidi muttered, took a step back, drove her boot into the door and the ancient wood crumbled.

The door burst open to reveal Inverdale and Mala sitting together behind the desk as though they were preparing to interview someone for a job, but in Adam's hand was the gun. The short barrel was pointed at the head of Stacey Logan who knelt on the floor at his feet, hands in front of her body, a cable tie binding them.

'Oh my God,' Ben said. 'Stacey!'

'That's far enough,' Adam warned.

The officers froze, unsure how to handle the situation. Heidi glared at Adam and Mala, eyes burning with hatred.

'Inspector,' Adam said. 'How do you feel now, having broken into a church, a sacred place of worship? They could have made good use of you when Henry VIII was ransacking monasteries.'

'We're not ransacking,' Ben said. 'We've come to arrest you and Mala, so release Stacey and watch while we take this place apart to find out what you've done with the children.'

'Children?' Adam feigned surprise. 'I don't know what you're talking about.'

'Yes, you do,' Heidi muttered, 'and you will tell us.'

'Will I?' Adam sneered. 'Are you going to make me?'

Heidi stepped forward and Adam waved the pistol dangerously. He pointed it back at Stacey, then poured two glasses of a pale liquid into two wine glasses. He handed one to Mala who smiled and touched his glass with hers before drinking.

Adam glared at Heidi. 'I answer to no one but God,' he said. 'I have walked with Him for years, Mala at my side. I am not of this world and have been sent to bring human souls to God. Help them discover the rapture for themselves. Am I a prophet? Possibly, but like to think I am more than that.'

'You are,' Mala said and brushed his cheek with a long finger. 'You are so much more. Why else would I have served you for so long, given you my only daughter?'

Adam caught her hand and kissed it. 'Beloved, my faithful Mala. We will travel together to God, find peace, the rapture, the spirit of God and He will welcome us to sit by his side at the high table.'

Heidi spluttered with laughter. 'Bloody hell, you've completely lost it, haven't you? That's what happens when you surround yourself with people you've brainwashed using this sort of rubbish, you end up believing it yourself. You sad, deluded little man. You don't enrich souls, you destroy them and I promise you, I am going to destroy you.'

'I'm the one with the gun,' Adam said and grinned nastily.

'God not enough for you?' Heidi sneered. 'It's not God who makes you brave, not love, but fear. You control others with fear. Tell me where those children are. Tell me who bought them.'

'No one bought them. They are God's seed and I am his conduit. The children were adopted by loving families, but they weren't sold. What makes you think that?'

'The money in your bank account.'

Ben cut in, 'What have you done to the people upstairs? If you have hurt them…'

'Why would I hurt them? I love them. You really don't understand what's going on here, do you? Authority always looks for the bad, never for the good. If you did, you'd understand.'

'Stop this crap,' Ben bellowed. 'Tell us what we need to know – this minute.'

Mala suddenly fell back in her chair, bent over and held her stomach, groaning loudly.

'What's up with her?' Ben asked.

Adam shrugged. 'The Rapture is close.'

'Poison,' Stacey spluttered. 'They've taken poison. Tried to make me drink some too.'

Adam swiped at her forehead with the barrel of the gun, she yelped, lost her balance and sprawled in an untidy heap.

Adam chuckled mirthlessly. 'Now you understand why I don't feel threatened by you. Very soon, Mala and I will leave this veil of tears behind and find true freedom. There is nothing you can do to us.'

'What about the others?' Heidi snarled. 'Have you fed them poison too?'

Adam shrugged, a sheen of sweat broke out on his skin, face flushed crimson, his breathing laboured and air whistled in his lungs like a leaky set of bellows. Mala bent over for a second time, whimpered and suddenly vomited on the floor. Stacey used the diversion to drive her shoulder into Adam's knees and tip him off balance. Caught by surprise, Adam lost his grip on the gun and it skittered away across the floorboards. Erica executed a neat rugby move and snagged the revolver, as Heidi launched herself across the desk and delivered a vicious punch to Adam's throat. He hit the floor, coughing and retching as Mala groaned and released another deluge. Stacey wriggled across the dusty floor away from her tormentors and Ben cut her hands free.

'You're bleeding,' he said, removed a handkerchief from his pocket and pressed it against her temple. 'Are you OK, Pumpkin?'

'Fine, don't fuss. Deal with them.'

Heidi grabbed Adam by the shoulders and shoved him against the desk.

'You coward!' she spat. 'You disgusting, despicable example of humanity. What have you used to dose the others?' She raised her fist but Ben snatched her hand in mid-air.

'Enough, Heidi,' he said. 'Back off and let us do our job.'

'Not until I know about the others… he will tell me.'

Adam was struggling to breathe, never mind speak, but still managed a smirk. Heidi slapped him, hard, before reluctantly moving away. She stood, looked through the window and spotted a fleet of ambulances tearing along the drive. She grabbed Erica's hand, headed towards the front of the house to guide the paramedics to their patients and prayed the commune members could be saved.

Chapter forty-nine

Lizzie waited in her car on the main road next to the picnic area while the bomb disposal crew defused the last home-made device. She rested her head on the steering wheel and moaned. How had things gone so wrong for her?

Before she'd been sent to Wales to deal with these bloody stupid people, she'd been on the way up. A rising star. She knew without being told her career was ruined, as much use to her as a pair of knickers without elastic.

The brass in Brecon had been in touch, they wanted a meeting before she left for Bristol and guessed she had already been removed from the investigation. She wasn't wanted here… maybe not in England either. A tap on the glass shook her back to the present. She buzzed down her window and Connor looked in.

'You OK?' he asked.

Lizzie nodded. 'What do you want?'

'The lads have made the bomb safe and are going to take it away with them. They think they know where the TNT came from, but will know for certain when they've run their tests.'

'Where do they reckon it originated?'

'The slate mines in the north, left over stock perhaps. That's more than likely what Daffydd was up to when he went to visit his granddad, he picked up explosives. At least we can finally nick the old man.'

'Where are the Jones brothers?'

'Cardiff central. CTU officers are dealing with them.'

'What about us?'

Connor shook his head. 'They don't want us. After you've been debriefed in Brecon, we can leave. Go home.'

'But this was our investigation,' Lizzie grumbled. 'We've spent hundreds of man-hours on this. They can't just send us away.'

'They can, and let's be honest, boss, we didn't achieve very much. Perhaps we should have tried harder.'

'We weren't given the resources,' Lizzie grumbled. 'Over half the available staff either walked away or were seconded elsewhere. This case was never taken seriously by Dyfed Powys.'

Connor shrugged. 'What will happen when we're back in Bristol?'

'No point asking me. I guess a lot will depend on what the bosses here say when we meet them later.'

'Yeah, I guess.'

A bomb disposal officer walked up to the car.

'All safe,' he said. 'We'll take the whole shebang to our main facility and run some tests. I'll ring the results through. Glad we could defuse the thing, be a shame to lose all these beautiful trees.' He wandered back the way he came.

Lizzie snorted. 'The trees? He's worried about the bloody trees? I tell you, Connor, if I never see Wales again I shall die a happy woman. Fetch your car, I'll meet you in Brecon.'

* * *

A bright log fire burned in the grate and warmed the library. Heidi and Erica lounged together on an old leather sofa, while Freddie made sure he kept the brandy glasses topped up. Angus perched on the brass fender and fed the fire.

'Bloody good to be home,' Heidi said. 'You really did pull a blinder, Freddie, everyone says so.'

'Not difficult when you have the right name and the right contacts. Thank God the commune members were OK, drugged not poisoned.'

'Where are they now?' Erica asked.

'Local hospitals,' Heidi said. 'They'd been overdosed with benzodiazepine and are being treated with flumazenil, an antidote of sorts. They should all be fine.'

Freddie sipped his brandy. 'Inverdale and Mala didn't last long,' he said. 'They'd taken aconite, also known as Monkshood or Wolfsbane. It was growing in the herb garden and had been made into a tincture. A teaspoonful would have been sufficient, never mind half a glass. Died of asphyxiation when the poison paralysed their lungs.'

'Good,' Angus muttered. 'I'm glad they're dead, and I'm glad their death was unpleasant. It could have been us.'

'Bollocks!' Heidi said. 'I told you Freddie would rescue us.'

'I'm glad they're dead too,' Erica said. 'They made my skin crawl, the pair of them.'

'Where's Pixie?' Heidi asked.

'Upstairs with Greta and Miriam.' Freddie said. 'They're helping her and Felix to settle back into the world. Clover is coming to stay tomorrow.'

'Is she?'

Freddie nodded. 'Poor little thing has nowhere to go and with her mother being dead… Miriam is wonderful with Pixie and says she wants to help Clover too.'

Heidi humphed. 'She's got a nerve, couldn't look after her own child – and what? She's trying to make amends now?'

'Maybe,' Freddie said, 'but I do need help, won't be able to manage on my own.'

Heidi's mobile chirruped breaking the tension. She peered at the screen and her eyes widened. She uncurled from the sofa, padded to the desk, woke up her laptop and battered the keys.

'Eureka!' she yelled and jumped up from her seat.

'What?' Erica asked.

'Thanks to Angus, the program has finally produced riches.' She turned to face the group. 'I've found Clover's baby,' she announced, 'and the other two!'

'That's fantastic!' Angus said. 'We can bring the child here, so when Clover arrives tomorrow…'

'Won't be anywhere near that easy,' Erica warned. 'The dreaded Social Services will be involved and of course we'll need to handle the surrogate parents gently.'

'I don't see why,' Heidi muttered. 'They must have known buying babies was illegal.'

'We need to interview them with an open mind. We have no idea what Adam told them at the time, they could be victims like all the others.'

The library door opened and Miriam hesitated in the doorway before she entered and perched uncomfortably on the end of the sofa. Freddie handed her a balloon of his best brandy.

'How are the kids?' he asked.

'Work in progress,' Miriam said and sipped her drink. 'Pixie is struggling, she doesn't understand why she contacted Adam and tipped him off, she's so ashamed. I asked her and Felix to come down here with us, but they refused.'

'We've good news,' Freddie said. 'Heidi has tracked down the missing children, including Clover's little one.'

'Really? That's wonderful. Can we reunite them tomorrow when Clover arrives?'

'I doubt it, Mrs Holtz,' Erica said. 'There will be mountains of red tape to wade through first, but eventually – yes.'

'A baby in the house. How lovely.'

'Really, Mother?' Heidi snapped. 'You like the idea of a baby, but you sold your own.'

The group fell silent, an awkward silence which lengthened and deepened. Miriam took a gulp of her drink which set off a coughing fit. Freddie patted her on the back and passed her a handkerchief to wipe her streaming eyes.

Miriam took a deep breath. 'Heidi… I'm sorry, truly I am. I was young and scared, didn't know what to do for the best and made a mistake.'

'A mistake?' Heidi huffed. 'Foisting an unwanted child on a couple in a foreign country could not – in any circumstances – be called a mistake. How could you do such a thing?'

'I was terrified I'd lose your father, sure he'd never take me back with a cuckoo in the nest.'

'Cuckoo! How bloody dare you! You were thinking of yourself, as always.'

'I know I can't put this right,' Miriam said, 'and I also know you will never forgive me – don't expect you to – but I must be allowed the chance to redeem myself, make some form of restitution.' She sipped more brandy. 'I am not a bad person and not the person I was… none of us are.'

Heidi cracked her knuckles and stood. 'I'm tired and off to bed. You coming, E?'

Erica nodded. 'Right behind you. I'm not letting you out of my sight, not until I'm used to having you back with me.'

'Where do you think I'm going to go?'

'Don't know, but I'm not taking any chances.' She snagged Heidi round the waist and squeezed. 'Night all. See you at breakfast, sleep well.'

They left the room and headed upstairs. Heidi snuggled under the quilt and wrapped herself around her partner's body.

'I've missed this,' she mumbled. 'Thanks for rescuing me and Angus.'

'Wouldn't have left you,' Erica said. 'Although, if you had your own GPS device hanging from your neck, it would have been much easier to convince Gloucester you were inside New Eden.'

Heidi groaned. 'Not that again, E. I wasn't using it to spy on you. I'm not good at emotional stuff, you know I'm not, but I do love you. I've always loved you and don't want to be without you. The tracker was only because I wanted to keep you safe.'

'I know.' Erica kissed the top of Heidi's head. 'And I'm so glad you wanted to.'

Chapter fifty

The kitchen was crammed and Freddie was enjoying himself. He'd sent Cook home and press-ganged Angus to help with breakfast. Miriam had been able to coax Pixie and Felix downstairs, they sat together at one end of the table looking uncomfortable and out of place.

Greta bounced in and waved copies of the morning's papers. 'Hey,' she said, 'New Eden made the dailies.' She dropped the thick bundle on the table.

Heidi snatched *The Guardian* and spread it flat. The two inches tall headline screamed from the front page: COTSWOLD CULT RAIDED – TWO DEAD.

Heidi chuckled. 'Looks like Stacey Logan finally hit the big time, listen to this:

> *In a joint operation, close to the sleepy Cotswold village of South Hatherop, Gloucester Police, together with officers from Dyfed Powys, raided a manor house owned by a group calling itself, 'The Church of New Eden', and released thirty-two individuals. The residents were discovered unconscious, having been drugged by their self-styled leader – Adam Inverdale – assisted by a shadowy woman known as Mala. Commune members are recovering in hospital. Their condition is not life threatening and all are expected to make a full recovery.*
>
> *Inverdale and Mala were not so fortunate. Both died yesterday after ingesting tincture of aconite, harvested*

from plants growing in the herb garden at the property.

'It goes on a bit, but Stacey's done a good job of warning the public about dodgy new religious movements, how to recognise those who have been converted and how to care for those who have escaped.'

'Good piece,' Angus said, scanning one of the tabloids. 'This should wake folks up. Bloody shame Inverdale got away with it though. Too easy him quaffing poison, should have lived out the rest of his life under lock and key. Evil bastard.'

'When will Clover arrive?' Miriam asked.

'Not sure,' Freddie said. 'Sometime today.'

The front door bell clanged, Greta went to answer it and returned a few minutes later with DI Ben James and DC Oliver Langdon.

Freddie glanced up from the range as they entered. 'Gentlemen, marvellous to see you and just in time for breakfast. Can I interest either of you in a bacon sandwich?'

Ben smiled. 'Both of us I should think, sir, thank you.' He pulled up a chair. 'Coppers never refuse a bacon sarnie. We've dropped in to see how things are with you before we head off to Wales.'

'We're fine, Inspector,' Freddie said, 'now everyone is where they should be. Have you recovered Clover's child?'

Ben nodded and took a steaming mug of coffee from Greta. 'Yes, we have. The parents are in custody while we investigate the circumstances and the baby is safe. We've explained the situation to Social Services and have been given assurances they will speed up procedures so we can reunite the baby with her mother as quickly as possible. Are you still willing to take Clover, Mr Holtz?'

'I've told you, it's Freddie. I'm only Mr Holtz in Whitehall, and yes, more than willing. My wife has agreed to stay on to help with our unexpected guests and they can remain here as long as they need.'

'That's very generous, sir, it would certainly help enormously.'

'Anyone would do the same,' Freddie muttered and placed overstuffed sandwiches dripping butter and bacon grease in front of them. 'Tuck in.' He settled himself at the head of the table. 'Now, tell me about Cenedl Cymru. How do things stand?'

Ben reluctantly put his butty back on the plate. 'One dead – Daffydd Owen – five directly involved with the attack in custody, including the dead man's grandfather. He supplied the explosive. Nasty piece of work, Granddad Owen, dreadful racist and was heavily involved with The Sons of Glyndŵr when they were burning cottages. We've never been able to nick him for anything until now. It's no wonder Daffydd grew up like he did, indoctrinated from birth.'

'Another form of brainwashing,' Freddie said. 'Just like the methods employed by Inverdale at New Eden, both groups actively recruited others.'

'Yeah, you're right,' Ben said and finally took a bite of his food.

'I guess they'll be charged under the Terrorism Act,' Freddie said and stirred his tea. 'If we're lucky, they may not see the light of day again. I'm in London next week and I'll have a word in the right ears. Banning Cenedl Cymru is a priority and once the group is on the proscribed list, you can round up the rest just for being members. We don't want extreme right-wing groups on the streets of the UK and if we don't stamp out the movement now, there will be worse trouble later.'

'I'm with you,' Ben agreed. He glanced at Heidi. 'DI Wild has gone, sent packing last night. I wondered if you might consider returning to the force. I've been sidestepping the bosses ever since you went AWOL and can probably smooth your way back in. We miss you, Heidi, you're a good copper.'

Heidi laughed. 'No, I'm not. I'm a crap copper. Don't play by the rules.'

'That's true, but you get results. We need clever people like you.'

'Clever? I'm a bloody genius.'

'OK. You're a genius. Now, are you coming back?'

'No, sir. The police force doesn't really fit me, too many rules to prevent me getting the job done. If I'm not a copper, I'm not bound by the rules.'

'What do you think you'll do? Do you have a plan?'

'Working on one, but in the meantime, I shall be more than happy to work for you in the capacity of special adviser… should you need anything hacked for example.'

'Hacking is illegal,' Ben said.

'Only if you get caught,' Heidi giggled, 'and I won't.'

Ben grinned. 'I'll keep your offer in mind.' He glanced at Erica. 'Are you going to desert me too?'

'No, sir, I'll be back. I need the money and only ever wanted to be a copper, so you're stuck with me.'

'Glad to hear it,' Ben said and stuffed the last of his sandwich in his mouth.

'I had a call from Jon Williams,' Erica said, 'the builder guy working on Brecon cathedral. He's concerned about his nephew, Matthew. Is he in custody?'

Oliver nodded. 'Yeah, on remand. He rang Jon on Friday when he realised what was going on, he was the escort for the bomb destined for the second crossing. Shame the lad didn't find out about it earlier, but he did call in the information like he said he would. Meant we were able to get the team in place at Magor to prevent a potential disaster. Matthew will be charged with aggravated burglary and ABH for his part in the attack on the Cardiff newsagent. He'll do time, but not as much as the others.'

'How is Stacey?' Heidi asked.

Ben smiled. 'At home with a stinking headache, but she'll live, thank you.'

'No loose ends then, Inspector?' Freddie asked.

'No, sir, and if you succeed in banning Cenedl Cymru we will arrest the other members. As you say, if we don't deal with the XRW, the problem will grow.'

'I'll do what I can, but I'm sure you're aware how slowly government moves.'

Pixie suddenly stood and cleared her throat: 'I want to say something.'

'What is it, my dear?' Freddie asked.

'I want to apologise to Heidi and Angus. I never meant to put them in danger and don't understand why I told Adam what they were planning. I don't feel much like me and can't really remember what me felt like before. Everything's mixed up and doesn't make sense.'

Miriam rested an arm across the girl's shoulders. 'That's because you haven't been you for a long time. New Eden damaged you, Adam damaged you. He took away your mind. It wasn't your fault and I'm sure Heidi doesn't blame you.'

Heidi looked up from the pile of newspapers and smiled. 'Don't sweat it, kid. Everything turned out OK in the end.'

'But…'

Heidi held up her hand, anxious to avoid another Pixie-hug. 'All I'm interested in is happy endings and well… isn't that just what this is? A really happy ending?'

Epilogue

Greta stood at the bathroom window, forehead resting on the cold glass and stared at the wintry parkland surrounding her family home. There had been a sharp frost during the early hours, the countryside looked as though it had been dusted with icing sugar and sparkled in the early sunshine. A pair of crows flapped lazily by and Greta wondered – not for the first time – how birds managed to survive the cold nights. How was it their feet didn't freeze solid? And crows were big, what about blue tits?

The room was warm and steamy, condensation misted the surfaces. Greta had run a deep bath and added bubbles to the water, realising too late she had probably overdone it as foam slithered slowly over the roll top and onto the floor. She was so glad to be home. Milebrook was the only place she really wanted to be and decided to try to fit in a little better, not cause Freddie any more grief; after all, he'd welcomed her home without a single awkward question. Yes, Milebrook was the place for her, not a commune run by religious nutters, and not prison run by a different sort of nutter. She replayed the last few months of her life in her mind and wondered if she should write the story down, maybe a book, but where to end the tale? She knew it wasn't over yet.

She turned from the window and picked up the small piece of plastic she'd balanced on the shelf beneath the mirror. Taking a deep breath, she turned it over, held it under the light and stared at it, unsure how she should feel, delighted or distraught? She'd never considered being a mother before – maybe she should have – especially as it appeared she was going to be one in the summer.

List of characters

Governor Hughes – HMP Heatherlea
Maria Cole – chaplain at HMP Heatherlea
Greta Holtz – DC Heidi Holtz's sister
Frederick Holtz – father of Heidi and Greta
Miriam Holtz – mother of Heidi and Greta
Adam Inverdale – messenger at The Church of New Eden
Mala – Adam Inverdale's right-arm
Clover – Mala's daughter
Eleanor – church member
Pixie – church member
Felix – church member
Alex – victim of attack
Daniela Stoica – victim of attack
Geri Skinner – 999 caller
Jon Williams – witness
Matthew Williams – Jon's nephew
Lottie – Easter Europeans' social club patron
Jonesy Francombe – skinhead
Peter Leech – skinhead
Daffydd Owen – spokesperson for Cenedl Cymru
Rhys and Geraint Jones – prominent members of Cenedl Cymru
Stacey Logan – reporter at *The Mid Wales Times*
Angus Hickman – DC Holtz's old friend
DI Ben James
DS Erica Bevan
DC Heidi Holtz
DC Tegan Hedges

DC Oliver Langdon
DI Lizzie Wild – Bristol Counter Terrorist Unit
DS Connor Haskins – Bristol Counter Terrorist Unit
DCI Andrews – Gloucester Police
DS Colin Amos and DC Andy Boswell – Gloucester CID
DS Dan Briggs – Builth Wells station
DC Will Deacon – Builth Wells station

Acknowledgements

With special thanks to Ian Haworth, founder of the Cult Information Centre in the UK. Plus, my hard-working reading panel: Bill, Sue L, Helen, Pauline, Sue P, Erica and Kerry; The Writer's Circle at the Cammarch; and of course, The Book Folks.

If you enjoyed this book, please let others know by leaving a quick review on Amazon. Also, if you spot anything untoward in the paperback, get in touch. We strive for the best quality and appreciate reader feedback.

editor@thebookfolks.com

More fiction by Nicola Clifford

NO REFUGE – book 1

Reporter Stacey Logan has little to worry about other than the town flower festival when a man is shot dead. When she believes the police have got the wrong man, she does some snooping of her own. But will her desire for a scoop lead her to a place where there is no refuge?

THE CONSORTIUM – Book 2

Whilst reporter Stacey Logan is investigating illegal raves in the Welsh countryside, her boyfriend DI Ben James is dealing with a suspicious death. When drugs enter the picture, their two separate inquiries will collide. Can they find a way to collaborate and catch a dangerous killer?

NOT FORGOTTEN – Book 3

When journalist Stacey Logan's policeman boyfriend disappears with little more than a note, she suspects he has been abducted. But his colleagues refuse to pursue her leads. She'll have to go it alone, but must brace herself for the worst.

CODDLING MOLLY – Book 5

A teenager is found dead after a fall from a bridge on a winter night in Brecon. Nobody knows who she is and identifying her proves a challenge. DI Ben James and DS Erica Bevan manage to connect her to someone else with ties to a drugs gang. But when these crooks bother someone dear to ex-detective Heidi Holtz, she too will jump on their trail.

www.thebookfolks.com

Printed in Great Britain
by Amazon

81070056R00171